Contents

Preface

A few years ago I read an article about Stephen King in *The New Yorker*. The author had interviewed the humor writer Dave Barry, a friend of King's, and a colleague in a truly awful amateur rock band. Barry said about King that his talent is telling stories and that everyone in the world likes stories, except literature majors.

When I was growing up I loved the work of great story tellers like O. Henry, Roald Dahl, Jack London, Ring Lardner and others. I didn't want current fashions in literary criticism to get in the way of a rollicking good tale. I started writing stories when I got out of the Army in 1953 but soon put them aside for a career as a History professor and it was more than 40 years, with my first computer, that I once more tried my hand as a story teller.

I like strong plots, but I can't take all the credit for them. When I get an idea for a story I seldom know exactly how it's going to end., I like to create memorablee characters and let them determine the direction the story is going. Often they just take over the action and even add surprising twists to the plot that I had never sspected when I started writing. This may sound odd, even surreal, but authors I respect admit to the same lack of control over their characters. Elmore Leonard said he gave a name to the main character in *Bandits*that didn't seem to motivate him, "but when I changed his name to Jack Delany, I couldn't shut him up." My characters—actually I think of them as friends—come from the same dimension. It's time to meet them.

To this second edition I have added two new stories — with two new and memorable characters: Dorothy, the space child and Detective Mulkey and his 9/11 case.

GERSHWIN'S LAST WALTZ

Karabakh had been trying to sell a vintage poster to a couple who had wandered in off the street but didn't seem very involved. Now, to his annoyance, his concentration was broken by the sight of an old woman outside, a raggedy old woman, peering through the window, her hands framing her face and her nose almost against the glass. He had a sudden painful memory of people like that back in Russia, looking into a bakery, or a restaurant, freezing out there on the street. But this was New York in the springtime and there was nothing here but art, posters, old photos. The couple abruptly decided that not even that interested them, and they left. Karabakh was on his way to the front of the store to shoo the old woman away, but she had caught the door as the couple left and was now coming in, looking around with great interest.Karabakh had an opportunity to study her more closely and the brisk dismissal he had been phrasing died on its way to his lips. Ragged she may have been, in shapeless clothes, her gray hair windblown, but now he could see that his visitor had been a beauty, maybe many years ago, but a beauty, even a great beauty.

"Can I help you, madame?" He had tried for a tone that would discourage his visitor, but her wide green eyes suddenly fastened on his, her full lips opened into a warm smile, and suddenly he couldn't help sounding as if he'd been waiting all day for her visit.

She paused, then looked around the store again, as if expecting to see a familiar object. She turned back.

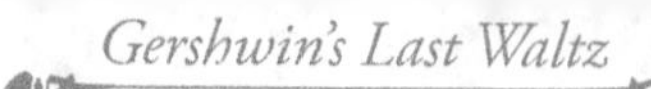

"I'm sorry to bother you—"

"Not a bit, I—"

"But in your window it says, ah..."

"Yes, madame?"

"It says, 'Gershwin memorabilia.' What can that mean?"

Karabakh smiled back. Maybe there was a sale here, unlikely as it had seemed. "Yes, Gershwin memorabilia. Over the years I have made a specialty of collecting items: old sheet music, letters, but particularly photographic material having to do with George Gershwin. Are you familiar with his career?"

The lady inclined her head slowly to the left and laughed softly, a beautiful, gentle laugh.

"I knew George Gershwin."

A shock ran through Karabakh and he calculated quickly. George Gershwin had died in 1937 at the age of 39. If this woman had been, say, twenty years younger than the composer, she would be, eighty, no, at least eighty-two years old right now. It was possible. But his store was right in the middle of the Village and the streets were thronged with frauds and loonies. He forced himself to concentrate, stay with the sale.

"Ah, of course. But you, madame, are far too young to have—_"

She laughed again. "You are so kind. But yes. I am...I am almost eighty. You won't tell a soul?"

"Of course, madame," he said, savoring the little lie. "Would you...is there any particular sort of Gershwin memorabilia that you would like to see?"

The woman stopped smiling and shook her head.

"No. Actually..." she stuttered a bit. "Actually, I have some old photographs and I wondered if...if they had any value. You see—"

Karabakh quickly cut off any despairing claim of poverty and urgency that she might be about to make and held up his hands. His heart was racing, but he managed to keep his voice professional.

"I would be delighted to see your photographs, madame, but I have to assure you that the market for Gershwiniana at the moment is—"

His visitor pealed with laughter, real laughter this time. "Gershwiniana! How George would have loved that!" She grasped Karabakh's arm suddenly, intensely.

"Yes. Yes! I'm so glad I found this store! It was completely by hazard. I'll have to...have to find those old photos and I'll come by tomorrow. Will that be all right?"

Karabakh agreed, trying to stay calm. He knew that the estate of the Gershwin family would pay top prices for any original Gershwin material and he was wondering if he would encounter a real treasure, at a bargain price.

"I'm afraid these are in an awful mess," she was saying the next day, taking sheaves of old, mismatched black and white glossies out of a large grocery bag. She had changed into a long dark blue dress that could have come directly from the racks of the "formerly owned" clothing store down the block. But her silvery gray hair was neatly tucked back into a bun and she was wearing tiny earrings that, if Karabakh was not mistaken, were sapphires.

But he was disappointed at the pictures that shuffled out of the bag, sending a cloud of dust into his shop: edges worn, some quite browned by age, most of them amateurish, none of them novelties. George Gershwin had been the most outgoing of men and had been photographed tens of thousands of times. And the value of a photograph depended on the venue and the provenance. A professional photo of Gershwin at a famous club, sitting in for the pianist, a blond bombshell beside him on the bench, all correctly credited with names and dates, would be worth thousands. But all these poor prints were anonymous. One couldn't tell where they'd been taken, or by whom; they were of mediocre quality, and some of the 8 x 10s had actually been folded. The one he was looking at now showed Gershwin seated on a piano bench, pointing to a piece of music on the piano, a big smile on his face, across which, unfortunately, the photo had been folded.

"I took this one," said the lady, sadly." I wish it was in better condition, but I've...I've not been well for a long time and my things—"

"You can see my problem," said Karabakh. "There is no way that I can authenticate the background. There are so many photos of George exactly like this, pointing to 'I've got Rhythm,' or 'The Man I Love.' It was one of his favorite poses."

"Oh, but this was different. You see, George and I were...close. And he had just written a little waltz for me. He played it, and then I insisted that he write it out, you know, so I could keep the music, but I forgot to take it with me and all I had was my photograph. And then he was always so busy after..." She fell silent, her face in shadow betraying an ancient sadness. "And then I read in the papers that he died out on the coast. It was so sudden."

It took Karabakh several moments to completely comprehend what she had just said. If she was actually telling the truth, he had here a worthless picture of George Gershwin—but an image of that rarest of objects, an unpublished Gershwin tune, worth well into the millions, at auction. He struggled to keep his voice neutral, his heart pounding.

"Madame...I'm sorry, I never got your name?"

"It's Gisele. Gisele Morgan. It was, ah, Gisele Bernheimer in those days."

"Yes. Mrs Bern— Mrs Morgan. You will understand that there may be a certain value for the piece of music." He stood up abruptly. "May I keep this overnight? I will write you a receipt, of course, but I wish a colleague of mine, a distinguished composer, to look at the music, to see if it actually can be read." He leaned down peering at it closely through his thick glasses.

"It goes, 'tah da dee dah, dada tah da dee dah...,'" sang Mrs Morgan in a not unmusical voice. "But I'm afraid that's all I remember of it."

"Yes, yes, of course. A beautiful melody. But you see—"

"Oh, of course you may keep it. And have it looked at. Oh, this is so exciting! I've been waiting forever for something like this to happen!"

She had barely disappeared around the corner when Karabakh quickly stepped out, carrying the photo, locked his store and rang a bell in the next doorway. The name card was scrawled in pencil: ARTHUR HERSH. COMPOSER-ARRANGER-ACCOMPANIST. PIANO LESSONS. PIANO TUNING. He was buzzed in and he ascended a flight of stairs to a large airy studio, a tiny kitchen in one corner and a bed in another, where a young man with wild dark hair was busy scribbling music on the stand of an old Knabe grand piano strewn with sheet music.

"Arthur! I'm so glad I found you in! I have a favor to ask... in fact, a commission. I'll be glad to pay you by the hour if you'll look at this picture and see if you can read the piece of music in the background."

The young man did not look excited by the offer. He gave Karabakh a long look, then took the old folded photo and inspected it carefully.

"It's Gershwin, of course."

"Yes, of course. But the photo is virtually worthless. You see the crease goes directly across his nose, of all things, and he had a big nose. If I can identify which one of his tunes is in the background, it could be worth maybe a hundred...in fact I'll give you ten percent of the sale, whatever it is."

Arthur turned and looked at the photo again. Now he got up and looked through a jumble of papers on his kitchen table, finding a magnifying glass. He leaned down.

"Hum, hum, de dum. Yes, I can make out just a few notes. It's just the melody line, with a few chord symbols overhead. And I can see the three-four time signature. It's a waltz, of course."

Karabakh's heart nearly stopped. He counted to ten, then said, as if he had lost interest, "Yes, of course. Anything else?"

"Let's see. A waltz. You know, just thinking about it, I can't remember any Gershwin waltzes. I play his popular songs all the time. A waltz? I don't know. From *Porgy and Bess*, naturally— 'My Man's gone now,' for instance. Three-four time...not really a waltz. I'll have to look through my references. The man had an enormous oeuvre, you know. A lot of it pure junk, just Tin Pan Alley stuff ground out day after day, never played anymore." He went back to inspecting the photo.

"You know, I can't make out most of this." Karabakh's heart fell.

"But... Can I keep this for a bit? I think I'll scan it into my computer and then try to grow it a bit." He looked at his watch. "But I'm running late. I have a lesson in five minutes and then I have to rehearse for a job tonight."

As soon as he was back in his shop Karabakh was on the phone, punching in numbers furiously, remembering to keep his voice as calm as possible.

"Leonard...? Morris here. I have an interesting offer from a customer who says she has an original Gershwin tune.... Ha, ha, yes, I know. 'I-like-a-Gershwin-tune..., da-dada-*Dah*.' Anyway she claims he wrote this little waltz just for her. I know you knew the family well, all the old stories. Did you ever hear of something like this?"

The old man on the other end of the line finally stopped laughing.

"Morris, my old friend. This is ancient history. First you have to know that George was a first-class lover boy. A real cocksman, you know what I mean? He never married, but he had some beauty in bed every night, or after lunch, even before. We all heard the story about George's waltz. If he found a girl who was reluctant— if you could believe it—he would *patz* around on the keys and then play some romantic little melody, looking at her with those soulful eyes, and say 'Darling, I don't know what you did to me this never happened before but just looking in your eyes this song suddenly came to me...,' some nonsense like that, and next thing they're in the sack. You could check it out, it's in all the books, that story. Bennett Cerf told me, ages ago."

"But could it be possible? That she actually had the music?"

"Morris, if she has the music, actually a piece of music in her hand, and it's a waltz, even a good tune, still, how do you authenticate? Does it have his signature? Hah! Impossible to prove. Does it sound like Gershwin? So what! Everybody stole from Gershwin, just like George stole from everybody else, when he was coming up. So, good luck, my friend!"

They exchanged cordialities. Karabakh had neglected to mention that he had an unquestioned photograph of George Gershwin sitting at his piano and pointing to a piece of music that might or might not be legible. He could hardly sleep that night.

Bearing in mind that Arthur had worked in a club the night before, Karabakh managed to restrain himself from calling his neighbor until 10:30 in the morning. An irritated voice came on the phone.

"Yes?"

"Arthur, this is Morris Karabakh. I'm sorry if this is too early, but..."

"No, Mr. Karabakh, it's okay. It's just that I haven't finished yet. Maybe after lunch we could get together?"

An hour later, Arthur was still peering at his computer, jotting down notes on manuscript paper at his side. He straightened up suddenly, muttering to himself, "Ah, of course! It's a repeat. That's the bridge coming in again, and in a minor key! Brilliant! And then finishing in D-flat. Beautiful!" His doorbell rang.

"Who is it?" he blurted into the intercom, abrupt, thinking it was Karabakh again.

"Oh...I'm sorry, Arthur! It's Claire. Maybe I'm too early. I thought—"

"No, no, Claire! Please come up! Early is fine! I thought my neighbor..." and he buzzed her in.

Claire was a gorgeous but virtuous piano student. She had little talent but because of her spectacular good looks Arthur kept her on, hoping some day to get past her reservations about dating her teacher. She burst into his studio, a fresh, outdoorsy girl with a guileless smile and boundless energy, seemingly unaware of the amazing body that was obvious even under heavy layers of winter clothes and now on a warm spring day, in a flimsy cotton dress... Arthur had difficulty swallowing.

"Hi, teach!" she cried. "I finally got the fingering on that Chopin. You were right! I just had to keep doing it over and over." She spotted the computer and the hasty notes Arthur had been writing.

"What's that you're working on?"

"Oh. That. Actually, it's a nice little tune. I've just about figured it out. See here?" And he showed her the old photo and the music on the piano and how he had blown the page up on his computer. "It's supposed to be by George Gershwin, the guy here in the picture."

"Gershwin? Oh, I love him. Didn't he write 'Summertime'?"

Arthur cringed inwardly, thinking of all the women who came to clubs and wanted to sit in and sing 'Summertime.'

"Well. Yeah. And some of the most beautiful songs in the whole world, too. The music is really hard to make out, but I think I got it now. It's a little waltz. Would you like to hear it?"

"Oh gee! I'd love to! I hardly ever get to hear you *really* play, Arthur."

Karabakh was about to call Arthur again when his door jingled open and Gisele Morgan came in. She had made an effort to dress up a bit more today, although her suit was completely wrong for the season and at least three decades out of date. She had a hopeful look on her face.

"Mr. Karabakh? Have you heard anything about—"

He shrugged, managing to convey the greatest resignation.

"My dear, what can I say? My friend next door, an eminent musicologist, says the notes are virtually illegible, and that what can be read seems to be a waltz from..." he thought hard, *"Porgy and Bess?* Yes. I'm sure that's what he said." He was about to go on but suddenly they were surprised to hear some tentative notes from a piano and then music flooded the street outside. Arthur was playing his grand piano and all the windows in his studio were open to the spring morning. Dappled sunlight falling through the mulberry trees found a tableau of suddenly still figures on what had been a busy pedestrian byway. Couples had stopped to listen, their arms around each other. Shopkeepers were coming out of their doors, smiling and looking up, mystified at the swelling melody that filled the block. A taxi driver picking up a fare heard the song and quickly got out of his cab to help the elderly passenger with heavy packages. And now all traffic had halted. Strangers looked at each other and laughed with wonder, hearing a captivating melody of pure happiness and love. An old man and his wife turned to each other and embraced; onlookers smiled and hugged each other. Even the birds in the trees began a counterpoint chorus as the first refrain ended. Then the bridge repeated in a minor key, sending an anxious tremor through the crowd below. But now it modulated magically into the majestic finale in the key of D-flat and their spirits rose and rose to hear the haunting lilt of the waltz at its climax.

Mrs. Morgan had tears streaming down her face. Karabakh was standing there with his mouth open, speechless, desperately thinking of something to say.

After another half chorus the music stopped abruptly.

She was now smiling through the tears, smiling in a rather calculating way.

"Yes, that's my little waltz. I'm sorry to be so...to lose control like this. But I told you, didn't I?"

"Uh...Mrs Morgan, he must...my neighbor must be playing something for his girlfriend. He often does. I'll go over there—"

"No, Mr. Karabakh. I know my waltz. And if he was playing for his girlfriend just now I wouldn't go over there for a little while. In the meantime, let's talk business, shall we?"

Gershwin's Last Waltz

Frank Frost

Note to the music of Gershwin's Last Waltz

I wrote this story years ago and was always frustrated, having written about a beautiful song and not being able even to hum the melody. But then one day, listening to one of my favorite Bach compositions, I realized that I could switch some parts around, write a little original material and compose a lyric. So that is what you will find in the following pages. It should actually be entitled : an adaptation of J. S. Bach, Flute Sonata "Sicilienne." I would never venture to invent a Gershwin tune but I thought, maybe George Gershwin, entertaining a beautiful woman and needing inspiration, might very well borrow a Bach tune. So that's what I did.

The lead sheet I wrote is simple to play. But if music notation is a foreign language to any reader, you will find the song performed on YouTube, by Tierney Sutton.

STORY TIME

When the girl heard Missy coming she quickly hid her writing pad and pretended to be watching television. Missy came in with a big smile on her face, went over to close the blinds against the afternoon sun fading the rug.

"We've got a surprise for you today, Amy." She came over to Amy's wheelchair, took a hairbrush off the dresser and began to brush the girl's long brown hair gently. Missy nodded at the television.

"You'll like your surprise better than 'Miss Brooks' I bet," she said.

Amy couldn't figure out what Missy was talking about for a moment. Then she realized the show she was pretending to watch was called 'Not now, Miss Brooks.'

"I'm through watching," she said. "You can turn it off if you want."

Missy turned off the television, then came back to tuck Amy's blanket around her. Her hand encountered the writing pad under the blanket and she pulled it out.

"Oh, have you been keeping your diary again, Amy? Can I peek at it sometime?" she asked archly, one eyebrow raised.

"Maybe some day," said Amy, seriously. "But I'd rather you didn't right now. Okay?"

Missy smiled primly. "I'm sorry, honey. I didn't mean to pry." She tucked the writing pad back down under the blanket again.

She wheeled Amy down the hall and into the library, sunny and light with the sun streaming in.

"And there's your surprise!"

Amy saw a gleaming, cream colored computer on a new desk with a keyboard mounted just below and a printer to the side. Her mouth fell open but she couldn't say a word.

"Doctor Bob thought you might like it. Your teacher from last year said you were the best at the computer in the whole sixth grade."

Missy wheeled Amy over and carefully pushed her in until her knees were under the keyboard. Amy immediately picked up the mouse, pulled down the menu to the left of the screen, and studied it intently.

"Has it got Story yet?"

"Story? You mean a word processing program?"

"Uh huh. I had Story last year. It was fun and I wrote some stories. I'm a good typist."

"Well. Doctor Bob said he had some things to add. He needs to use it sometimes himself. Maybe he'll put it in later today." Missy did her best to sound as if she knew computers and all their habits.

"In the meantime, Doctor Bob left you a bunch of games." She held out a handful of CDs. Amy took them, shuffled through them rapidly. *The princess and the goblins, Treasure island, Animal farm...* A bunch of junk, she thought. But she smiled.

"These look neat. I'll have to try them." She did her best to sound enthusiastic.

As soon as Missy had left Amy pulled out her writing pad. She'd filled almost four pages, single spaced, since yesterday and her fingers were beginning to cramp. She propped the pad up behind the keyboard and started trying to find the built-in simple text that came with the computer. It wasn't a very good writing program but at least she could type her story so far and then when Doctor Bob put in Story, she could transfer it and make it a Story file.

Amy looked over the first page of her writing pad. It was messy, she'd corrected some spellings and crossed out things here and there. Now she could make a neat copy. She liked to start stories by taking a situation in some TV commercial. Commercials showed you interesting people, people you'd like to meet, but the minute you got involved they would drink beer or drive off in a pickup or something. Amy figured she could give them more exciting lives than that.

She began to copy her text.

Hank pulled his dusty red pickup off the highway and into the restaurant parking lot. He got out wiping his forehead. The sun was almost overhead and hot in the sky. He clomped towards the little cafe in his well worn boots. An old brown dog lying in the shade of the gas pumps looked up at him and wagged his tail lazily.

Janey saw him come through the door first. She was behind the counter, hot and sweating, just waiting for lunch to end so she could go somewhere else boring. She saw a tall, slim young guy just standing there looking around, pushing his hat back, the old guys in the room checking out the newcomer, them in their overalls and tractor caps. Then he saw Janey and he gave her a big smile that lit up the whole room. The old guys went back to their coffee and chili and it was like there was just the two of them there.

Hank came over to the counter and sat down on a stool, sighing. He propped his tan arms on the counter and cocked his head at Janey.

"I got tired of all this fast food stuff, last couple of days, you know? It's about all you can find on the highway anymore."

"It won't be fast, but it'll be food anyways here," said Janey, laughing. She had a teasing way about her.

"You mean good old home-cooked American food?"

"It's like home-cooked but in this place it's Indian," said Janey with an arch grin.

"Indian? You mean curry and like that?"

"Never heard of the Curry Indians," she said, "Round here you're going to get Blackfoot... Ray!" she called over her shoulder.

A face appeared at the window to the kitchen, high cheek bones, flat. black eyes expressionless. The cook had a long black braid hanging down his back.

Amy heard a door open and Doctor Bob came in saying something over his shoulder to Missy. He turned to Amy.

"Hi there scamp! What are you up to today?"

Amy quickly put her file away. "I'm just writing some stuff, Bob. Thank you so much for the computer. I just love it!"

Doctor Bob looked embarrassed.

"You don't have to thank me, honey," he said. "That's all provided for by…" He stopped for a second. "All provided for, and just about anything else you want."

Provided for by the insurance, Amy thought. She was going to change the subject but Doctor Bob spoke first.

"Missy said you asked for a Story program. I had this disk at home and I thought I'd just bring it by and we'll put it in your machine. You're supposed to buy a new one every time but we won't tell, Okay?"

Amy laughed. "I won't. Anyway sometimes the older programs are better…simpler at least."

They put the disk in and followed all the installing instructions. The computer was strong and fast and almost immediately it told them *Installation Successful.*

"There we go!" said Doctor Bob. "Now what are you going to write? And can I read it?"

Amy squirmed. "Well…I don't…"

Doctor Bob saw her discomfort and cut in, "Now don't you worry, Amy. You write anything you want. If you want to show us, that's fine. If you want it to be private, we'll never, ever pressure you. I know some of the greatest writers *never* showed their work to anyone until it was done."

And sometimes even after it was done, thought Amy. But she just smiled and started asking the doctor other questions. He helped her transfer her document to Story and made a point of looking away rapidly when her story came up on the screen for a moment.

"There you are, honey. You know this program, don't you?"

"Oh yes! We learned it at school last year. In fact, I had to show Daddy how to use it for his reports."

Doctor Bob smiled, patted her on the shoulder and walked out of the library into the hallway. Missy had been waiting there for him.

"I heard what she said...about her Daddy. I want to cry every time she..." The doctor shushed her and they walked down the hall for a bit.

"I know, I know what you mean," he said. But it's good that she can talk about them. And the writing is excellent therapy."

"You don't think she's writing about..."

"No, it's just a story. I saw 'Blackfoot' in there."

"A black foot? What in the world...?"

"No, no. 'Blackfoot' as in Blackfoot Indians." The doctor saw from her expression that she still didn't get it. He sighed and went on alone into his office. Convalescent home nurses were not always intellectual giants. But at least Missy was sweet and kind.

"Hey Ray, what's best today, the chicken fried steak or the chili size?" Janey turned to Hank again. "It's one or the other. Everything else here is lousy." She made a face and giggled.

Hank looked her over carefully. He saw a happy face, a wicked grin, mischief in the eyes. She was average cute, but he was attracted by her kidding. He liked women who were happy and kidded around. There were too few of them these days, he thought. Janey was wearing an extra large T shirt and short shorts under her apron. She started tapping her fingers on the counter.

"Okay. I think I'll have the steak. I get biscuits with that?"

"Unless we ran out. I'll see. And cream gravy too."

One of the men at a side table called to her. "Hey Janey! I get some more coffee here? Or you gonna spend all day with your beau?"

Janey called into the kitchen. "It's the steak, Ray. Biscuits with the gravy, if we got any left." Then she drew a cup from the coffee machine and walked from behind the counter to take the man his coffee. Hank checked out her figure. She had a nice behind and long tan legs. She looked back suddenly, caught him checking her out, and wiggled a hip at him, smirking.

Amy stopped writing for a moment. She was remembering how her father would watch her mother walking across the room. And her mother would whirl around and say, "Caught you, you dirty old man! What are you thinking about? What would your wife say?" And then maybe she'd wiggle her behind and they'd both laugh. Then sometimes if they both started laughing and kidding around after awhile they'd go upstairs. Amy was wondering if she would have Hank and Janey doing something like that. It seemed like so much fun, but once when she'd written a story at school about a girl and a really neat guy her teacher had this worried look on her face and she must have told her mom because her mom told her to write all the stories that came into her head, but to keep them secret.

"For school, just make up stories about things we've seen, you know, everyday things," she'd said. "And you can add makeup things to make the stories more interesting. You know, like the other day at the market when that lady got mad at the woman with the food stamps."

So Amy had written a story about a nasty lady who got mad at poor people using food stamps, but when the lady started checking her own things out the manager caught her shoplifting a bottle of vodka. It was funny, but her teacher didn't like that story either.

"What would your wife say, she saw you looking at other girls like that?" said Janey, laughing, coming back behind the counter.

"She'd say I still had a dirty mind," said Hank, grinning. "But I don't have a wife anymore. Did, but she picked up and went."

Janey's face fell. "Oh, I'm sorry. I didn't mean to...."

"No problem." Hank sort of looked down into his cup of coffee. Guess it was just one of those things, you know, college sweethearts."

"Yeah. I know all about your college sweethearts deal," said Janey, and for once her smile sort of twisted into a scowl. "I did a couple years at Boise State and had to get away from there because..." She shook her head, smiled again. "Enough of that stuff. Tell me, what're you doin' on the road, old pickup like that?

"Movin' on, movin' on," said Hank. "Left all that hurt behind. Got a pretty good chance at a job in Seattle. Turns out I do the kind of computer programming they're looking for, so they said come on out and let's see what you can do." He looked up directly into her eyes.

"I'll be there tomorrow. Want to come with me?"

Janey met his eyes, started taking her apron off and called into the kitchen. "Ray? I'm outta here." She turned back to Hank, her face alight. "Let's get going, Mr. computer dude. Seattle's fine with me."

Hank was getting up, his face suddenly unsure.

"Won't your boss get mad?"

Janey laughed, turned to the kitchen. "Hey, Ray? You mad at me?"

The impassive face appeared at the kitchen window. He looked at Janey, over at Hank, then back.

"No. Hell no. Good luck." Then he disappeared.

"I mean, your boss, the owner here..." Hank began to stutter.

"Ray is the owner, big guy." Janey grabbed him by the arm, steering him towards the door. "What's the problem? You getting cold feet?"

Hank took her by both arms, looked seriously into her face. He realized he didn't even know her name.

"No, no cold feet. You and me, babe, forever. I'd kiss you but I don't even know your name."

One of the old ranchers spoke up, "It's Janey, you dumb jerk, and if you two kids don't get outta this lousy town quick, you'll be stuck here forever." The whole room burst into laughter.

"I'm Hank," said Hank. "Don't you want to get any clothes?"

"I hate all my clothes," said Janey. She reached up and kissed him and they walked out to the truck.

Mrs. Largo was concerned. She was the director of the convalescent home and had to answer to a board of directors so that's what her normal look was, concerned. But now she was extra concerned. She had Doctor Bob with her looking at Amy's story.

"I really don't think Amy should be getting involved with stories about...about, you know...well, it's obvious what's going on in this story!"

Doctor Bob owed his appointment to Mrs. Largo so he had to look serious too. But he tried to calm her down.

"Well. I can see what you mean. But I think it's really harmless, I mean, it's just romance, and a girl her age is going to think about romance." He chuckled.

"But that's just it," said Mrs. Largo. She was a thin woman with a thin face, who wore very pale lipstick on her thin lips and had big hair a disconcerting shade of caramel.

"Can't you see? The poor girl isn't going to be able to have any kind of...you know, romance, with her injuries. Why encourage her to fantasize...Don't you agree?"

Doctor Bob obviously didn't agree. In fact, he looked very angry. But he forced himself to adopt the expression of a true scientist, considering every contingency..

"Well. You could be right, Dorothy. But she is a darling little girl. Who can tell what's going to happen in her..."

Mrs. Largo was not used to other contingencies than the ones she herself had selected. "I want you to monitor her writing very carefully," she said. "If this obsession goes on..." And she considered the subject closed and left the room. Doctor Bob carefully restored Amy's story to the file name on the screen: "Janey and Hank," and then paused, as if thinking very carefully about something. Then he left too.

Janey and Hank were driving down the long country road in the dusty red pickup. It was getting dark and the surrounding mountains were shading from tan down into dark purple. They hadn't stopped talking since they'd left the restaurant.

"Hey, wait a minute," said Hank. "We keep telling each other our life stories we won't have anything else to say and we'll be like boring old married people."

"You doofus!" said Janey, punching him on the arm. "Didn't you know old married people can know everything about each other and be even more in love?"

Hank looked over at her for a long moment. "Only one way to find out," he grinned. "How about getting married?"

Ahead of them a few miles on the winding road, coming their direction, was a big lumber truck. It started climbing a long grade and began to slow down. Behind it was a smaller truck. Its driver was annoyed and looked ahead down the road. Looked all clear, so he pulled out to pass. The lumber truck driver didn't feel like getting passed by another truck so he accelerated as much as he could on the hill. The two trucks mounted the slope straining, side by side, up towards the crest, neither one giving an inch.

At that moment, Janey spotted a sign ahead. THE TIMBERS MOTEL.

"It's like the Bible says," said Janey. "*And a sign appeared to Abraham.* You know, there's nothing else ahead until Shelby, 'bout an hour or so."

"My name's not Abraham," said Hank. "But a sign is a sign." And he pulled into the Timbers.

Mrs. Largo was looking at the computer screen, her tiny lips pressed angrily together. She hesitated, as if about to go call Doctor Bob again. Then she smiled to herself grimly, sat down at the keyboard and changed the last few lines to

"Then we'd better get on to Shelby and find a minister," said Hank"

Then she left for home.

Amy screamed in her sleep and woke up. Once again she could see the hill ahead of them on the country road, and then suddenly the two trucks coming over the crest and roaring down on them...

"No, no!" she shrieked and threw herself out of bed, her poor legs flopping on the floor. Hand over hand she clawed her way over the rug to her wheelchair and desperately pulled herself up into its seat, then frantically wheeled her way through the doorway and down the darkened hallway to the library.

Her computer was asleep so she pounded a few keys."Please, please!" she whispered, willing the screen to light up again. And there was the terrible sentence!

Amy's fingers had never flown so fast. Boom! She deleted the horrible invader's words. *Tap, tappity tappity tappity tap!* She restored the last sentence.

"My name's not Abraham," said Hank, "But a sign is a sign." And he turned into the Timbers.

Amy punched the window key and a box came up saying "Do you want to save the changes you made to "Janey and Hank"?

"Yes, yes, yes!" she moaned and clicked the "save" box. The screen went blank and she sank back into her wheelchair, tears of relief pouring down her cheeks. "Oh, yes, yes, thank you, thank you!"

Mrs. Largo was on her way home down a country road. Ahead of her a dusty red pickup turned into a motel and for a moment it reminded her of something. But it must not have been important so she put it out of her mind, driving up toward the crest of the next hill, self righteous to the last.

THAT OLD BIG SUR

Christian crested the last hill on the yellow dirt road, wrestling the wheel on the old ruts, coming over the top unexpectedly, and suddenly the whole blue Pacific smacked him in the face, forcing him to pull the old Jeep to an abrupt halt and absorb the visual impact of half a hemisphere receding into the distant haze to the west. From here there was nothing but ocean until Japan, seven thousand miles away. He was up over a thousand feet and the steepness of the slope almost gave him vertigo, looking down at the blue-green sea crashing against the cliffs, miniature waves at this distance, he couldn't even hear the surf.

So this was the Big Sur. Nothing but a huge cliff, from Monterey to what? The Hearst Castle? Two hundred miles of coastline? Something like that. He'd left the map on the back seat of the Jeep. But he'd read the guide book. The west coast here had been forced up out of the ocean millions of years ago in the geologic past and had remained perfectly remote, inaccessible, until the road was built by the WPA during the Depression. Now it was California Route 1 and famous for its wild cliffs, savage ocean, refuges for seals, sea otters, poets, the few millionaires who could afford houses on crags, and a few very protected and limited resorts.

Christian was headed for Ninkopo Kai, an old collection of hot springs right on the coast, recently a famous and fashionable refuge for damaged human beings. Ninkopo Kai was said to mean "Circle of Peace" in the Miwok Indian dialect. He'd had the recommendation from a counselor, had phoned and explained his situation. Although they usually had a waiting list eight months long the woman to whom he spoke accepted him immediately and he was amused that she had never asked for assurance that he could pay the $450 per day charges.

The road down the chaparral-covered hill wove through a collection of switchbacks until it finally joined California Highway 1 a little south of the tiny cluster of Lucia. He stopped for a cup of coffee at what looked like the only cafe in town, had to go back into the kitchen, finally into the adjoining house to find a woman, flustered before a visitor, who led him back into the cafe.

"Didn't expect anyone this early. I can fix you some toast too, if you want. Nothing else this morning. Truck from Cambria didn't get here yet. Okay?"

"That's fine. I got up early in King City, had breakfast there."

"Came over the mountain? That's a hard drive."

"Well. I'm sort of taking other roads these days. More interesting."

"There's your coffee. Here's the sugar. Oops, it's empty, just a second..."

"It's okay, really. I don't take sugar."

An hour later he saw the big rugged wooden sign. NINKOPO KAI. GUESTS ONLY. A gravel road led down toward the ocean. Now he could hear the surf booming on the cliffs below. He could also smell the faint rotten-egg odor of the famous sulfurous hot springs. The driveway led through a circle of wooden buildings and he saw the sign, RECEPTION.

He was expecting to meet the head guru, or at least some enthusiastic disciple, but there was only a spotty teenage girl in the office wearing engineer overalls from which her fat arms sprouted like white sausages. She showed no interest, avoided eye contact, gave him two towels, a white terrycloth robe, and the key to cabin 6.

"I probably don't need a key here," he chuckled. "Who am I keeping out?"

"Suit yourself," the drab replied and went back into the office.

Margot had been checking out the new arrivals. Most of the women fit into the Hapless Recent Divorcée category. She had to admit that she could almost fit into that group, except her two previous divorces had given her some perspective. The few men seemed to be a complete loss. At a place like this you could count on at least one scrawny guy in his fifties, half-bald, but with a brave gray ponytail, glasses, and a distressing compulsion to tell anyone in earshot how liberating this whole thing was. She'd seen the first one come in an hour ago, followed shortly by someone who could be his twin, except they were complete strangers to each other. Then there was a plump younger man who had been wandering around in a black bikini since he got here. Nobody would have to explain their life stories until tonight. It wasn't as if she couldn't wait.

And then, hello?! A dusty Jeep pulled up to the reception and a slim young guy got out, stretched, and walked into the office. He could have been a hot young hunk in a beer commercial.

Margot instantly looked around at the circle of cabins to see if anyone else was checking out newcomers. They were. Across the oval of the driveway she could see the young girl—what was her name? Penny, or something—staring a hole in the man's back. Penny was one of those fragile beauties without a bone in her body, had to have someone to cling to, it was obvious. She'd started to tell Margot her whole story at breakfast and had been discouraged gently at first and then almost rudely. *She looks like she's going to run over and attach herself like a refrigerator magnet,* thought Margot.

Now she saw a movement behind the window of the next cabin. That would be Deirdre, a tall mountain woman in jeans and a leather jacket, hair in a long braid.

The two women who'd come from Berkeley together were walking up the rocky path from the beach when the man came out of the office and they froze in their tracks, watching him stride across the compound looking for number six, pack slung over one shoulder, discovering his cabin, and disappearing into it. *So,* thought Margot, *maybe they're not lesbians after all.*

Christian found himself in a one-room cabin, all old knotty pine, gingham curtains on the windows. The single bed was covered with a threadbare chenille spread. There was a nightstand, a wooden desk with a chair, and an old dark brown naugahyde recliner. A small dresser stood next to the door of the bathroom. He unpacked his two changes of clothes rapidly and stored them neatly in the dresser. Then he took the Bible out of his pack and sat down in the recliner. He looked at his watch. They said drinks were at five, supper at six, and the big meeting in the hot spring at eight. Time to consult his Bible.

Hungry for companionship, the new group at Ninkopo Kai heard the bell announcing cocktail hour and rushed over to the main building, where they circulated eagerly, milling and clustering like dogs just unleashed at the beach. They adhered to the written rules: first names only, small talk only, no politics or sexual innuendo, absolutely no biographical details. That was all left to the big moment, the moment in the huge heated pool after dinner, when they'd had a chance to digest their food a bit. Nothing had been said about drugs, and Christian noticed a plump young man with sleek dark hair in Gucci warmups trying to pass around a joint, being politely turned down by everyone except a scrawny man with a gray ponytail.

And into their midst bounced the guru, Hans Katzen, a small, almost shriveled old man, but radiating good cheer, wearing a floor length Egyptian *gelebiya*. He rapidly made the circle of the twelve guests, addressing them by name, stopping by Margot for a second—"Glad to see you again, my dear, good luck!"—flashing her a splendid smile, and off to Christian.

"Christian, Christian! So good to see you! I read your application. You'll be one of our stars in the hot spring later!" And then on to the plump young man, saying something quietly that made him stub out the rest of his joint and slip the roach into a pocket of his warmup jacket.

Dinner was simple and adequate. Rice, broccoli, and carrots on a big platter with an olive oil and lemon dressing, and another platter of baked chicken and onions, sprinkled with fresh herbs from the kitchen garden. Lots of brown bread cooked in Ninkopo Kai's own outdoor clay ovens. Something for everyone. Carafes of white and red wine were passed and drunk. There were no dietary laws at Ninkopo Kai, no prudery.

After dinner Hans Katzen shooed everyone out into the evening air. "Walk around! Enjoy the moon! Listen to the waves crashing below! Relax, free your minds of anxiety, stress, give up all the silly rules you have set yourself. And remember, this is the hour of silence. Smile at each other but do not talk. In one hour—actually now, forty minutes—we meet at the great pool, the place of peace! Wear your bathrobes to the pool, but if no one told you yet, when you get there you have to take all your clothes off, all your old attitudes, all your childish whining, any phony baggage you might have brought here by mistake...and get in the pool of peace the way you were on the day you were born!" There was general nervous laughter. Christian had felt discouraged so far. Now he was impressed by Katzen's manner and he wondered, *How good can he be? How does this compare to the confessional?*

The great pool had a shingled roof supported on redwood logs set upright like pillars in the concrete pad, but it was completely open on the sides and the fog had begun to blow in from the Pacific. A few overhead lights shone down on the steaming surface, gurgling at the north end where the natural hot spring funneled the sulfurous water in. There was a small raft tethered in the middle of the pool, covered with candles of all sizes and shapes, flickering, but staying lit despite the breeze.

Christian slipped off his bathrobe and climbed quickly down into the pool to escape the frigid air and welcome the heat of the water, which always remained five or so degrees above body temperature. There was a shallow seat in the concrete, he found, and he could sit with his head just above water while his legs stretched out along the bottom of the pool. He'd been concentrating too much on undressing and getting into the pool to observe anyone else, except a blond nymphet on the other side who took her time submerging, oohing and ahhing, and splashing water up onto her small breasts. He thought she was the one who hadn't said anything at dinner, just looked defeated and hurt. Hans Katzen appeared, nude, at the end of the pool, still short and wiry, standing for a moment at the edge to look over his flock. Then he stepped gradually down into the steaming water. There was complete silence, broken only by the cries of gulls out over the water. Then Hans spoke.

"Please hold hands with your neighbors, don't be shy."

There was some squirming, as the twelve-plus-one bodies in the pool nervously searched for a neighboring hand.

"That's right, get closer together. The pool is shallow, and there are no monsters in the middle." Nervous laughter again.

"Now, the rules you have agreed to. First, let me stress the subtitle in our literature, 'a place for damaged human beings.' Do you all fit that model?" All heads nodded.

"Then I should remind you that 'damaged human beings' in this case, means California human beings, not, for instance, Rwandans or Kosovars."

There was dead silence. Margot thought, *That was brutal. That little reminder. Good for him! Better than last time.*

"Next, there are no religions here except the religion of humans living together in peace and, whenever possible, love of each other. If you are true believers in some creed, go happily back to it when you leave, but do not speak of it here. You are on spiritual sabbatical." Chuckles, and the plump young man said, "Right on!"

"Finally, we hope nevertheless to repair some of the California-type damage you've suffered. Tonight we will take a little test, like a college test. I'm sure you've all been to university? Hold up your hands?" All hands went up.

"All right, the test question we ask here is, in three minutes, identify yourself and explain your significance."

There was general laughter. They'd all taken those ID tests.

And we'll start with...Penny!"

Margot thought immediately, A *stroke of genius! Get rid of the worst, whiniest, boring casualty first!*

Actually, Penny surprised them all. She'd been in med school with this guy and they'd gotten married and like one of them had to work to keep med school going so she quit and worked as a nurse and he got his MD and started to get rich and then he dumped her. She poured all this out in about five minutes, although everyone had figured her as a half- hour whiner, and people actually wanted her to go on. But the rules were, no questions, no rebuttals, just go around the circle. There would be two more nights, after all.

Most of the others were boring: he dumped me, women always reject me, Margot was almost going to sleep when one of the scrawny ponytails came on with this story about the lab he worked in and he had done the work and the research and then they told him he was out, the company owned all the proprietary stuff he'd developed and he was causing problems. This sounded like a real-world problem, not a Ninkopo Kai-style bruised psyche.

Margot told her carefully rehearsed story, which got as little attention as it deserved, and then Hans Katzen looked over at Christian, pointedly skipping over the plump young man, who had desperately tried to break in after the last four life stories.

"Christian. Or should I call you 'Father'?"

There was an intake of breath all around the pool. Christian felt his hand squeezed by the woman next to him—Margot, was that her name? The man on the other side almost let go his grip.

"Please, no fathers, no brothers. That's all over."

"Marvelous! I love your name, Christian. So appropriate. Can you identify yourself and give your significance?"

"Well." *Here it was. Could he go through with it?* "Well, I was raised a Catholic. The whole thing. I was an altar boy, then went to seminary up in San Rafael, then on to Loyola and I guess I never really considered there was anything else to do with my life until one day, there I was, a Jesuit priest."

The audience was quiet and respectful. The world was full of Jesuit priests who had left the priesthood. Everyone knew at least one.

"So then I had this big crisis. Here I was, twenty-six years old. And Iraq and Rwanda and Darfur in the papers every day, massacres and war everywhere, and things seeming just to get worse everywhere in the world, even in the inner cities here in California. Anyway, one day it just hit me in the face. I didn't feel I could go on one minute longer just teaching history and theology at this little college because...because the history and the theology just seemed to contradict each other. And when I asked for guidance my superiors...anyway, you don't all want to hear that stuff. And I'm not going to knock my church, even though I left it."

He stopped and there was silence until Hans asked quietly, "And what have you been doing since then, Christian?"

He chuckled sheepishly. "Nothing, actually. I told my order that I was resigning, I got into my Jeep and came here."

Somewhere in the world, hidden in some precious, protected wonderland, there might have been a female who didn't immediately understood what Christian was saying. All the women in the pool at Ninkopo Kai felt something like the jolt of an electric current go through them, the current amplified by the hot water in which they were all sitting. And the questions began, in spite of the rule against them.

"So, Christian, you've always been a priest until just now?"

"Well, yeah..."

"And before that, you were always studying for the priesthood?"

"Right." A beat or too in the silence of the night. "So," Margot finally said it. "You've never made love to a woman in your entire life?" There it was.

Christian laughed nervously. "I guess so. I mean, no. Not that...not that, uh..." he went on quickly. "Not that I don't know all about sex, men and women, and men and men, and you name it...after all, I heard confession for quite a few years. But no, you're right. I never actually had sex with anyone, although I sure felt like it sometimes and I had to confess that and do the penance and try to put it out of my mind."

Hans Katzen had been listening intently instead of enforcing the no-questions rule. Now he broke in.

"Christian, that was some identification and you really explained your significance. But we're going to go on and leave the interaction until tomorrow when we get into some heavy group stuff, okay? Now, Wendell, you've been bursting with your story. Let's hear it!" And he turned to the plump young man who began talking immediately, and no one heard a single word he said.

Margot walked up to the door of her cabin and just waited there, watching, until she saw Christian coming down the path, turning, then going up his steps. She immediately walked quickly across the lawn and was at his door before he had closed it all the way. She pushed in after him and he turned in surprise.

"Christian," she said. "You didn't think you could say what you did and just come in and go to sleep, did you?" She grinned at him maliciously.

He cocked his head, gave her a blank look, a glimmer of a smile. "You know, I'm not dumb. Jesuits aren't. Ever since I decided to come here I knew that when I said...when I said what I did, that it would cause at least some reaction."

Margot closed the door behind her, then turned and locked it. "Okay, Christian, if you're not dumb then you won't be surprised. Here's the reaction." And she let her bathrobe slip off her shoulders. They'd just been in the pool naked together. Naked in a small room with a bed in it was different. Christian was petrified, helplessly staring at her body, so Margot stepped forward, took his hands and placed them on her breasts. Then she parted his robe, placed her hands behind his back, and pulled his hips to hers, held him tightly. She was almost a head shorter so she had to stretch her head up.

"Kiss me, you idiot. You must have heard how to do that in confession." It was a long kiss, and he got his arms around her, and then finally figured out the tongue part, and then Margot pushed him back onto his bed and got on top of him.

"Get ready for prime time," she said, and reaching behind her, guided his prominent and by now very unpriestly member into the right place.

Margot had expected it to be fast but the action took longer than she expected and she was quite thrilled by the time a ragged cry burst from his throat and the grip of his strong arms threatened to crush her. They lay for a while in silence and when he started to say something she shushed him. "This is the time that the first person who speaks says something stupid," she said.

But after they'd eased apart, still holding each other, they talked, and he seemed in a rush to explain that this wasn't what he'd expected—maybe he'd hoped to meet someone, get to know her, and then, maybe... Margot had to explain that the unexpected presence of a twenty-six year old man, a good-looking man with a great bod (and she ran her hand over his tight buns and his thigh) who had never had a woman, might conceivably cause a violent reaction in some women, maybe even many women. So Christian asked her why she was here and she told him about the kind of men who were attracted to her and why it always seemed a fatal mistake. He couldn't stop looking at her, "Your belly is like a heap of wheat," he said. "And I shall lie between thy breasts all night."

"What's that?" Margot asked. "Gibran or someone?"

"A little older." He smiled. "The Song of Songs, in the Bible."

"Oh," she said. "But I'm Jewish."

"That's okay. It's in the Jewish part of the Bible." They both laughed.

"Shows you how good a Jew I am," Margot added.

And then, just as she could feel him becoming aroused again, there was a soft knock on the door.

"Don't move," she ordered him. Quickly moving to the door she opened it a crack and saw Penny standing there in a lacy nightgown, wispy blond hair outlined by the moonlight, a rose in one hand and a bottle of wine in the other.

"Beat it," Margot said and closed the door.

"What was that?" asked Christian.

"Room service," Margot said. "What did you expect?" She snuggled down next to him, kissed him, whispered in his ear, "That first time was the basic model. Now we're going to customize you. Give me your hand a minute..."

First light was coming over the Big Sur to the east when Margot finally slipped out the door and walked quickly back to her own cabin. It was noon before she finally appeared for lunch. Christian was nowhere to be seen Most of the guests had chosen to drive into Carmel to shop or eat lunch, so she was stuck with Wendell and Deirdre and one of the Berkeley women. She wondered how many of the group had heard about where she spent the night. The four of them managed to stay on neutral topics.

As the afternoon wore on Margot had to admit to herself that she felt like a high school kid again, a kid with almost a painful crush. She couldn't wait for Christian to get back.

But cocktail hour arrived and Christian never came back.

"Oh, he checked out this morning," said the creepy girl in the office, where Margot had finally gone in desperation. She slumped. *Dammit, I came on too strong! But he fucked like a hero all night! What could have happened?* She was trying to imagine something she'd said or done. And then came the terrible blow.

"And that girl, Penny? She checked out the same time."

Margot managed to stick it out that evening in the pool, avoiding the eager group repartee. Hans tried to get her involved but he'd obviously heard about her adventure and Christian's disappearance so he didn't press it.

She checked out herself the next morning before breakfast, unwilling for any of the rest to see her go.

Margot produced the eleven o'clock news on a big television station in Los Angeles. She threw herself back into work, thinking she'd get over the Christian thing. But it kept bugging her and her mind kept going to the back of a business card in her wallet where she'd scribbled down the license number of his dusty Jeep. Finally she couldn't help it. She called an old friend at the Los Angeles headquarters of the California Highway Patrol.

"Conrad? I got a license number. I need the name and address, okay?...I know you're not supposed to...I know...Okay, let's say I'll owe you one...No, nothing'll come back on this...No, no, it's not political, it's personal..."

Two minutes later she was jotting down, "Townsend, Christian," and the address, obviously an apartment, in Santa Clara. "Thanks so much, Conny. I'll call you later."

She waited two days, then couldn't stand it any more. She called in sick first thing in the morning. By early afternoon she was looking up streets on a Santa Clara street map. There was the apartment building, a nice one, with lawns around it, a swimming pool visible in the interior courtyard, spacious balconies on all the upper floors. She couldn't see an old Jeep parked anywhere. She was standing on the walkway below, just figuring out where apartment number 207 would be when a woman came out on the balcony and started watering plants. Margot couldn't hide. It was obvious she was staring right up at that apartment.

"Are you looking for someone?" the woman asked. She was a slim brunette and did not appear to be in a good mood. She took off her sunglasses and inspected Margot carefully.

Margot was an experienced reporter. She didn't make many mistakes locating addresses. And yet she nursed a faint hope that she'd got the wrong number, the wrong block.

"Uh, does Christian live here?"

The woman didn't answer for the longest moment. Silence filled the hot afternoon.

"Okay, what was he this time? Was he a priest again?"

Margot couldn't face her. She walked slowly back to her car. All she could think of was Christian's face, contorted in passion, as he pretended that he was having his first...

But the woman wasn't through. She called to Margot's retreating back. "And listen, if you're Penny, don't bother leaving any more poetry on the e-mail." And she went back into the apartment.

THE RABBIT FARM

Julio began to worry about the offramp they'd taken twenty minutes or so after they'd crossed the George Washington bridge. But it didn't bother him too much because Mrs. Shapiro had the map, after all. He was still cruising on a couple of tokes of the killer weed his pal Nigel had given him back at the garage before he took the bus to the school to pick up the kids. He figured the teacher, Mrs. Shapiro, would straighten it out. After all, he was only the bus driver, she was the boss, this was her class, and the kids were all happy in the back of the bus, singing some songs now. Only problem was, Mrs. Shapiro had been moaning the last half hour about her bladder infection and Julio wasn't sure she was paying attention to what was going on.

After leaving New York City you really get into some pure country in a hurry, the other side of the river, and Julio began looking around on those little roads for any kind of street sign, name of town, whatever, even if it wasn't his job. They were driving through lanes of trees with turning leaves in the early fall, red, yellow, the kind everybody talked about. And then Mrs. Shapiro said, this must be it, the third left, so he turned the bus and now the road was even narrower, dark, trees on all sides, and Julio would've suggested going back and asking someone, anyone--even behind that good dope he was getting worried--and then they saw the sign: MACDONALD'S RABBIT FARM.

The kids saw it too. They were third grade after all, they spotted the sign as the bus slowed down and they all cheered. They were all smart kids, from that private school up on Riverside Drive. Parents all tops in the professions. Julio liked the kids and drove the bus a lot for the school even though it paid less than some other assignments. Little guys were funny, could joke with him, told him about vacations they took in places he never heard of. The kids were carrying on now,

"Old MacDonald had a farm. Ee-aye ee-aye oh," and so forth.

Mrs. Shapiro had thought it was McDougall, or McDermott? McDermott's Bunny Farm and Petting Barn, a famous day trip for all the younger grades in Manhattan private schools. But at the moment she felt as if her urethra was transfixed by a red hot needle. She was in agony, and when she saw the pleasant faced middle-aged woman standing by the driveway and waving her hand her only feeling was relief, this must be the place, finally. She forced herself to her feet as Julio opened the bus door.

"Hi, hi, hi! We're here!" she said, trying to sound half way alive, bright, in control, a responsible teacher.

"Great! Sounds good!"

"Okay, kids! Out of the bus, we're at the Farm!

They needed no encouragement, scurrying down the bus steps, spreading in all directions, desperate for any kind of activity after an hour clustered in the yellow bus.

"You must be...uh, Mrs. McDermott?"

"Hi, hi. Yes. Great, great! Sounds Las good!" The woman came up, took both of Mrs. Shapiro's hands in hers. She had such a warm, friendly face, such trust..."

"Mrs. McDermott, you'll have to forgive me but I've suddenly had an urgent attack of a...a problem with my bladder, and I'm going to go back to Patterson or somewhere with my driver, see if I can find a clinic. I hate to miss the orientation, but I should be back in an hour. Do you think you can handle the kids until then?"

"Great, great! Sounds good!" The woman's face lit up in an enthusiastic smile. Mrs. Shapiro was just barely able to wave at the children, yell to them, "Take care now!" and then she was back in the bus, telling Julio, "Let's get out of here, back towards the bridge, there's got to be a walk-in clinic in Patterson somewhere, maybe before, we'll look in the phonebook.

The bus drove off. The rollicking of the children gradually tapered off and they started to mill around the nearest identifiable adult. As the pleasant woman at the edge of the driveway showed no signs of leading them off, or signs of anything, for that matter, Peter Maddy spoke to her. Peter was a leader, or a trouble maker, depending on the day of the week, but he always seemed to be able to grasp what what was going on, even though he was one of the younger ones, at eight.

"So. When do we start the tour?" he asked the pleasant woman. She looked down at him, smiled, then turned back to the road as a car went by. She waved, said, "Hi, hi. Great! Sounds good!" She paid no more attention to the children.

Peter looked mildly puzzled, which wasn't normal for him, and Alexandra, who could sense any stray emotion wafting around, instantly seized his arm.

"What's the matter, Petey?"

"I don't know, I don't think this is Mrs. MacDonald, or something! Maybe..."

But at just that moment all the children saw a large man walking up the driveway. If they had been slightly worried about the place they had been dropped—"dumped" is the word for it, said Bobby later—they were immediately reassured by the appearance of this man. This was a farmer. He was huge, larger than anyone's father, older too, he was wearing overalls and a blue work shirt, and he had a big tan cap on his head and hair growing out of his ears. At the moment he was smiling and trying to get the attention of the woman at the end of the driveway.

"Christina? What's going on here? Come on child, time to go inside for a while."

The woman turned and obediently took his hand. He was looking around at the crowd of children, over twelve of them, near as he could tell. They started walking back to a complex of buildings nestled in the pines.

"Now, who can tell me what all of you are doing here?" he asked, still grinning. "I'm Mr. MacDonald."

"We're from the Walton Riverside School," said Peter, appointing himself the leader in this uncertain situation. "We have the day tour today." He looked around. "Mrs. Shapiro should be here but I think she was sick."

"Her inside was burning," said Alexandra, dramatically. "That's what she was saying."

"Mrs. Shapiro?" said farmer MacDonald, his forehead creasing to indicate thought processes. "So Mrs. Shapiro would know what was going on?"

"We know too," said Leah Green. "We heard about it in class. We're going to see the bunnies and pat the animals." She gulped in embarrassment and tried to sink into the ground. Leah did not like to talk out of turn.

"Well, Lord, you can sure look at the bunnies! Take all day if you want! Is this one of those County Mental Health things?" The children just looked at each other. Farmer MacDonald was thinking it over. "'Cause they were saying Christina needed more visitors and they were going to arrange something, I don't know."

Seeing the children's bewildered expression he put on his cheerful expression again.

"That must be it. So you'll be Christina's visitors and I'll show you all over the farm. I'm sorry. I must've missed a phone call from the County or something. Come on, let's go!"

"Why does Christina have to have visitors?" asked Bobby Kooper. Christina beamed when she heard her name spoken and waved to Bobby, saying, "Hi, hi. Sounds good!"

Farmer MacDonald put his arm around Christina, who immediately put her head against his shoulder and smiled sweetly at the children.

"Christina's my daughter. You see, she's simple. She's a big woman, you can see, forty years old, but inside her head she's your age, maybe even younger. But she's a good worker, aren't you honey?"

"I'm a good worker, Daddy, sounds good!"

"So. We're all set! Let's go see the rabbits." But Christina interrupted. "Hot chocolate, Daddy! Time for hot chocolate!"

Farmer MacDonald stopped and looked back. "Darn, child! You're right! We should all have some hot chocolate. And maybe somebody needs to use the bathroom too?"

With this, Farmer MacDonald won the hearts and minds of the Walton Riverside third grade. Some of the children had never had to feel anxiety about the availability of a bathroom before and were just beginning to feel the first pangs of urgency, perhaps influenced by Mrs. Shapiro's fairly explicit complaints all the way out here on the bus. So the pace picked up as they all walked towards the ancient, two story frame house, grey and weather stained.

* * *

Dr. Singh looked at Mrs. Shapiro gravely. She had managed to find an emergency clinic in the first town they'd come to, which to her surprise was Pompton Lakes, rather than Patterson. Dr. Singh had taken her temperature and a urine specimen and then quickly took some blood and rushed into his lab. Now he was worried.

"Mrs. Shapiro. You have a temperature of one-hundred-and-two degrees and your bloodcount is much too high. I worry that your bladder infection may reach your kidneys, and then you have problems!"

"But Doctor, I have to get back to my kids, they're on a day trip and..."

"My receptionist will call your school to tell them the situation. I am sufficiently worried that I will drive you to the hospital myself. You are in risk of toxic shock and the sooner the better. Nadine!" he called out the door, "I'm driving to Saint Luke's. Will you kindly take the information from Mrs. Shapiro's driver?"

And he bustled Mrs. Shapiro, protesting, but not very vigorously, out the door.

"What's going on? What was that all about?" Nadine asked Julio. She was a plump blond young woman and they had been discussing a recent salsa special on MTV while the doctor was examining Mrs. Shapiro.

"Hey, ain't no big deal," said Julio. "I'll go back to the farm and wait for the kids. Coming out here I know the roads now. Can I give you a call later, maybe? Could go dance some salsa, you know." He gave her a splendid smile and was out the door before Nadine remembered to ask for the number of the school.

* * *

It was Marla who caught the call at the Walton Riverside School. There was a breathy voice on the phone.

"Hi. This is Antonia at the McDermott Bunny Farm. Did we get our wires crossed or something? I thought your third grade was coming in this morning?"

"Well, sure. They'll be there any..." and then Marla looked at the clock and saw the time, almost two hours late.

"Oh my God!" she said. "They left here at eight-thirty! Our bus company is always..." and then she realized abruptly what she had to do. "I have to check immediately. I'll get back to you! Sorry about the..." And she hung up the phone.

Like all staff at the Walton Riverside School Marla knew the first thing she had to do was check to see just who the parents were of the children on board the missing bus. Third grade, let's see, here we are.

A. Buffington, that's Alexandra, of course. Father is...partner in Rentschler Buffington Schnee, brokerage, a Wall Street address. Not so good.

P. Maddy, son of Jane Maddy, separated from father P. Emerson Maddy, attorney.

E. Smith, um..um...no one important, thank God.

L. Green, that would be that dumb little daughter of...oh my God... the US ambassador to the United Nations. Ulp! Getting worse!

McF. Erickson, that's McFee--where do they get these names--daughter of the divorced wife of the Secretary of the Air Force? Jesus Christ!

And now, R. Kooper, that would be Bobby, the little klutz, and he's the son of...the Attorney General of Connecticut.

Marla saw there were still eight names left, considered her options, including pretending she'd never taken the call and going out to lunch. But she knew that wouldn't work and that the prudent thing was just to pass off to higher authority. She pressed a button on her console.

"Mrs. Walton, I believe we have a problem here. Could I come see you for a moment?"

* * *

"Well, here's the rabbits," announced Farmer McDonald. Some of 'em anyway. We got two other sheds."

They were all standing inside a long roofed structure with only partial walls. Down each side was a long row of cages, four feet off the ground, and the children could see white creatures in every cage. Underneath the cage rows was a long carpet of straw beginning to fill up with rabbit pellets. There was no mystery about the source of the pellets. The cage bottoms were of wire mesh and the children could see pellets falling from here and there, and now and then a flash of urine.

"These are the mommies," said Christina, proudly.

"That's right," said her father. "These are all breeding mothers, or about to be. You can see them charts on every cage, tell when they're going to have babies. The bigger young ones, they're all in the north shed. We let them run around together."

"Peeyou!" exclaimed Alexandra, who like all the others was amazed at the amount of excrement on the ground.

"Oh, peeyou, peeyou!" Some of the boys mocked her for her daintiness. "It's just rabbit poop," said Everett Chung.

"Rabbit poop! Of course that's what it is!" exclaimed Mr. MacDonald and Christina giggled. "But you see we're all organic here. We let all the poop and the pee fall on straw instead of on the ground. Rake it up every day, every pellet, and store it in that big composter over there by the woods. Come spring, every year, there's better'n a ton in there."

"But what do with it?" asked Alexandra, making a face.

"Fertilizer," said Bobby. "They put it on plants."

"See! Is he a smart kid?" MacDonald said to his daughter. "Fertilizer is right! And the part what's worked down to the bottom gate is the best stuff in the world. It don't smell and there's not a germ in it! We sack it and sell it all over the state. If you've ever eaten New Jersey strawberries you've had a bit of MacDonald rabbit poop in there, somewhere."

The children were tickled pink at this choice nugget of information. They all giggled and nudged each other and many of them began trying to imagine where they could first display their new knowledge.

A horn sounded and a white refrigerator truck turned slowly down the gravel lane next to the sheds. A sign on the side identified it as *Butler's Meats. Wholesale Restaurant Supply and Catering.* A cheerful young redhaired man in white coveralls got out.

"Mornin' Mac! You got that order ready?"

"By golly, Billy! I forgot you were coming this morning! But the order's ready, we just gotta box it..." He looked around at the children.

"And we got some great little helpers here, don't we? You all want to help us load this gentleman's order?"

Few of the children had ever been asked to help do some real grownup thing that working people did. So they all nodded eagerly and followed Mr. MacDonald to the end of the shed, where there was a big walk-in cold room.

MacDonald indicated a long stainless steel table just outside the entrance to the cold room..

"Christina, honey, you get the boxes ready there at the end. You kids, just line up along the table and we'll make a bucket brigade, just pass the little darlings along. Chris, she knows how to pack 'em just right."

And before the children could react here came the little skinned rabbit bodies, pink and scrunched up, cold and dry, and the children had to pass them along the line to Christina, who was unfolding waxed cardboard boxes with great concentration, her tongue sticking out of the left side of her mouth as she tried to remember which side of the box pulled out and where the slots fitted.

Farmer MacDonald kept talking, which helped keep the more horrified children from thinking about what they were handling.

"Half the rabbit you're going to eat in a New York restaurant comes from here. They know they can count on MacDonald rabbit. You know, years ago, they had laws, you had to leave the rabbit's head and paws on, so customers would know it was a rabbit instead of a cat."

"A cat?" expostulated Leah, in spite of herself. "Eat a kitty?"

"Well, of course, no one wants to eat a kitty, that's the whole point. But back when I was your age, we were real poor, down there in Newark, lots of people were really poor, and if you could catch a poor cat in an alley and kill it and skin it, cut the head and the paws off, it wasn't that hard to pass it off as a rabbit, maybe make forty cents or so. Not very good eating, I should say. Tasted part of one once."

"You ate a kitty?" This from Bobby. There was dead silence from the other children.

"Didn't mean to. My sis went to the market instead of Mom. Mom was sick, actually dying then, though we didn't know."

MacDonald gave sort of a rueful chuckle and shook his head, as if just thinking about all those jokes life could play on you.

"Sis thought she was buying a rabbit at a real good price. Those days we'd put a rabbit, or a chicken if we were lucky, in the pot, a lot of onions and water and boil it up. Potatoes too, if we had one or two left. Turnips sometimes. They were real cheap but we were sick of them. Whole thing was to stretch everything out so all five of us could eat something. Momma was in bed and she was hungry. She was eating her meat and potatoes and soup out of the bowl but Pa, at the kitchen table, he put his spoon down.

Time Momma got through he went and took her bowl and kissed her, told her to go back to sleep. Then he closed her door, came back in the kitchen, and told us in a soft voice.

'Mother needed her food, so I didn't say nothin'. But that was a cat we put in the pot. I can't eat it and you don't have to either.' Well we all knew something was wrong with that taste so that night we all went hungry. And now we're all done! All the little guys packed away! We couldn't have done it without you, could we Christina?"

"That's right, Daddy! Great, great! Sounds good!"

The meat truck had gone, Farmer MacDonald let all the children wash their hands at the faucet, and then Esmé Smith, against all odds, was the one who asked the question uppermost in all minds.

"Mr. MacDonald? Who kills the bunnies?"

The farmer bent over to look closely at the little girl, a colorless girl who could get lost in a crowd, wispy light brown hair, a sort of heavy face and lumpy body, but right now, very intense eyes, dark brown eyes.

"Well, honey, we have to kill them. They're our friends, we raise them up, feed 'em, and all, and there's only one reason we raise 'em. So someone can eat them. So we don't like to do it, but we do it. Doesn't hurt them a bit, they don't know it even happened."

"How do you kill them?" asked Peter Maddy.

"We gotta do a dozen or so today." MacDonald looked doubtful. "You sure you're supposed to see all this?

Half the children were goggle-eyed and silent, mouths open. The other half, mostly the boys, immediately responded.

"Oh yes! We're supposed to see everything!."

"Well...okay. Christina, let's go over to the next shed and start on that batch."

There was an ominous machine on a bench. Christina brought a rabbit out of a big hutch full of young rabbits running around.

"Old Chris! She's great with the young ones! They come right up to her fingers when she wiggles them, she can pick 'em right up, not scared at all. Now we just take this little guy, and you know, all rabbits like to go into holes, so we put his little head through here, he starts to stretch out, and..."

The machine made a click and Farmer MacDonald brought back the twitching body of the rabbit, missing its head and bleeding furiously at the neck. One glance at the faces of his audience was enough for him to decide that perhaps they weren't supposed to see everything. Only Peter Maddy ducked around the other side of the machine to see where the head had gone.

"Christina, honey. It's getting along to be lunchtime. Why don't you take your friends into the kitchen for some lunch. I think we'll fry up that bag of rabbit wings."

This was a fortunate phrase. The image of the headless rabbit was driven from the children's minds by the mention of rabbit wings.

"Uh, Christina," asked Alexandra, as they were walking up to the house. "Did your father say rabbit wings?"

"Rabbits don't have wings!" exclaimed Everett Chung. Some of the girls giggled and Bobby Kooper flapped his arms.

"They're the best part," said Christina, calmly. "You wait and see."

The mystery was solved when farmer MacDonald rejoined them in the large kitchen, where Christina had set out a big metal bowl and was now taking a plastic bag out of the refrigerator.

"They're just the little front legs. We call 'em wings 'cause they're like chicken wings. Bony and hard to eat, but they got the most flavor. Sometimes the restaurants only want the thighs and saddle. So we keep the wings, eat 'em all the time."

* * *

Jane Maddy picked up the phone.

"It's me, babe. What's it look like for tonight?"

"Oh! Mario! God! Thank God you called! I've been going crazy! The school called about an hour ago and said the bus never showed up at the...uh...whatever, wherever the kids were going today on this day trip. They said, 'Don't worry,' but Jesus! How can I not..."

"Where was Peter going?"

"Oh, some goddamn farm in New Jersey, they were going to pet rabbits or something. Now stop laughing! It's serious!"

"Hey, Janey, it's just a mixup of some kind. Kids at that school have such important families, something like this happens, everybody starts thinking 'Hostage situation!'"

"Well, it could be..."

"Come on babe! Listen, I'll make some phone calls, find out if the feds or anybody is alerted. I'll let you..."

"Oh God! If you would, Mario."

"Count on it! Now here's the picture. I got a serious final permit hearing this afternoon. About forty acres for a mall in south Jersey. It's going to be a dogfight, all your environmentalists out there as usual. I get through with that I'd like to get out of the combat zone and relax for a while. Petey gets home okay, what's tonight look like?"

"God! I'd love to see you! Petey will too!"

Mario chuckled. "I dunno, babe. I don't think your kid's warmed up to me yet, last couple of times I was over."

"Mario! Come on! Just 'cause he called you 'godfather?' He saw the video over at Alexandra's house last week, and I don't know how her crazy parents can let her watch stuff like that. You're the only Italian he knows!"

"American, American, babe! Third generation? MBA from Dartmouth? How WASP can you get? Look, I gotta run. Just remember, no hostage situation!"

* * *

"It's very possibly a hostage situation," said the Director of the FBI. He was on the phone to the Secretary of the Airforce, who had just called him again in a panic. "I've called the top state police people in New Jersey and they're trying to get organized, but in that corner of New Jersey, up there by the border, there're about forty little jurisdictions, one cop towns, you know what I mean?"

"My wife is going crazy! My ex-wife, that is. She's blaming it all on me, thinks I'm the target!"

"Mac, it's hard to say. I got the list of parents from the school the first time you called and we have three, maybe four parents, net worth up there in the mid-eight figures, couple others like you with national security exposure. We can't figure out who's the target. I'll keep in touch. Is there anything you can be doing?"

"Right now? I gotta tell you off the record, Fred, but I scrambled a U2 out of McGuire, soon as I heard, and the guy's up there now plotting every yellow bus in northern New Jersey on a computer map. He thinks it's a training problem."

"That's super, Mac. We get the reports on the normal local school bus traffic the computer should spot the odd one right away! Okay! I'll be in close touch!"

* * *

After an hour of frustrated driving on country roads Julio finally saw a familiar turnoff. A few minutes later he turned into the MacDonald farm driveway and parked under some big trees. He'd stopped for a large lunch at a burger joint on the highway and thought he'd be safe taking a little nap. He couldn't see the kids anywhere, they must be on the tour or whatever it was. So he went back to the long back seat and turned in.

* * *

The little rabbit wings were popping around beautifully in the big fat fryer. The children were enthusiastically dredging the last raw ones in flour and seasonings in the big bowl, shaking them off and passing them for Christina to put in the fat.

"Best thing to go with that is good farm bread and some cole slaw," said Farmer MacDonald. He was passing cabbage heads over a shredder into a bowl with a puddle of lemon juice, olive oil, and mayonnaise on the bottom. "The slaw here cuts the grease."

A few moments later the children sat down around the big kitchen table. A few chairs from living room and study had been dragged in to make up the number. There was a steaming pile of golden rabbit wings on a huge platter, a bowl of cole slaw, and a basket of bread.

"Christina, bring some forks for the slaw, honey." He explained to the children, "You gotta have a fork for the slaw, but you just grab those legs at the end and chew 'em like corn on the cob. Who wants ketchup?"

"Mr. MacDonald?" This was Leah Green.

"Yes, sweetie? What do you need?"

"I don't think rabbit is kosher. Maybe I shouldn't eat it"

Bobby Kooper laughed. "My folks are Jewish too, Leah. And I was at your birthday party when we had Chinese, remember? Nobody cared about kosher then! Your mother was joking about it!"

Esmé Smith put up her hand and spoke almost soundlessly.

"Mr. MacDonald? I have to eat kosher too."

The big man beamed. "Well, there's nothing simpler, honey! Christina! Why'n't you make a big plate of peanut butter and jelly sandwiches? Anyone doesn't want to eat rabbit can have one of them."

A few minutes nothing could be heard but the sounds of eating.

* * *

The director of the FBI was on a conference call with the Mayor of New York, the police commissioner, the deputy commander of the New Jersey State Police, Mrs. Ashley Walton of the Walton Riverside School, and six of the concerned parents.

"Let me get this straight," asked the director. "No one here, no one at all has received a ransom demand, no message of any kind?"

The answer was an agonized negative.

"My God!" cried Mrs. Buffington. "It'd almost be better if we knew someone had them. Safe, I mean. But not knowing..." and she began crying again.

"Well, then. This is a puzzle," said the director. "We have every agency in New Jersey out scouring the roads. We talked to the bus company. The manager says this guy Julio Villegas has been driving for them five years, no problems, good man, good attitude, very dependable."

"Vee-yay-goss," said Mr. Buffington, pronouncing it the way he'd heard it, "What kind of name is that?" "I have no idea," said Mrs. Walton, bristling a little. He's an American citizen and has a high school diploma here in New York. That's all the bus company requires."

"But it could be a Cuban name, said the police commissioner, "And if we find out this is a Castro operation, I'm going to…"

There were agonized cries from three of the mothers on the line.

"Let's try to be rational about this," said the Mayor. "We have no reason to believe there's even been a kidnapping, let alone some kind of weird foreign plot. We could be dealing with just a lost bus!"

Mr. Buffington immediately realized that his importance in this situation was being threatened and he responded with some heat.

"Well! In that case let me tell you that I am authorizing my law firm to start a suit for child endangerment in the amount of one hundred million dollars against, jointly, the Walton School, and the City of New York for inadequate licencing regulations!"

The amount of dollars caught the fancy of several of the parents and they chimed in that they would join the suit. The FBI director, although realizing that he had originally mentioned the magic word, 'hostage,' thought it was time to reassert control.

"Ladies and gentlemen, I don't think we should let our imaginations run wild here. Let me assure you that our people are covering every eventuality and that they will contact you the second we have hard information." And he closed the line in the midst of clamoring interruptions.

* * *

"Well, we don't have too many other animals, but I can show you our pigs, Mama and her little ones. But I don't know about petting…"

After lunch several of the children had asked Farmer MacDonald about the petting barn they had been told about. It turned out that he had no baby ducks, or lambs, or goats, and only two cows, who were out in a back pasture and tended to be antisocial.

They approached a large enclosure surrounded by a wall built of massive old railroad ties. Half of the enclosure was covered by a makeshift shingled roof, but the mother pig and her children were out in the sunny part as it was a chilly day. The sow was huge, and her tiny red eyes shifted back and forth between her little piglets dashing around and the visitors now clustering around the top row of railroad ties. Not even the most naive, romantic child believed that her rather calculating expression was an invitation to be petted.

"Now all of you be careful! Pigs aren't much for petting anyway. And if anyone fell in that pen they might wind up like old Barlow's dogs!"

"Who are Barlow's dogs?" asked Peter Maddy immediately.

Farmer MacDonald pointed to what the children had thought were two rugs hanging from an oak branch. One was black, the other sort of yellow.

"I warned Barlow a bunch of times not to let his dogs come over here. They killed a couple of my chickens and they were always trying to get into the rabbit hutches. They'd run around the big hutch there where the young rabbits all are, scare 'em to death, get 'em dashing around, a couple of times some of the little guys got crazy and killed themselves running into the wire."

The children were agog at this tale of dog misbehavior.

"So I told Barlow that my sow was having little ones and he should watch his dogs. He just badmouthed me as usual and one morning we came out here, me and Christina, and both dogs were on the bottom of the pen, just the way you see them hanging there. Flat. They'd jumped down into the pen to get at the little ones and old Flossie just chased them, squashed them up against the side of the pen and then tromped them flat. She's four hundred pounds if she's an ounce. She looks heavy and slow but she can move like lightning! She ate about half of 'em too, the soft parts. I called Barlow and told him he could come and get his dogs back if he needed a couple throw rugs." He chuckled and some of the children laughed uneasily too.

"You just don't want to mess with a mean pig, you know what I mean. Come on, let's go back up and check out the rabbits."

"Mr. MacDonald?" asked McFee Erickson. "If you keep, uh, killing the bunnies and selling them, how do you get new ones?"

MacDonald looked at Christina and they both laughed.

"We never have to worry about that, do we honey? We got some real bunny factories here. Chris? Do you think it's old Annie's time again?"

"'Bout a month, Daddy. Sounds good!"

They were all entering the third building. On one side were single hutches. On the other, a few cages with large rabbits in them and several empty cages.

"Okay," said MacDonald, "We're going to put Butch here, in what we call the honeymoon hotel." And he picked up a large grey and white rabbit from one cage and put him in an empty one.

"Now, we get Annie, here, and put her in with Butch."

The children had never watched anything with such rapt attention. They were as sure as anything in the world that what they were watching was forbidden. Butch and Annie ran around the cage a couple of times. Then Butch came up and sniffed Annie's behind. She ran off, let Butch catch up, ran off again, repeated this maneuver three times. Then suddenly they ran as fast as they could around the cage. Just as suddenly Annie stopped, raised her rump in the air. Butch was on her in a second, bounced up and down a few times, shrieked and fell twitching to the floor of the cage. Annie wandered off aimlessly and began chewing at a bit of celery that had been left in the cage.

"The bunnies are fucking!" said Christina, giggling. The children looked at her with wonder. All of them knew that she'd said a bad word.

"Well, that's strong language, Christina," said her father, chuckling a bit and patting her on the shoulder. He was looking around at the children, smiling and sort of shaking his head. "We like to say they're 'romancing.' Anyway. About a month from now Annie's going to have a litter. Twenty-nine days, thirty days, usually. Now come along here and I'll show you. See this cage? Betsy's about two days from having her little babies. See? She's pulled a lot of fur out of her chest and put it in that box full of straw, just getting ready to keep her young ones warm. Now over here is Jackie, just had her babies five days ago."

The children could see the rabbit lying on its side in the nest of fur, with five tiny, hairless, blind babies rooting at her nipples.

"And over here is Susie and her kids. One of them died but the rest are real healthy and ready to go in the big pen." The children could see a large lethargic mother surrounded by very active baby rabbits the size of a child's hand, all rushing around, carrying on, trying to unearth their mother's nipples, which she was carefully lying firmly on top of.

"So. That's the story of rabbits! You saw the young ones, you saw them grow up, go on to be our dinner, you saw the bunnies making new bunnies, you saw the whole picture! You even had some rabbit wings for lunch! You got any questions, or maybe it's time for you to go on back home?"

Farmer MacDonald had spotted Julio, now woken up from his nap, strolling casually back into the yard and waving at the children. It was three o'clock.

* * *

Mrs. Walton answered the door and let in a flood of parents.

"Yes, yes, hello, hello Mrs. Buffington, Mr. Chung, yes. Hello Rabbi Smith. All of you! Please go into the reception. We've got a TV set up in there and we've got our switchboard on direct to the FBI and the Mayor's office. This is agent Hameed from the FBI and over there is Lieutenant O'Brien from the police." Agent Hameed was huge and black and he did not smile back at the parents.

The parents had all seen innumerable African Americans playing FBI agents in movies and on television dramas; they were not reassured to see a black man with an Arab name in charge of the crisis in which their children were involved. Lieutenant O'Brien was large himself, but old, red-faced, fat. He grinned awkwardly, waved a hand, and said "Harya doin?" The old New Yorkers in the crowd sighed. They were certain that if there was a hostage situation it would not be resolved by an old doughnut snarfer like O'Brien.

"Oh my God!" said Mrs. Walton, looking out the window. Just pulling into the street in front of the Walton-Riverside School was a big television van. As the parents clustered at the window another van pulled in across the street. Crews piled out of vans and started setting up their cameras. A tall young man with wavy hair began combing his hair while looking at a script and on the other side of the street they could see a hard faced young woman checking her makeup in a mirror held by an assistant.

"What the hell is going on!" demanded Mrs. Green.

* * *

The bus was on its way back through the wooded countryside of northern New Jersey. The children were still singing "Old MacDonald had a farm" and were making up sounds that rabbits made while "romancing," or dogs being stepped on by pigs, giggling and getting a little disorderly, saying "Sounds good! Sounds good!" in imitation of Christina. Some of them were repeating what Christina had said about the rabbits romancing until it didn't even sound like a bad word anymore. They were all still enchanted by their day and rehearsing in their minds all the wonders they would describe to their parents. Peter Maddy was sitting next to Alexandra Buffington.

"If I show you something, can you keep a secret?" he asked.

She looked at him skeptically. Everyone knew Peter was a piece of work.

"What? And where is it?" she finally asked.

Peter opened his little fanny pack slowly.

"Ta da!"

As Alexandra started to scream he grabbed her and put his mouth right next to her ear. "You promised!" he hissed.

Alexandra was looking at a rabbit head. Its eyes were open and it looked completely alive, calm, looking out of the pack as if it had always lived there.

"I picked it up from behind that machine, you know? The one that cuts the heads off? I'm going to take it home and play a trick!" Peter giggled.

"Petey! You're terrible! You're going to get in trouble! What kind of trick?"

"I can't say just yet. I'll tell you tomorrow. But *no telling, you hear me*?" He whispered insistently.

"I don't want to know! I think you're disgusting!" she hissed back.

"Hey kids," said Julio, turning around and shouting back into the back of the bus. "I think we got a police escort or something!"

* * *

At the airforce base a woman with her eyes glued to a computer screen was talking to the U2 pilot up the air over New Jersey.

"Are you sure that's the one you're looking for?" asked the pilot.

"That's the one that's not accounted for by the local traffic," she responded. "And it's headed back towards the George Washington bridge. We just put local ground forces on it, New Jersey state troopers."

"So what's this all about?" asked the pilot. "Is this an exercise or what?"

"That's classified, Captain," said the woman. "Stand by to return to base."

* * *

"They're in heavy turnpike traffic," said the state trooper to his radio audience, which included the Director of the FBI, the Secretary of the Airforce, the Mayor of New York, and a dozen other public law enforcement agencies, as well as the link to the parents at the Walton- Riverside School.

"I don't think I should pull them over. They seem to be headed back to the school."

"Can you see any obvious terrorists controlling the bus?" asked the FBI Director.

"No. In fact, the kids all seem to be clustered in the back of the bus waving at me. Are we sure there's a hostage situation here?"

As the bus crossed over the George Washington bridge and took the winding offramps onto Manhattan streets it was joined by five NYPD cars, gumballs flashing, escorting it down Riverside Drive. At one corner two dark blue sedans pulled out in front of the bus and an arm from the first one waved to Julio, "Follow me!"

"Jeez! I don't know what's going on here!" said Julio. "Any you kids got any idea? We on the wrong street or something?"

The children stared at their escorts with wonder. But as the bus slowed, turned the corner and came slowly down the block to their school they could all see a crowd in front, television cameras...and there were some of their parents, waving frantically.

"Whoa!" said Peter Maddy, "Something's going on!" But the other children were delighted to see their mothers, their fathers, all gathered to welcome them.

The doors of the bus opened. The television cameras focused. There was a hush for a moment. Then little Esmé Smith, the quiet child, burst out of the bus, waving to her mother.

"Mommy, Mommy, we saw bunnies fucking!"

"Jesus, I wish this was live," said one cameraman under his breath.

"We ate rabbit wings!"

"Farmer MacDonald cut the bunny heads off in a machine!"

"His daughter's simple!"

"We helped her pack the dead bunnies!"

"His mother ate a cat and died!"

"There's bunny poop in our strawberries!"

"His pig squished two dogs!"

"And ate them too!"

The joyous news went on and on, recorded by four different television channels until the reporters, disgusted that there was no real story except a trip to the wrong rabbit farm, started packing up to leave. The cameramen all knew the parts of the footage that were going to make the all-time outtake file.

* * *

"Petey get to sleep okay?" asked Mario, coming up the stairs. Jane Maddy was standing at the top in her nightgown, a big smile on her face.

"He babbled all about today for about an hour. I thought he'd never run down. But he's out like a light. Must have been a big day for him!"

"You too, babe! You okay, no stress anymore?"

"No, no, not at all. You can't believe the relief we all felt. And then the parents' faces when the kids started yelling these unbelievable things. I was laughing so hard I thought I'd pee in my pants. I'll tell you the best parts when we get to bed."

A few moments later Mario emerged from the steamy bathroom, naked except for the towel around his waist. Jane was standing by the bed looking naughty.

"God, it's great to be here! After my afternoon, too!" said Mario. "I'll tell you later." And that was when he threw the covers back.

THE ROUND ABOUT

Harrison was on his way to the office when he remembered the article in the morning paper about the roundabout. The city had put in a European style roundabout at a troublesome intersection and despite two months of helpful reminders in the paper and on the local television station, drivers were still having trouble with the concept, *Yield to traffic from the left; otherwise don't stop.* Harrison had driven in France and Spain on vacations and it seemed absurdly simple to him. So he decided to go out of his way and try out the new roundabout.

At mid-morning traffic was light and his silver Lexus entered the roundabout without stopping. Halfway through the roundabout Harrison noted an old red Datsun stopped at the entrance to the roundabout to his right, the driver looking wildly in the wrong direction for some clue as to what to do. He chuckled at the typical Santa Barbara airhead drivers, then suddenly tensed, as he realized she was about to launch out into the intersection without looking. His car was just going by when she crashed into his right rear fender. Not really a crash, but that crumpling sound that means buckets of money to men in oil-stained blue coveralls at body shops, who can barely restrain their snickers as they scroll through their computer software to find the unbelievable estimate for a Lexus fender-bender.

Harrison rapidly exited the roundabout and pulled to the curb. He had expected the other driver to follow him but she had stopped in the middle of the intersection and was now out of her car, inspecting her damage. A few cars began to toot their horns behind her.

He trotted back to the scene of the accident, holding his hands up as she began to expostulate.

"Please miss, why don't you get back in and I'll push you over to the curb. Then we can talk about this."

She looked at him in bewilderment, a wiry looking girl, on the edge of tears. But she understood and got back behind the wheel. Harrison put his shoulder to the rear of the car to no avail, realizing that she hadn't depressed the clutch. Two young Hispanic men, who had been lounging against a fence watching the whole incident with amusement came to help. One leaned in her window, obviously telling her to put it in neutral, the other joined Harrison behind the car and very quickly they were able to push her car to the curb just behind the dented Lexus.

Harrison was calm. He wasn't in a hurry and his car didn't seem to be damaged very much. The young woman, however, was now in tears, her hands cupped over her cheeks, as she regarded the two cars. From beneath the old Datsun a steady flow of some dark liquid began to fill the gutter.

"Oh my God! I wrecked my car! And I banged yours too! I never could figure out this dumb intersection! And you're probably going to get some big time lawyer to—"

"Actually," broke in Harrison, "I am a big time lawyer. But I'm certainly not going to make a big deal out of this." He had been angry at the stupidity of the accident, but his bad temper receded quickly before the helplessness of a girl in tears.

She only sobbed louder. "And I was rushing home to phone in my orders. Now I'll have to close down my stand this weekend!" She broke down completely.

Harrison looked closely at his assailant. She was boyish, curly-haired, wearing an extra-large T shirt and cut-off jeans, a jaunty outfit, but right now she was simply vulnerable. He put a gentle hand on her shoulder.

"Actually, it's no trouble for me to drop you off at home, miss..."

"Oh, would you?" She gazed at him with amazement, almost disbelief. "But after—"

"It's no problem for me," Harrison said. "I'm not really in a hurry today. I'll take you home. And then we can decide what we're going to do about your car." He'd been about to say 'my car' but caught himself at the last moment. As they drove away he looked back and saw the two young men inspecting the car. "Let's hope it's still there," he chuckled.

Ten minutes later he was following directions up a gentle hill, past a school, down a street lined with trees, a nice neighborhood.

"It's that one, after that blue van."

Harrison was surprised at the prosperous looking two- story home, but she wasn't through.

"No, turn in the driveway and go all the way back."

Her home turned out to be a shack, obviously a former garage, turned into a cheap, and probably illegal rental. *Itould be cute inside,* Harrison was thinking.

But it wasn't. The one room contained a bed, unmade, an old stained couch, a small refrigerator, and a kitchen sink module with a hot plate on the counter.

She turned around and faced Harrison, her hands on her hips.

"Now we're going to figure out my payments for fixing your car," she said. "I don't make very much, but I can maybe give you a hundred a month? I'll write you a check for the—"Harrison stopped her. "Why don't I get an estimate for the repair. Then we can—"She was shaking her head. "No," she said stubbornly, "I want to write you out the first check right away. You've been so nice, and...and then I wouldn't keep feeling so dumb. You want some coffee or something?"

Afterwards Harrison was never sure how it had happened. Sitting and chatting on the couch, exchanging names. "Harrison Bradford? You're one of those two-last-name guys?" She was Ginger, short for Virginia, but she'd always hated 'Ginny.' And the 'Ginger' went with her reddish hair. Although she'd always wondered, because real ginger wasn't really reddish, you know? Against the squalor of the room she was bright, and funny, and sexy, with her long bare legs tucked up on the couch. And when he got up to go there was a hug that turned into more than a hug, and then a kiss that was more than a kiss, and then somehow they were on the unmade bed removing clothes.

Driving away, Harrison felt numb with disbelief. And yet there was the scrawled check on the seat next to him. In his office he tried to compose himself during what was left of the morning. And his wife was coming to meet him for lunch.

"Hi," she said, coming unannounced through the door, wearing her tennis togs and carrying her racket, a slim, athletic woman, looking much younger than her mid-forties. "What in God's name happened to your car, Harry? I thought it was someone else's car at first!"

And of course he'd never thought about her seeing the car, worrying that she'd detect something more related to his guilty secret.

"You know," he lied. "I stopped at the mall to get something and when I came back to the car, it was just a few minutes, but someone must have backed into me and then driven away."

"What did you need at the mall?...Never mind, we're going to be late." And she grabbed his arm and they left, Harrison thinking that as a lawyer he was supposed to lie a little more professionally.

In the lot she bent down to inspect the dent. "It's a red car, anyways."

That afternoon Harrison was busier than usual. An old client had been denied a building permit and was going to sue the City Council. Not an unusual case, but it took careful preparation and citation of all the right precedents. So he had almost forgotten the morning's adventure when his secretary put through a phone call from his insurance broker.

"Harry! Otis here. Heard about the little fender-bender! Madge called me from the club, asked me what to do."

Harrison was going to say he'd planned to get some estimates, but Otis was way ahead of him.

"Look, I called Tri-County Lexus already. Told 'em to go ahead and fix your car, send me the bill. You're all covered for hit and run. The shop said bring it in first thing tomorrow. They'll drive you to work, pick you up the end of the day when the paint dries. No problem!"

Harrison had always enjoyed his status as a recognized community leader, accepting the respect, the eagerness of others to make matters smoother for him than they might be for someone else. But now he was almost cross, wishing people would just leave him and his little problem alone.

His mood was not improved by finding two policemen inspecting his car when he left. A uniformed cop was scraping something out of the dent in his fender, supervised carefully by a wiry older man in jeans and a warmup jacket. The older man turned to Harrison.

"Mr. Bradford? Sorry we didn't call ahead, but we're rushed today."

"What...what's that you're doing?"

"Santa Barbara PD. I'm detective sergeant Kline, and this is officer Lopez. Sorry. We're taking a paint sample from the car that hit you. Put these little bits in the chroma...chroma...the machine they got in Sacramento and we got it all computerized. Ten seconds and we know from the paint what kind of car hit you." Detective Kline shrugged. "Of course, if it's a late model white Chevy, a Honda, like that, forget it. You're going to get twenty thousand registrations. But maybe it's an old car, or a rare model. Anyway, we just got the software and we like to try it out."

"Don't get too impatient," added officer Lopez. "The gas chromatography takes ten seconds, but we gotta get in line. Three weeks, usually, except if there's a fatal, they get ahead of us too."

Detective Kline spread his hands, smiled. "What can you do? We get the technology, suddenly we get half a million people need to use it."

Harrison shrugged, trying to appear casual. "Look. It's not a big deal. Some lady in the parking lot, maybe didn't even know she hit me."

"Maybe, maybe," said Kline. "Could you give us an approximate time? Your wife said you were on your way to work, so you musta known when you were gonna get there. So you go to the store, what was this? Maybe close to ten? We can ask store clerks there in the mall, they're all looking out the windows. We could get lucky."

Harrison made a dismissive motion with his hand. "What do we have here...a dent worth, what, three hundred bucks? You guys probably have other things to do."

Officer Lopez stood up, holding the little plastic envelope. "Three hundred? We talked to Lexus, Mr. Bradford, and they said twelve hundred, at least. That makes it a serious crime."

Harrison drove away sweating, wondering what the hell he could do. In three weeks they'd know what car they were looking for. They'd arrest Ginger, and she'd say...she'd say... He knew what she'd say. Should he warn her? He kept seeing her face, not really pretty, round and freckled, hair short and wiry, not really much of a chest... He decided to think about suing the City Council about the building permit.

It was two weeks later when he was stuck in downtown traffic on the way home and heard someone calling his name.

"Harrison? Harrison! Over here! The flower stand!" And there she was on the corner, selling flowers. She came over to his car, laughing.

"Hey, buy some flowers, big guy! What you been doin'?"

"Uh..." He was desperately hoping for the light to change. It did, but there was gridlock ahead.

"Here, take a bouquet. Surprise your wife!" Harrison started to fumble for his wallet, but she waved him off. "No, my treat. And I gotta see you. And soon. How about tomorrow, on your way to work? We know how that goes down, right?" She giggled, and the traffic began to move. "Nice looking fender!" she called after him.

All the way home Harrison worried why she had to see him. At the same time he kept remembering how she had felt under his hands, how she had sounded when...

He was in the kitchen pouring himself a drink when Madge came in from the garage with a bouquet of flowers.

"Harry? Did you bring these home for me? I found them in the front seat of your car..."

It was so ludicrous that Harrison was able to guffaw realistically. "My god! I got stuck in traffic by this flower stand and I thought, why not bring home some flowers." He slapped his forehead. "And then I started thinking about this case and completely—"

Madge was laughing too, but she looked curious. "What case was that? Pete said the other day that it was slow at the office, trust accounts and like that."

Once again Harrison wasn't lying well. "Yeah. Well. You know me. I can get preoccupied with anything…"

The flowers had put Madge in a romantic mood that night but Harrison was unable to perform.

"That's alright, darling, don't worry." She kissed him. "Just don't be like Bob Dole, telling everyone about it."

He had no such problems the next morning. Ginger met him at the door and almost tore his clothes off. She wasn't wearing any, which saved time. If anything, their lovemaking was more passionate and Harrison worried at the end what the banging of the bedstead against the wall sounded like outside.

Afterwards she cuddled next to him. "I've been wanting to talk to you for weeks, you know, but I didn't want to phone you, even at the office." He started to speak but she put a hand over his mouth.

"The big news is, my mother called from Oregon. My great aunt Emily died—she was almost a hundred or something— and out of the blue she left me five thousand dollars! Can you believe it? She always said I was her favorite of all the kids but I never thought she had any money. Who knows up in Oregon? Nobody ever acts rich, you know what I mean? Anyway—no, let me finish—here's the deal. I called Lexus and asked what a little fender-bender would cost and they said about a thousand, or more. Anyways, now I can pay you the whole thing, maybe even buy insurance from now on. I'm so happy!" And she reached down and squeezed him in an intimate way.

Harrison didn't know what to say. But Ginger went on anyway. "And you know the funniest thing? The other day? You were worried about those Mexican kids? Maybe stealing my car? Well, a friend gave me a lift down there to maybe call a tow truck, and those guys were there. You know what they did? They were so sweet! This guy says 'We popped your hood, lady, just to take a look, and it was only your radiator hose shook loose.' And they had put a new clamp on and filled the radiator. And you know what now? I want to get on top."

Driving away, Harrison felt enormously relieved. He'd been worried about a steady stream of mysterious hundred dollar checks coming into the office. He had tried to tell Ginger to forget about paying him but she had been firm. "No siree! Then it would be like, you know, tit for tat! Ha ha, so to speak." He figured he'd have to give Otis back the insurance money...but how to explain it? So he put it off, thinking about it, and then forgot.

It was a week later when he came down to find detective Kline and officer Lopez inspecting his car. They were not as pleasant this time.

"Mr. Bradford? Looks like you got your fender fixed."

"Uh...yeah. The next day, actually."

"That would have been at Tri-County Lexus?"

"That's right. Is something wrong?"

"And your insurance paid for it? Is that right?"

Harrison was trying to think how he could avoid the line of questioning. But he had the feeling they knew all the answers already.

"Because, Mr. Bradford, we got the chroma... the ID back on that car that hit you."

"It was an '87 Datsun," added officer Lopez. "'Toro Red,' the color, that's what they called it, that year."

"And, it turns out, CHP's computer shows one, just one red '87 Datsun in all of the county. You wouldn't know who owned that red Datsun, would you?"

Harrison started to say something, stuttering, but detective Kline went on.

"Actually, it's a Virginia Jones, right here in Santa Barbara. So we go to find Ms Jones, and you know? It's a funny thing, 'cause we were going to take her in, book her, for leaving the scene of an accident. But you know what she said?"

"She said she'd paid for the dent." said Harrison. He wondered if they could see him sweating.

"That's right. Now here's the big question: did she pay you for the dent?"

"Yes, she did." It was like in court. If they had you dead to rights you just had to tell the truth.

"And she shows us her checkbook and there were the checks made out to you, and she says there was some Mexican kids saw the whole thing, even fixed her car. So we went down to the roundabout and they're still hanging out there, and one kid says, 'Oh yeah, we saw the whole thing. And the guy drove off with her.'"

"That 'Toro Red' color, it's named after 'toro,' you know? In Japanese? It's the belly meat of the tuna," said officer Lopez. "It's the best part. I asked the guy down at Nissan and he's like, just go to any sushi place and—" Harrison looked at him, mouth open, a total lack of comprehension.

"Okay, Lopez," said detective Kline. "We're not trying to get Mr. Bradford confused, here. The thing is, we find some little grifter getting paid twice, it's insurance fraud. Now we gotta give you the benefit of the doubt, Mr. Bradford, someone like you in the community, know what I mean? Let me ask you, were you going to return the insurance money?

Harrison was stricken with a sudden thought. "Did you talk to Mr. Selig? Otis Selig, at my insurance company?"

Detective Kline and officer Lopez looked at each other. "A couple weeks ago to ascertain the claim was settled," said Lopez, in formal cop-speak. "Not since this new information came up," added Kline. "You want to go settle up with him? It's gonna make this whole thing simpler."

Harrison bridled. "Of course I was! You want to come along? Right now! Let's go see him!"

Otis was not as friendly as before. They were sitting in his little office downtown and he was shuffling through papers and staring at his computer screen. Finally he looked up at Harrison and his police escort.

"Harry, this is going to be a problem. No wait, let me finish. Because there is no way on this software program for anyone to give back money. The thought process on the software the company put together is that no one would ever give back a settlement without a court case." He looked at the police officers.

"Obviously we're not going to court over a fender- bender."

"Then Mr. Bradford here defrauded Ms Virginia Jones." said detective Kline. "Is that what we gotta go with?"

Harrison felt he had to speak up. "Now wait a minute! Ms Jones insisted that I take her check. She said that otherwise it would be as if—"

There was a dead silence and everyone looked at him. Then detective Kline gathered the papers before him into a neat stack, looked at Otis.

"You're satisfied there's no fraud, if Mr. Bradford here gives back the money to Ms Jones?

"No. No way. Listen. Harry here is covered for accidents. Doesn't matter whether someone hit him in the parking lot and drove off, or in the roundabout and he settled with her. It's just an accident. And it's just money. Okay? Why Harry wanted to say it was a hit-run I dunno." Otis was looking right at Harrison and was not happy.

Harrison figured the ball was back in his court. He forced himself to get a little hot.

"Okay! I said I never wanted to take her check. So let's go pay her back, if you're so worried I'm trying to defraud a flower girl."

"A flower girl?" asked Otis.

"Yeah. That's what she does," said detective Kline. "She buys flowers down at the greenhouses in Carpinteria and sells them on the street in town."

Recognition flashed across Otis's face, then a knowing smile. "Skinny girl, right? Not so pretty but always cheerful? I get flowers there maybe twice a week. Something we ought to know about you and her, Harry?" The smile became a smirk.

Harrison had been a lawyer long enough to know when not to say anything. Also, to realize when he was off the hook. He stood up.

"Gentlemen? I don't believe we have any remaining business. I was actually on my way to refund Ms Jones her money." He looked at detective Kline. "You are at liberty to check with her, to make sure I'm no longer in the business of deflowering fraud girls...I mean, oh crap! Goddammit!"

That hadn't come out exactly as he had wanted but he managed to maintain his dignity and stalk, as he thought of it, out of the office and over to his Lexus.

The three men in the office looked at each other. Otis was grinning.

"He's been screwing her."

"*Pinche*, man, no doubt," said officer Lopez.

"If that's what I think it means, you're right," said Kline.

Otis turned serious, leaned forward. "Okay. But let's keep all that in this room, okay? Harry's a big guy in town, got a great wife. This isn't like him. I think he learned a lesson. Okay?"

"My lips are sealed," said Kline.

Lopez was smiling, shaking his head, and no one knew what he was thinking.

Harrison drove up the hill still steaming about his ordeal, being pinned down by three miserable little shits, Otis of all people, who everyone knew took long lunch hours with any temp dumb enough to think it meant something. Now he was looking forward to seeing Ginger, giving her the refund in cash, all eleven hundred dollars of it. And then maybe celebrate a little.

He was dumbfounded, reading the note pinned to the door. "Hi Harry! I had a long talk with Mom and decided maybe I

should go back to Oregon. Business isn't so great here and other things are getting too 'hot to handle.' Thanks for everything!" There was a picture of a heart and a smily face.

He never thought he'd feel so crushed. This little romance, just sort of a treat on the side, he could take it or leave it. And now she'd dumped him. And he felt absolutely rotten.

He hadn't been paying attention as he reached the bottom of the hill and entered the roundabout without looking to his left. There was a scream of brakes and a crunching sound, he felt his Lexus lurch to the side and then his horn started to blow and blow and just wouldn't stop.doc

Keep the Change

Mr. Magnus circulated cautiously through the giant Food Bounty supermarket. He hated change. Food Bounty had recently done a demographic survey and found itself surrounded by a large pocket of ethnic neighborhoods. Mr. Magnus and other bewildered white middle-class shoppers now found themselves confronted with strange foods on every aisle. In the meat case they saw new offerings of pork tails and ears, *tripas de leche* in glistening lilac loops, beef tendons. There were strange plants in produce: lemon grass, bok choy, taro root, jars of kimchi and hummus. Worse, the marketing strategy had paid off and on certain days of the week the market was thronged with small people, generally of a darker hue, always accompanied by swarms of small children, sitting crying in shopping carts, otherwise usually out of control, running and screaming up the aisles, bumping into elderly shoppers. The air was rife with foreign tongues, from the familiar Latin staccato, to Middle Eastern gutturals, to singsong Oriental clamor. Even Mrs. Washington, a portly African American woman who had been shopping here as long as Mr. Magnus sometimes rolled her eyes at him to express her distaste with the new clientele.

Mr. Magnus had thought that the crowded days coincided with paydays for lower-class workers. No, sneered Edna, the bad-tempered checker, it was welfare check day. Mr. Magnus always tried to avoid Edna but her line usually seemed the shortest and Holly's was the longest. He liked Holly because when his bill was $8.61, or $12.76 she'd say, "I'll loan you the penny till the next time, sweetheart," and give him a big wink. Mr. Magnus didn't carry pennies and he made a point of it. Once when he left three cents behind and explained to the checker that everybody should just round off the price to the nickel a woman in the line behind him said sarcastically, "They do add up, you know!" He retorted, "If you save ten thousand pennies they'll add up to a hundred dollars. And it takes a hundred dollars a day to live at the poverty level in this town!" Which was true, but he knew he shouldn't have been such a smarty- pants.

Today Edna's line was shortest again so he went there with his package of skinless chicken breasts, frozen broccoli, and herbal teabags. The bill came to $6.91 and Mr. Magnus knew better than trying to wheedle Edna out of the penny so he just gritted his teeth and made a point of putting the four pennies back on the counter. An Asian-looking woman behind him said, "You left your change, mister."

"I don't carry pennies any more," said Mr. Magnus in a smug but good-natured way.

"Hey, I'll take them," said the woman.

"You're welcome to them," he said. But Edna had already raked in the coins and was plunking them in her register.

"Excuse me," said Mr. Magnus, "I told this lady she could have my..."

"Store policy!" snapped Edna. "Manager says we can't leave pennies lying around."

"But he already said I could have them," said the Asian woman, obviously getting angry.

"Too late now," said Edna, slamming the cash drawer closed. "Who's next here?"

"Hey, wait a minute!" exclaimed Mr. Magnus. "I said she could have the pennies and you just grabbed them up, took them right out of my hand..."

"Come on, for crissakes," yelled a man back in the growing line, juggling two six-packs and three frozen dinners. "Let's get it moving, okay?"

Edna's lips were clamped in a thin slit and she stared at Mr. Magnus with hatred. Then she turned on the Asian woman. "You wanna check out your stuff, or you think you can get pennies in some other line...?"

The woman jerked back as if she'd been slapped. "You think I am begging pennies? How dare you..."

Mr. Magnus was about to chime in but a big meaty hand came down on his shoulder. It was the assistant manager, a big foreign guy with a black mustache, the guy he'd had trouble with last week.

"What is trouble here? Not coupons again, is it, Edna?"

There had been a misunderstanding last week about an ad in the paper specifying a discount for three soap bars with coupons. Turned out it was only for *jumbo* soap bars and Mr. Magnus had made a fuss.

"He wanted to give his change to this woman," said Edna, making the word "woman" sound like "third-world slime," "But I already put it in the cash drawer."

Now three more people in line complained loudly.

"She insulted me," shouted the Asian woman. "She called me a beggar! You can keep your goddamn food!" She swept her purchases off onto the floor and stalked out of the store.

"Next customer!" announced the assistant manager loudly, gently kicking her cans and packages under the check-out counter, beckoning to the man with the six-packs. "Step right on up, sir! Is no problems here, folks!" Then he moved Mr. Magnus away from the check out counter, actually bumping him along with his sturdy belly, and spoke softly but intensely.

"Listen, Magnus, you make more trouble in here and we call police, you understand? Boss will get restraining order in two seconds, keep you out of store. Now you get out, you hear me!"

Mr. Magnus was livid with rage. He couldn't remember being so angry in his entire life. He started to sputter his side of the story but the manager just kept backing him up until the automatic door hissed open behind him and he had nowhere to go but out.

* * *

The Asian woman was named Phan. She got in her old Datsun and drove furiously the seven blocks to her apartment building. It was only eleven in the morning but her husband Prin had been drinking since breakfast. He'd been laid off two weeks ago. He looked up at her with reddened eyes. He was about to warn her not to bitch at him again but she slammed her purse down on the kitchen table and started talking viciously in their native tongue.

"That filthy sow at the market insulted me, called me a beggar, just over four cents. The same one who made the remark about my food stamps last week... And then the boss threw my food on the floor and told me to get out," she lied.

Prin got unsteadily to his feet. "She what? He did what?"

She told her story again. This time the manager had pushed her out the door and she almost fell.

Prin's eyes almost fell out of his head. He stared upward in disbelief and his hands trembled. Then a horrid curse erupted from his mouth. He dashed into the bedroom and she could hear him rooting in a drawer. He emerged with an insane grimace on his face and a large revolver in his hand.

"Where are the car keys," he screamed.

She pointed to her purse. He snatched the keys out and slammed his way out the door. Mrs. Phan silently watched him go, a little smile playing on her lips.

* * *

The assistant manager was standing in his cramped station by the window. He heard the Datsun scream into the parking lot and screech to a stop in the middle of a lane of traffic before he whirled and saw a frenzied Asian man scramble out of the car holding a pistol.

"Oh no!" he said and yelled, "Lookout! Is danger! Hit the floor!" Then he reached into the safe and pulled out his own automatic. The assistant manager had once been in a civil war and was a crack shot.

In the meantime, Mr. Magnus had been sitting in his car trying to settle down. He finally decided that he had regained some control and would now be able to speak without stuttering, so he got out intending to give the manager the tongue-lashing of his life. He was almost knocked down by an old Datsun swerving into the lot and lurching to a halt and he stared in amazement as an Asian man clambered out with a gun and dashed into Food Bounty.

"Oh boy!" he thought, and followed swiftly, not deterred by the sound of shots.

Prin started shooting the second he cleared the door. He was vaguely aiming at the assistant manager but managed only to hit a black woman and a little Latino boy. The assistant manager took dead aim and drilled him in the heart, killing him instantly. Prin fell and his revolver went spinning across the polished linoleum floor to wind up at Mr. Magnus's feet just as he entered. Without even thinking Mr. Magnus bent over and picked up the gun.

"It's all right..." he was about to say but the manager was taking no chances with other crazy people and shot him dead the next second.

Edna was out in back on her break, smoking one of the thirty cigarettes she permitted herself every day since she had decided to cut down on her smoking. She could hear the shots.

"What now? she wondered.

Mrs. Applewhite

Afternoon business was beginning to pick up at the giant Food Bounty supermarket. Holly always got a kick out of watching the people coming in from her position, the nearest checkout counter to the main door. Some were reluctant, resigned, ready to buy anything for families who only wanted to stuff something into their faces before returning to the TV. Then there were others who entered with their eyes sparkling, anticipating the treasures that awaited them. Holly saw a woman as broad as she was tall coming in, almost running. An elderly man had his hand on the first shopping cart in the rack but the fat woman ignored him, twisted the cart out of his hand and almost raced away down the aisles. Holly knew her type. She would show up later at the check stand with twelve frozen Slim Sweetheart dinners, but she would be eating the last jelly doughnut in a six-pack, girding herself for the ordeal of the Slim Sweethearts, guaranteed less than six hundred calories, whether the sole with broccoli or the turkey breast with summer squash tidbits. She would give Holly a messily written check, smeared with jelly and doughnut grease, that would stick to her fingers and the other checks in the drawer.

Then there were Holly's favorite shoppers, the real chefs, with their veal, or duck, Italian parsley, garlic, wine, always ready to tell her what they were going to cook. "Yeah, Holly, I just bone out the duck breasts, coat them with pureed garlic and Dijon mustard, grill them for a few minutes--just like a steak-- and serve them with a green peppercorn sauce with cream. You wouldn't believe...!"

And then there was Mrs Applewhite. This afternoon the regular routine was interrupted for a moment by the shriek of brakes outside in the parking lot. Some of the Food Bounty staff craned their heads to see out the windows. Manny, the hyperactive Chicano bagboy, just jumped and down, his back to the window.

"Mrs Applewhite! I betchou you a million dollars!"

Arkan Skanderbeg, the assistant manager, was spelling the manager at the raised desk by the window. He could see the old, enormous green finned Cadillac, maybe from the sixties, come cruising down the aisles of the parking lot, never stopping, swerving across lanes, cutting off legitimate traffic, until it finally wedged at an angle across two parking spaces. Other cars had screeched to a halt in order to avoid the old car and now drivers were getting out, infuriated, waiting to see who would get out of the Cadillac. At first it seemed that there was no driver at all. Then, when the door opened, they could see that the little old lady was almost too short to appear in the windows of the car. She stepped out, looked around at her audience with a serene smile on her face, then made for the door of the Food Bounty with a deliberate, bowlegged pace.

Mrs. Applewhite thought that she sort of blended in with the crowd in the Food Bounty. She had a shopping cart that she almost had to reach up to push. She was surrounded by crowds of people who were almost certainly ethnic minorities, she thought, therefore the security people in the store would be watching them, not her. Mrs. Applewhite cruised down the produce lane and picked up two red potatoes and three onions. Up the cereal aisle, where she collected a box of All Bran and some corn flakes. She never ate corn flakes but she didn't want people to think she just needed the All Bran to do...you know what. In the meat case she picked out a slim package of pork chops. Then up in Paper, she got herself a four-pack of paper towels, and paused. This was always the most embarrassing part of her shopping. But she had to do it. She was completely out. So she picked up a package of four rolls of toilet paper, blushing, although she knew no one was watching her.

Actually they were watching her. Back in the room next to the employees' lounge was a row of closed circuit television sets covering every inch of the store. They had been designed for three security employees to monitor but for financial reasons the store management had reduced the number to one, and only now and then. No one watched produce. But they always watched the meat case, seeing the shopper looking right and left and then slipping the steaks into the purse or overcoat pocket. It was never a chicken, or stew meat. Steaks. And of course the liquor section was always watched. It used to be cigarettes but now the cigarettes were all under lock and key since state taxes had made them more expensive, pound for pound, than caviar.

And they watched people they knew were thieves and Mrs. Applewhite was a thief.

It had been three weeks ago when she wandered into the liquor section. Edna, the bad-tempered checker, had been on duty at the TV monitor back in the employees' lounge at the end of her break. Mrs. Applewhite looked around and took a great interest in little jars of cocktail onions. She made a big production of selecting a bottle and putting it in her cart. At the same time, with miraculous speed, her left hand snapped up a half pint of brandy on the next shelf and, zip, it was in her large purse. Edna yelled in triumph! "We got a live one!" And everyone on break in the lounge ran to see.

"See! That old lady just grabbed a half pint of some kind of booze and slipped it into her purse!" And she went out to tell Arkan.

Mrs. Applewhite eventually wandered over to Holly's checkout counter. It was the express counter for fewer than twelve items, no checks. Holly was chatting with her last customer.

"Yeah, hon, I know. But what can you do? Now you have a good evening, you hear!"

She saw Mrs Applewhite coming up to the counter, putting out her various food purchases and her paper products. Holly knew Mrs. Applewhite's hangups so she grabbed the toilet paper first and hid it in a plastic bag.

"Hi there, sweetheart! How you doing tonight?"

"Oh, I'm just fine, Holly. Except, you know, the aches and pains. Don't ever get old, dear!"

"I'm doing my best, hon!" By now Holly had swept all the items across the magnetic bar-code reader and had all of Mrs. Applewhite's purchases in plastic bags.

"That'll be eleven-fifty-seven, sweetie."

Mrs. Applewhite was getting a ten and two dollar bills out of her wallet when Arkan walked up to the checkout counter. He was an imposing man, well over six feet and with a big black mustache and an intimidating foreign accent.

"You maybe forgot something in your purse, lady?"

Mrs. Applewhite shrank away. "Oh my goodness! No, no, no! Why would you say that?"

Arkan simply grabbed her purse, reached in and pulled out the half pint of brandy. He held it aloft as if it had been a strangled child. "So! What is this? You steal liquor?"

Mrs. Applewhite covered her face with her hands and burst out crying. "Oh! No! No! I never meant...!"

A crowd had formed around the checkout counter. The next person in line, a big burly red-faced man burst out, "Oh, for Chrissakes! A half pint? What could that be? Five bucks or something? Shit! I'll pay for it!" And he waved a handful of money.

Many others echoed him. "Yeah, what's the big deal!" "It was only a mistake!" "Come on, man, don't be a Nazi!"

But Arkan was adamant. "No. It is policy. Food Bounty always prosecutes. We saw on monitor in back, how she stole. We called police already.

And here they were, two large men in navy blue, serious as hell, walking into the store, coming up to the counter.

"We charge this woman with shoplifting," said Arkan. "Stealing liquor!" making it sound like a vile and depraved act.

Ten minutes later Holly was on her break back in the employees' lounge, still carrying on.

"I can't believe Arkan, that jerk, calling the cops like that!"

"But you gotta admit, she did steal the bottle!" said Doreen, who'd been watching the TV monitor.

"Yeah, but *cops?* If I'da caught her I'd just tell her, 'Oh, I think you forgot to pay for this, Mrs. Applewhite. And then...'"

"Maybe she's too cheap to pay for her liquor," said one of the bag boys.

"Maybe she's an alcoholic," said Edna. You could always count on Edna for a grim diagnosis.

The door opened and a policeman came in, one of the arresting officers. A burly man with ginger hair and a mustache. Arkan was following him, looking more glum than usual. The cop looked around the room.

"Who was the checker at the counter where Mrs. Applewhite got arrested?"

Holly stood up quickly. "It was me, officer and it was bullshit! She was going to pay for..." The officer held up his hand as if holding up traffic for the parade of a visiting dignitary. "No. No, no, no. Just one thing I need to ask. When the manager accused her of stealing the bottle, exactly what did he do?"

"What did he do?" asked Holly. "I'll tell you what he did, the big Armenian asshole, he grabbed her purse and took the bottle out of it. And you know what? She was going to pay me for it, she had just told me that..."

"Albanian! I always tell you, I am from Albania," shouted Arkan.

The cop held up his hand again, still directing traffic.

"No, no. You don't need to go into all that. You know what it is, we asked your manager there, the--uh--Mr. Skanderbeg, and he said the same thing. He took the bottle out of her purse. Thing is, that'll never stand up in court. Illegal search and seizure. Me and my partner talked it over with the lady, Mrs.-- uh--Applewhite, and we're just going to take her home, going to see she gets home okay. I don't think she's up to driving that car of hers right now..."

"Hey meng!" cackled Manny the bag boy. "She ain' no tief, but you chould jerk her focking licence, meng, the way she drive. Almos' ran my ass over today! Hee hee."

The policeman smiled wanly. "Well, yeah. Okay, take it easy you guys." And he left.

Most of the people in the lounge cheered. "Hey, Mrs. Applewhite!" yelled Manny, and went around high-fiving the employees who responded, like Holly, and Doreen. *Whap, whap!* went the hands...but not Edna. She was still pissed, hoping for a real prosecution.

* * *

That had been three weeks ago and now the Food Bounty employees who were in the lounge were all clustered around the surveillance TV, almost as if they were watching a police show.

"See!" said Doreen. "She hates to buy toilet paper! She brought it up to my stand once in a huge black garbage bag!"

"Toilet paper!" Several employees burst out. Manny was laughing like mad. "Hey, meng! You can do widout every sing in dis store. Every sing--'cept toilet paper, Hey, think it over, meng! Hey! Whatchoo goin' use?" and he went into a paroxysm of chuckles. Edna was in charge of the surveillance and she almost cackled.

"Guess what, everybody! Applewhite's in the liquor section again."

Doreen, Roy the produce manager, and the others watched the monitor.intently. They saw the grainy black-and-white picture looking down from overhead on this tiny woman with a monster shopping cart, standing in the narrow aisle between two rows of shelves and looking around nervously, no idea that the camera tracking her every movement was overhead.

Holly had come into the lounge just long enough to see the screen.

"Oh shit!" she said and ducked out the door again. No one noticed her go. They were all too entranced watching Mrs. Applewhite's act. She seemed to be gazing at a shelf of cocktail accessories, bottled olives, pickled onions, corkscrews, martini mixing glasses.

"Here goes the old cocktail onion routine again," chortled Edna. And indeed, Mrs. Applewhite went through the entire routine again, carefully picking up a bottle of pickled onions with her right hand and then her left hand, almost too fast to see, striking like a snake for a half-pint bottle of brandy and slipping it into her purse.

"She slam-dunked that sucker!" said Roy, with admiration. "That old lady got some chops!"

"I'm calling Arkan," said Edna. "This time the bitch is going to the joint!" And as the figure of Mrs. Applewhite exited the screen she turned and picked up the store intercom.

Holly caught Mrs. Applewhite moving down the produce counter, just by the eggplant.

"Mrs. Applewhite? I gotta talk to you!"

The old lady made an effort to focus through her thick glasses. Then she smiled beatifically.

"Well! Hello, Holly! How are you my dear? And why aren't you at your counter?" And she began pushing her cart down the aisle, nervously.

"Mrs. Applewhite. I have to tell you! They saw you take the bottle of brandy!"

Mrs. Applewhite's face froze and she pushed her cart quickly down the aisle. "I don't know what you're talking about," she said angrily.

Holly grabbed the cart by the push bar and stopped it. She looked around. Luckily they were surrounded by women picking out lettuces, chiles, cucumbers, their children running around, making noises.

"Mrs. Applewhite, I'm only going to say this once! They just saw you on the TV--and she pointed back to the liquor section-- and they know you have a bottle of brandy in your purse!"

Incomprehension turned to tragedy on Mrs. Applewhite's face and she started to cry.

"Oh! Not again? They won't arrest me again? Holly--please-- what can I do?"

"It's simple, hon. Just take the bottle out of your purse and put it in your cart and..." And now it was the old lady's turn to grab Holly's wrist and blurt out her complicated explanation, that in her day a decent woman would never buy spirits, how her maid had once done her shopping and had brought her home just a tiny bottle now and then, and then how all the money situation had changed, she didn't know how, and she couldn't afford her maid anymore, Maria, had been with her thirty years, and how she needed just a little drink now and then, just for her arthritis, she could afford to buy it of course, but she was so embarrassed--even with the toilet tissue it was so awkward--and a bottle of liquor? She just couldn't do it!

Holly was a smart woman. She got the cart turned around and they headed back to liquor again.

"Now listen, hon! Those little bottles are really incriminating! They really look like you're tippling. But you buy a big bottle of brandy, it's the sort of thing anyone would have around--you know, entertaining, even cooking with it, for God's sake!"

They were next to the brandy now and Holly reached into Mrs. Applewhite's purse and took the little bottle out and put it back on the shelf.

"Now," she said, "I know they're all looking, and I don't care. But let's get you a half gallon of the store label brandy. Here it is, 'Food Bounty Napoleon Brand.' See, hon, anyone would have brandy on hand, nothing to be ashamed of, and this bottle only costs--let's see--$11.99! See! That's almost eight times as much brandy as the little bottle, and the price is only about twice as much!" And Holly looked up at the TV camera and gave it a triumphant finger.

Arkan was now in the lounge looking at the monitor.

"That Holly!" he said. "She's going to get in trouble!"

"Why you say that?" asked Doreen. "I dunno what she was saying back there but she stopped the old lady from shoplifting. That's a good move, right?"

"And she made her buy a beeger bottle!" crowed Manny. "She's makin' money for the store, meng!"

* * *

As chance would have it, Mrs. Applewhite wound up at Edna's checkout counter. Holly's intervention had put Edna in a worse mood than usual.

Mrs. Applewhite plunked her purchases down on the counter, finishing triumphantly with the large half gallon of brandy.

"I don't know what I'll do!" she said to the shoppers on all sides. "I've got so much entertaining to do this next week!"

"Hey! I'm coming to your house!" said the man standing behind her, and everyone laughed. Mrs. Applewhite looked around wildly for a moment, then realized that everyone was just joking about her skills as a hostess--having a lot of brandy on hand, so she laughed too. Thank God for Holly, she thought.

Edna couldn't let it go. "I see you got a lot of toilet paper too!" she said. Mrs. Applewhite blushed furiously.

"Yeah, Edna," said Holly from the next checkout counter. "Four rolls. Would last a tight-ass like you the next ten years!" And everyone around dissolved in laughter again.

Edna would have attacked Holly but just then the two cops called by Arkan came hulking into the store and marched up to the counter. Arkan came to meet them.

"No. Sorry, officers. We made a mistake. Dere was no shoplifting." And in the confusion Mrs Applewhite quietly paid her bill and left, with Manny bringing up the rear, carrying her bags out to the big Cadillac.

Later on in the employees' lounge Edna started to get on Holly's case again but everyone started yelling.

"Hey, Edna, give it a rest!" "Yeah, that's a nice old lady!" "Come on, we all gotta live together! Forget it!"

Two days later they were all shocked by the front page headlines.

"Elderly widow found dead. Overdose of alcohol suspected." And the story went on to say that Mrs. Applewhite had been found almost as if asleep in her lounge chair, a smile on her face and a huge empty brandy bottle at her side.

Dorothy

The asteroid hurtled into Barnswallow, Kansas, and turned it into a crater thirty feet deep and a mile wide. The crater was filled with a shallow layer of smoking debris, the remains of Barnswallow and everything around it.

After remote instruments indicated a perimeter temperature 100°C or less and the level of radiation hovering under 5,000 millirems, the first responders wandered in through the rubble wearing their hazmat suits and helmets, not expecting to find anything. With the world's television cameras focused on them, they found a child. The child was reported to be female, approximately eight or nine years old, dressed in underwear appropriate for a child, dusty, dirty, scraped and scratched, but otherwise healthy. Except she could not speak.

The asteroid was not unexpected. It had been picked up by observatories all over the world weeks ago and was expected to boil a lot of Pacific Ocean water, until a sudden weird deviation aimed it at the center of the North American continent. A hole in northwestern Kansas was judged by a relieved world to be not much more loss than a bunch of Pacific water, excepting of course the regretted 329 inhabitants of Barnswallow. And now, here was one.

The news cycle during the approach of the asteroid had been dominated, to the exasperation of televangelists trying to get their oar in, by the Center for Extraterrestial Events, whose many media connections had alerted the world to possible dramatic developments from an earth visitor and had heightened expectations across the planet. And now, other than several thousand tons of fuming rubble, there was a single Barnswallowite to witness. Or was there?

The Center for Extraterrestial Events—or CXTE—was an unusually popular and well known non-profit, followed by everyone from right wing conspiracists to Green activists. The actual founders and patrons were two aerospace billionaires, one American, one British, who had discovered that their commercial profits were so huge that they were almost forced to create a non-profit to cushion their tax exposure. Having alerted the world to the asteroid, CXTE now believed that they owned the Barnswallow space child franchise. The girl had been moved to a Kansas hospital with armed guards keeping the curious crowds at a distance. She had been cleaned up and her scratches and bruises repaired by fascinated doctors and nurses. Kansas had recently declared bankruptcy and couldn't afford an extra bandaid, let alone sophisticated medical care, so the authorities were relieved when the Center descended in a sleek, shining private jet and spirited the child away to its campus and research estate along Rte. One north of Princeton.

A spacious dormer with every facility had been prepared for the girl with bewildering speed. She must have been happy to be met, not by a bevy of scientists and officials, but by warm and friendly nurses and psychologists, all female and dressed in casual civilian clothes. The room was filled with dolls and toys and nine-year-old-girl clothes. The little girl smiled for the first time and went to sleep almost instantly hugging a furry green dinosaur.

No one else was tempted to sleep across America and the world. All media claimed that survival from an asteroid landing was utterly impossible and speculation was feverish about the origin of the space child, as she was being called. But the FBI had not been idle. Someone had slipped a swab into her mouth at some time and within a few days the FBI's DNA lab identified a number of possible relatives, distant perhaps but still within parameters, in northwestern Kansas. Space child was from Barnswallow.

Boyish Rick Doulton, whose famously tousled hair and youthful energy belied his 61 years, was president and founder of Spastek, a space shuttle and satellite company, as well as one of the patrons of CXTE. He now took up almost permanent residence at the Center in his modest suite and began inviting the world's foremost astronomers, astrophysicists, and pediatricians to come and consult. He was accompanied as usual by his gorgeous companion and publicist, Katie Masters. As a young girl, Katie had accurately identified every advantage in the free market open to brains and beauty. Now with her face and figure on every screen, she enjoyed weapons-grade celebrity. Katie inspected the Barnswallow space child tenderly and kissed her sleeping head.

"Rick, this adorable girl needs a name. How about Dorothy?" Laughter rang through the hospitality lounge and space child became Dorothy. The girl woke to find a 60" television playing cartoons and, at an inviting child's desk, a computer, on the off chance that she was cyber competent. A motherly nurse, flown in from a children's home in Dodge City, bustled around bringing her pancakes and sausage, fried eggs and hash brown potatoes. Everyone was happy to see that Dorothy had a heathy appetite.

"That's an interesting earring you have, sweetheart," ventured the nurse. "Can I take a closer look?' Dorothy clapped a hand over her left ear. But then she relented and removed her hand a bit and smiled, letting the nurse—and all the surveillance cameras—see a round black stone, about the size of a pea. A Kansas physician, who had examined Dorothy under sedation when she was first discovered, had written a note: "Plain black non-gem stone, evidently inserted all the way through lobe."

"Examine earring" was added to the list of queries prepared for the coming group of scientists and select donors. Once again the televangelist community fumed at being ignored, but the Center had always rejected and proscribed any mention of divinity in their research; it was in their charter.

Another sleek, silvery jet discharged the noted British astronomer and billionaire Sir Alistair Spilhouse. The old gentleman had made a fortune in high tech stocks, which he seemed to predict with uncanny precision. He then, in a wry gesture of contempt for the world's economists, announced during an interview on Fox News that he had been entirely guided by astrology. He was instantly dropped from the rolls of distinguished scientific societies, but remained content with his post as chair of the Board of Directors of CXTE. "Come see my little girl," said Rick. "She's a darling. Katie and I might just adopt her."

The research group was now assembled, boasting three Nobels and a host of other distinctions. But the subject was still not talking. She did, however, seem to understand and could be seen laughing at cartoons. Rick and Katie sometimes ate meals with her and tried to attract her with family chat. Dorothy listened and sometimes smiled but didn't speak. To a room of frustrated scientists spoke a young physicist, hemming and hawing before the illustrious company. "I can't help it…I have to advise something… I have three young teenagers, girls, and they would all give an arm and a leg just to be on TV. You want to open her up, get her on some show. That just might do it." Heads nodded and the experiment was set up. Katie Masters entered Dorothy's room and after a bit of fussing about asked her, "Dorothy, how would you like to be on TV?" Immediate nod. "OK, then, let's look at some shows." It was assumed that any of the top celebrity shows would take Dorothy in a hot minute.

Using clips from YouTube, they went through Fox (hard headshake), Kimmel, Fallon and others (a yawn) until they finally hit Stephen Colbert (big smile and nod). The Colbert show was immediately phoned and offered Dorothy the Space Child. The producer was helpful. "Stephen is featuring another eight-year-old prodigy chick, a tap dancer. Could we get them on together?" The deal was signed.

Seven men were huddled in the lounge of a radio station deep in Tennessee. They were intent on the words of their leader, an obese man in a white suit. His face appeared young, but in the weary late hours it had come undone.. He was talking relentlessly. "That earring... This is a violation of freedom of religion... Being ignored like this. They are deceiving us. It must the temple stone... From *Revelation* 21:19. I ransacked the Holy Book for stones, even thought about the stone that David killed Goliath with. Too big. Anyway, that one is locked up in some rubbishy church in Poland. But *Revelation*! *The first stone was Jasper...,*' said the Saint. That's it. All the other twelve stones are light colored."

"Jasper is red," said one of the men.

"Red, yes. But black jasper is famous. I Googled it. It has fabulous health properties. It must be the Message and we must have that stone. The Lord has sent the first jewel of the temple to us back from space!"

"I've read about the security at that joint; it's air tight, they say."

"Nonsense, and we have the Lord with us to help recover his Message. We have a network of brave workers, some even in New Jersey. It is nothing to incapacitate a caregiver or attendant, assume his identity and infiltrate the area." The leader was named Homer Spode and he was calling on years of experience during his youth as a bank robber in the South before he found Jesus and a more profitable line of work. "I was thinking of sending our Deacon." They all looked over at the Deacon and back quickly. The Deacon was a spooky looking medium sized man whom people tended to turn away from. Some said he had done time for child abuse before he found Jesus. Nobody wanted to know the details.

"But we've got somebody on the spot, get in, try to get the stone out quick an' skedaddle."

The Center entourage could scarcely wait for the show, three days away. Dorothy remained silent but spent hours at the computer, showing experience with typing and browsing on the powerful Mac. Although the computer had been skillfully programed to transfer all her content, there must have been a glitch. Nothing she did or listened to on the Mac produced anything more than a pixilated screen and a farting sound. So feelings were high on the given evening, as she rode with Rick and Katie in a limo with the governor of New Jersey, escorted by four New Jersey Highway Patrol vehicles and trailed by the scientific cordon. At the Ed Sullivan theater on Broadway an enormous crowd was waiting. Security forces lined a passage to permit the space girl and her company to pass. Crowd excitement came to a peak, not over the small figure of Dorothy, in $289 GrlFrnd pre-torn jeans and a George Floyd T-shirt, but over their close contact to the almost nuclear celebrity glow of the semi-clad Katie Masters and tousle-haired Rick Doulton. Then they were up in the Green Room. The tap dancer, eight-year-old African American Tiffany Gardner, was already there, with parents and agent ready to do battle over precedence. Tiffany immediately ran across the room and embraced Dorothy, who responded gracefully but still did not speak. Colbert stepped into the room, joked at bit with the rather large crowd and left to prepare.

Tiffany's agent had insisted that she go on first and so the giant nationwide audience was treated to an extraordinary selection of Fred Astaire choreography, from "I'm Old Fashioned," originally with Rita Hayworth, in which Tiffany did parts of both dancers, including Rita's backward-and-in-high- heels bits'; and a solo from "Puttin' on the Ritz." The audience forgot all about space girl and went wild. When the applause died down, Colbert called both girls before him and asked, "You two girls are unique. Eight years old! Tell me, where are you going from here?" The Dorothy entourage held their breath. Would she speak?

Tiffany: "I'm going to be a star!"

Dorothy, after a hesitant moment: "I *am* a star."

Colbert, flustered: "Well, of course you're a star, but darling, you haven't performed anything. What can you impress us with, other than remarkable survival qualities." (laughter)

Dorothy: "No. I *am* a star. This part of me you see is just for appearing and speaking. The star is this black stone in my ear. It is now actually a black hole but otherwise is a giant star with a mass of 6.5 times 10 followed by seventy-two zeros. That's kilos."

Colbert, never at a loss: "And my mother-in-law is dieting!" (troubled laughter)

Colbert goes on. "I'm thinking I should be discussing the work of Stephen Hawking with you, Dorothy."

Dorothy: "I've been reading his work lately. It's amazing how much he gets right."

Tiffany, not to be ignored: *Tippity tappity tap*

The producer, seeing audience members checking their watches, is flailing his arms at the band to start cueing a break. The Dorothy entourage is exchanging glances that all mean: Let's get back to the Center! Rethink! Holy shit! But on the way back Dorothy fell asleep in the limo on Katie's lap so they put her to bed right away. Questions in the morning.

Benny Persons figured about 4 a.m. or a little earlier. Some burglars were impatient, went too soon after midnight and ran into insomnia, nagging money worries, or just plain ill-timed sex. He managed to follow an off-duty Center guard to a bar, bought him a drink with something in it, took his uniform and credentials and left him in a dark corner of the parking lot in his underwear. They were both African American, making confusion easy. As it was, no one even checked the cheerful, whistling security man with the easy smile. Benny figured he'd see if he could pop the earing out without waking the kid and disappear into the night. From down a long hall he could spot the target door. So he waited, and waited until a nurse emerged and went down the other way. In a second he was in the room, found the big bed and... the wrong side of her face was up. *She's dead asleep*, he thought, and he spoke softly: "Turn over sweetheart, y'hear? Gonna pull your blanket up." and he tugged it gently. Dorothy turned over obediently. The ear was there. The stone was there.

How hard could this be? Benny's skillful fingers gently encircled the stone and began to push it through its hole. Except there was no hole. Dorothy suddenly said "What!" And Benny disappeared. One second he was there, the next...nothing. Dorothy put her head down and went back to sleep.

Katie seemed to have the best rapport with Dorothy so far, so she brought in Dorothy's breakfast and ate a pancake with her (cringing at the thought of the hours on the stair- master to get it off her creamy thighs). Katie had also been selected as the best person to ask the girl a question on everyone's mind. In between bites and as casually as she could contrive, she brought up the former town of Barnswallow and its residents.

"We're all wondering what you can remember about, uh, your folks and your town and like that." She was prepared for tears or worse, and was surprised when Dorothy simply cocked her head to one side and concentrated, as if contemplating a classroom problem. Finally she shook her head and answered haltingly at first.

"I wonder, myself. You know...everyone asked. You know, the...the doctors back in Kansas...people on the plane. That was before I could talk, and that was funny too. It wasn't like I forgot to talk, it was like all a blank, like I never talked before. Then when Mr. Colbert asked me who...uh, what I was, it wasn't me who answered. It was my star and I could feel it moving my lips and talking, and then I could talk myself."

Katie: "But Barnswallow—"

Dorothy: "That's all still a blank. When I try to remember, just anything, it's like a flat white wall."

Katie took her hand. "Honey, I bet it'll come back. And now, would it bother you to have a little chat with Rick and the guys? We can do it in here or in the conference room."

"I guess we're going to talk about stars."

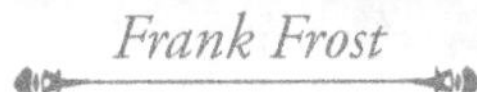

Katie laughed "Well, you sort of brought up the subject, last night."

"Can I wear those jeans again?"

Rick and Sir Alistair were joined in the conference room by all three Nobels, two astrophysicists and an arcane mathematician. An aide brought in a big pillow and Dorothy climbed up onto her chair. Rick led off the interview. "Dorothy, our group here is sort of split. Some, I have to say, really don't believe you are a star. I do, myself, and therefore my first question, the obvious first question is, why did a star come to visit our solar system?"

Dorothy considered solemnly. "You are assuming purpose. A woman going to the store to buy something has purpose. In the universe there is no purpose."

"I *knew* it!" exclaimed one of the Nobels. Nobel number two started to argue but Rick shushed them.

Dorothy went on. "I guess I was just a little girl. But over the past few days I've become aware. Things just come in my mind, slowly. Names and things come up and I Google them. And I can read real fast now. Mr. Hawking explained about Newton and Einstein and some of the rest my star filled in."

"If I may ask a question," ventured Sir Alistair. "It's about that black hole. Why isn't it just sucking the whole solar system into it instantly?"

Dorothy thought again, scratched her head. "I'm trying to think of the words. "It's in, uh..., null entropy. It is in fact a star but at some, uh, location in spacetime it is, was, became a black hole. It escaped gravity and can be anywhere at any time. Mr. Hawking speaks of wormholes and wrinkles in spacetime. I think he got a bit beyond me." She gestured helplessly.

There was a round of "hmms," glances exchanged and adjusting of eyeglasses.

"So your vigintillion-pound gorilla can just waltz through space and time?" chuckled the mathematician. They all laughed.

Dorothy's frowned. "Vigintillion. That's 63 zeros. Actually my star has 72 zeros. I don't know the word for that." She rubbed her earring. "Anyway, it says that being here is just 'ex-ist-ent-ial.'"

"Existential," pronounced Sir Alistair. "The oldest alibi in the world. "Might he not be investigating one of what you call 'wrinkles' in space time?"

"Why do you call my star 'he'? After all, I'm a she." Dorothy looked over at Katie and grinned. "But you raise a good question. Why did the star choose me to be its...uh... spokesperson? Maybe there is a purpose? I don't know."

"None the less," murmured the third Nobel, a minute Indian man, "a mass more than twice that of our sun, just lurking around our neighborhood...you're sure there is nothing we should be worrying about?"

Second Nobel: I'm still working on the bit about 'escaping gravity.' You mean to say that gravity is not a universal field?"

Sir Alistair: an entity that can escape gravity can reacquire it. That mass could immediately destroy the solar system."

Second Nobel: "Escaping gravity... acquiring it! Little Miss, all these ideas are totally beyond any theories we know. Is there some force your star enjoys of which we remain innocent?"

Dorothy played with a strand of her hair, contemplating. "Well...there is always *nous*—"

"*Nous!?* What the—" the refrain went around the table. "Of course, said the mathematician. She is speaking of νοῦς in ancient Greek. Meaning mind, or a sort of cosmic intellect. First proposed by Anaxagoras in the fifth century B.C. as the force that started the universe moving—"

"Oh bullshit!" exclaimed the second Nobel and a round of similar, if more diplomatic expressions echoed through the room.

"Please, gentlemen," cried Rick, striking the table with the flat of his hand. "Consider the feelings of our guest!"

"No," said Dorothy firmly. "That was correct, what you said… about starting the universe moving. It was *nous* and is always *nous*. It's always there and…my star says it…uh, sort of *tunes* things, like a…like a musical instrument."

Rick, anticipating another explosion of scorn, broke in swiftly, "But Dorothy, everything we believe in science is based on observation, or prediction tested by experimentation. Can you, or your star suggest any evidence for the existence of *nous?*

Dorothy: "May I ask a question, Mr. Doulton?"

"It's Rick, darling. We're all family here. And ask away!"

"Okay. I know you have space vehicles in your company."

"Boy, do we ever! We have six shuttles out there in the pine barrens. We can put satellites in orbit, contract to shuttle folks up to the space station—"

"And he takes silly rich people up for an orbit or two and charges a few hundred thousand dollars." Katie spoke up for the first time. "Would you like a ride?"

"We've got a wedding going up sometime in the next few days, if they can come up with the check. But we can put them off for a bit. That vehicle can take four of us—"

The girl clapped her hands gleefully. "Oh! Oh, could we?" She looked round the room, assumed a bit more gravitas. "My star is saying there *is* evidence but we have to be out in orbit to…uh measure it."

"That's fine for you—." All three Nobels started protesting at the same time. Rick put his hands up. "No, no, wait! We're all set up in that vehicle to Zoom all observations right back here on the big screen. If there is some *nous*-inspired wrinkle visible or measurable, everyone here will be right on top of it, and with two-way communication."

"I hope you'll include at least one real astronomer," grumped Sir Alistair. "Of course," answered Rick. "You, me, Katie and Dorothy. I'll call the launch pad right away, set it up for day after tomorrow!"

Homer Spode was ranting away in that church basement. "Nothing! Nobody's seen that burglar. If that son of a bitch ran out with that jewel—"

"My guy inside says the girl still has the earring. Something happened to Persons. Cops found his car in a lot a half mile away."

"Think he's in custody, they're keeping it a secret?"

"Negative. Cops found the security guard he drugged wandering around in his underwear. They're still working on his story."

"That settles it! No more half measures. We're leaving for New Jersey. Deacon, you think you can steal an earring?"

The next day was a flurry of activity for Rick. His Spastek operation had taken over the old Fort Dix and all the pine barrens between it and the sea. Spastek could launch two shuttles a day if they had a NASA contract and they could arrange a civilian orbit, with TV and a wet bar in a day, easy. Dorothy had her head in the computer most of the day and the rest of the time picking out her clothes, once Katie told her that they would be Zooming live back to earth on cable news.

The scientists congregated in the conference room and snarled at each other, citing wormholes and singularities until they could barely agree on Newton and Einstein. A good dinner put them all to sleep well before Colbert.

The televangelist attack was sudden and vicious. Wearing New Jersey highway patrol uniforms, the Deacon and a massive ex-wrestler leaped out of a waiting van and forced a door, then sprinted down the hall. Dorothy awoke to find her head clenched in hard hands. The Deacon felt the tightness of the earring, swore a terrible oath and with his penknife simply cut off the bottom of Dorothy's earlobe. Then they were out of the door and gone.

Dorothy's anguished cry woke everyone. Guards rushed to see a black van disappearing in the distance. Katie dashed in to find the nurse cradling the poor child in her arms, her hand over her ear, blood and tears streaming. A doctor hurried in, quickly applied a local anesthetic and bound the wound, but Dorothy couldn't stop crying.

"My star, my star! He took my star! He cut me! Oh, oh, oh!" The medic finally sedated her and she went to sleep in Katie's arms, Katie crying herself and trying not to mutter "Fucking bastards, fucking bastards," too loud as the place filled with police.

The televangelists had driven as swiftly as possible out of New Jersey and to a reserved suite on the 49th floor of the Times Square Marriott. Only there did they finally relax and examine their bloody trophy. "Cut that fucking meat off it, Deacon!" cried Homer Spode. "That's the holy jasper, first jewel of the temple!" They all agreed that the normal Baptist injunctions against alcohol couldn't apply at such a triumphant moment and ordered up a few bottles of Jack Daniel's, a decent Tennessee beverage. They finally all went into a boozy slumber, the "sacred stone," a small, silent very black stone resting in the center of a table, waiting.

Rick, Katie and the scientists were all standing around in the conference room early the next morning having coffee and doughnuts when Dorothy marched in, still in her nightgown.

"Darling, I've called off the launch—" began Rick. But Dorothy interrupted in a clarion clear voice that froze the group in mid-breath.

"No, Rick! Now of all times we must get out into orbit. We must! It's absolutely...it's— You will see something...*perceive* something so incredible—"

"But Dorothy!" cried Katie. You're still hurt...and your star... we have to get your star back! The FBI says—"

Dorothy shook her head calmly. "I'm not hurt. A tiny cut. And I know where my star is. It has told me. And it's too late... there's nothing that..." She stopped. "My star is now running things. Rick! Katie! Call Fort Dix again. If we can launch by...uh, 1030, we'll be in place by, let's see, about nine minutes and then... Let's say 1100. That will do."

Her voice was so hypnotic in its urgency and authority that no one thought to object, only the small Indian Nobel muttering, "She has the true performative function of speech...Barthes was right!" And of course, everyone desperately *wanted* to see whatever wrinkle of space-time Dorothy's star might be planning.

With not much more than a change of clothes—"*Warm* clothes! *warm* clothes!" Rick counseling—Dorothy, Katie, Rick and Sir Alistair were bundling into a R66 turbocopter and winging off to the pine barrens of Fort Dix. The launch was back on again, had barely started to stand down, in fact, and the ground crew helped the presumptive astronauts into the luxurious space capsule with its bubble canopy of aluminum glass, stronger than titanium and offering 360° visibility. The Zoom screen showed the tense faces of the scientists back at the Center.

"Get ready for three Gs," warned Rick. "We have to get up to over 17,000 miles an hour in under nine minutes." There was a howl of exploding fuel and Dorothy felt herself pressed back into her take-off pod by an enormous weight. The capsule quickly outdistanced its own sound and they were in the silence of space. In a few minutes Katie unbuckled Dorothy and then they were all floating around the bubble. Rick cautioned them all to find a mooring handle and Dorothy found herself able with just a little effort to keep a stable position with a great view of what looked like an ocean below her...or was it above? "This is so cool!" she marveled, now back again with her little-girl voice.

The televangelist-burglar brigade woke late and groggily. They ordered a huge breakfast and another couple of bottles of their Tennessee beverage and for a while ate silently at the big table, contemplating the tiny black stone in the center.

"Don't look like much. Sure it's jasper?" mumbled a bleary chap through a mouth full of pancake.

"This," orated Homer, "is the first stone of the temple. Men, Look on it and wonder at the glory!" He hurled the heavy curtains back and held the stone up to the rays of the morning sun streaming in the window.

The sunlight hit the stone. His hand burst into flame. The stone tore its way through his hand, fell onto his large stomach, continued down through it as it acquired gravity, then through the concrete floor and thence through forty-eight more floors, gaining speed, three garage floors, through the granite of Manhattan and started its descent to the center of the earth three thousand nine hundred and fifty nine miles away at a speed of several thousand miles per hour. Once there it bathed in liquid iron at a temperature of eleven thousand degrees Fahrenheit.

As her companions raved at the vistas of the earth passing before them Dorothy suddenly said, "Uh oh!" She quickly had their undivided attention.

"My star is loose," she said. It's got back gravity and is heading for the center of the earth." As they slid over Japan with its glistening cities in the night suddenly all the lights below went out.

"How did it do that?" Katie squealed. No one answered for a moment. Then Dorothy murmured, "It's two hundred years ago. No lights." Then they were in sunlight again and the earth glistened white. There were no cities.Another rotation and the earth tunred green and brown, then white again.

"It's not possible," said Sir Alistair calmly.

"What's not possible? None of this is possible! What is—"

Sir Alistair went on: "Your star, my dear, has reversed time. Turned back the clock he did, she did, whatever. First the lights went out; they hadn't been invented yet. Then, speeding up, the glacial ages began. You saw the snow and ice. 'Borne back ceaselessly into the past.' as it were. That star has more piety and wit than Omar Khayyam counted on."

"It's not changing space," said Dorothy. "It's using all its energy to turn time back instead. It's going to fix the wrinkle by going back to when it started, then start over again." Drawn by the high shrill voice, all stared at Dorothy, who was now an toddler of three or so. "We're caught in the wavelength too!"

"My boobs, where are my boobs!?" They all saw a fifteen year old Katie clutching her quite boyish chest with both hands. Rick's youthful hair grew out and pushed off his tousled hairpiece, which went floating around the capsule.

"If you have a moment, do you have any idea what's going to happen to us?" Sir Alistair asked. "Is this the end of the universe?"

"This one, I don't know." lisped baby Dorothy, "There are others, you know, all together, like pages in a book—" and *blip*, she was gone.

The outlines of the others grew indistinct, and smaller, as the shuttle continued its journey. California sank below the waves; the Mediterranean opened at both ends; South America lurched across the Atlantic and nestled into Africa's gulf of Guinea; India tore off and headed south to join Antarctica as *nous* guided his star in fixing the tiny wrinkle, not in space, but in time.

In Barnswallow a woman leaned out the kitchen window of a bungalow. "Dorothy," she called. It's getting dark, sweetheart. Better come in for supper."

The little girl skipped in the door. "Mom, I just saw a shooting star! It was the coolest thing."

The asteroid hit the planet's atmosphere, turned bright red and burst into flames as it hurtled on westward into the sunset, where it finally splashed harmlessly into the ocean.

* * *

THE OLIVE TREE

Spencer was walking around in the garden, deep in thought, spooking the redstarts who were accustomed to rule the yard this time of day. Rosalind had been watching him and when she reached a stopping point in the article she was typing on her laptop she went out and joined him.

"What's on your mind, big guy?" She put an arm over his shoulder. They had made love the night before and she was still feeling extra chummy.

"An olive tree," Spencer said, still concentrating on a spot on the ground in front of him. "An olive would be just right here in the corner. It would sort of balance the cherry over there. And the sun's just perfect. We could get a small one and it would grow like a bastard in this soil and climate."

"It would be nice," Rosalind agreed. "But do we need an olive? How about an oleander? They flower half the year here."

"We could have olives. You know, olives from our own tree. Like we did back in Napa."

Rosalind thought about it, remembering picking the olives every fall, slicing them with fingers turning purple,, brining them, changing the brine every few days, finally serving them to guests, with Spencer bragging about *his* olives, from *his own* tree, although she usually did most of the work. And the guests politely tasting the obligatory one or two before turning gratefully to the smoked salmon. Sometimes she'd thrown out whole quart jars because they'd molded, Spencer could never figure out why.

"But the olives here are dirt cheap, Spence. Last time we were in St. Rémy? You know, the market? The olive stalls had a thousand different kinds—we have some in the frigo right now"

But Spencer had convinced himself.

"We're in Provence, babe. We ought to have an olive!"

They had bought the old, stone house four months ago. Spencer had figured out that he could handle his investments anywhere in the world on the net. Rosalind successfully wrote travel articles. After thinking about it a bit she had decided she could work anywhere too. Napa valley had gotten smog-bound and awash with tourists all year long. And Provence was much closer to London, where she'd been born and grown up. She still had withdrawal symptoms.

After fifteen years with Spencer Rosalind knew better than to argue. Besides, she thought, an olive tree would be nice. Maybe they ought to have a grape vine too, train it over an arbor to make some shade on the terrace. They could buy both plants at the same time. But their trip that afternoon to plant stores was frustrating. The grape vine was the easy part. But even in the garden section of huge discount stores the little olive plants were absurdly expensive. Spencer was fuming.

"Three-hundred-fifty francs for a goddamned olive! That's more than fifty bucks. And did you see what a tiny thing they all were? Like a pencil! It'd take ten years before they'd bear!"

She agreed, tactfully, standing there with her grape vine on her hip in its five liter plastic pot. They both remembered transplanting root stock from an old derelict olive grove back in northern California, just chopping volunteers loose from the growth around the base of an old tree and planting them in full sun overlooking the Napa valley below their ranch. Olives were like weeds. In two years the trees had grown eight feet and started bearing fruit.

"You know," said Spencer, "I've seen neglected groves around here. I bet we could rescue some volunteers from there."

"I don't know," said Rosalind. "Maybe we should ask Jeannot."

So that evening they walked down to the cafe and put the problem to Jeannot. He was a former rugby player, huge and battered, a legendary star for France twenty years ago, when they'd won the Five Nations championship. He owned the cafe and some local real estate.

Spencer and Rosalind had bought their house through him and had found him marvelously friendly and helpful in dealing with all the complexities of French house-buying and furnishing. They sat in the bar facing his trophy wall with its montage of posters and photos of his greatest rugby triumphs, his desperation score against New Zealand in 1980, his impossible tackle of the Irish fly half in 1986, all the photos surrounding his old jersey from his last game, the number three on it, still unwashed, with the copious blood stains drying black through the years.

"Ahah," he said, after hearing their story. "You don't like the price so you want to steal from a neighbor. So soon you have become true Provençaux. Congratulations!"

Spencer started to protest but Jeannot put up a huge hand. "No, no, my friend—I am joking. But you must realize, in France all land belongs to someone and to take something from someone's land is a serious crime. Ever since the Revolution, when they gave the peasants the land."

"But there's all sorts of neglected land around here," protested Rosalind. "All that church property outside the village. It's full of trees and fields."

"Yes, and not one olive," said Jeannot, smiling. "You see, when the brothers went bankrupt the next day you couldn't find a small plant anywhere on the property. It was all dug up and carried away during the night. The cherry trees are still there, of course, they're too big to carry away, but in cherry season the kids here in town pick them bare. No," he said. "You have to find a small tree on someone's property. But not a real olive grove. Only a tree someone is not taking care of. Otherwise you are in trouble. Last year old Arnaud took his neighbor to court because he picked one cherry, just walking past the orchard while Madame Arnaud was peeking out the window. And the Malécot woman was fined five hundred francs because she went in Pillod's vineyard in February, of all things, and picked up the leftover vine prunings. You should have seen her in the court, crying. 'But I just wanted to grill the sausages!' The magistrate didn't even look at her. 'Five hundred francs.' Bam! And everyone in the room knew Pillod was a sour old bastard but they were thinking, 'What if it were my field?' Here in France you can cross anyone's field. But don't take anything!"

Spencer looked deflated but Rosalind was beginning to look stubborn. Jeannot recognized the attitudes.

"Alright, my friends. I'll tell you. Walk around the neighborhood, then tell me what you find. Maybe there are some deserted properties no one is taking care of." And he winked.

The next day Spencer set out for a long walk, having borrowed Rosalind's bird-watching binoculars as cover. He had already thought of a target. On the hill behind town there was an old, derelict *mas*, a country house surrounded by a two-meter high stone wall. The owners were rich old people in Paris who never came here. He and Rosalind had often walked by on the path that led up the hill, then through Fouquet's cherry orchard, then down a country road to the main road back home. Once they had stopped to peek through the locked and chained gate across the driveway. They saw nothing but overgrown brush, trees, vines, going every which way. As they turned away they had been confronted by a little old man who had emerged from a tiny cottage across the road.

"*That is private property,*" he had shouted in heavily accented Provençal French. "*I am the caretaker. I can call the police at any time!*" It was old Raymond, Jeannot told Spencer. A mean old man, as nosy as an old woman

This time Spencer kept to the back side of the property, concealed by the heavy underbrush along the path. He'd remembered a spot where a low oak tree limb overhung the wall and he thought he'd take a look into the property, see if he could spot any old olive trees. Rosalind had warned him about the wall.

"They put broken glass in the mortar on top of the wall when they're building it, you know. Mind you don't try to jump up with your hands on the wall." She told Spencer the old estates in England had broken glass on the walls too.

"My God! What if someone cut their hands...the insurance..." Spencer had been about to say, when he realized what a typically absurd American reaction that was.

When he reached the oak he was looking for, he did, nevertheless, feel the top of the wall gingerly. Yes, his fingers told him, there was broken glass on top of the wall. So it was up the tree then.

He had been thinking of his youth, when he had scampered up tree trunks, branch to branch, to look into the next yard, where the neighbors' teenage daughter from time to time lay in the sun with her top off to get an all-over tan. Without that sort of incentive, and now suddenly conscious of twenty extra pounds and what he thought of as a firm and muscular stomach that still seemed to get in the way of narrow spaces between tree limbs, Spencer attained the branch he was looking for panting, sweating, and with a long bruise on his thigh from a sharp stub of a branch. He inched out along the limb until he was over the wall. To the left he could see nothing but rank underbrush. He turned to the right. There, in full view, was a small, miserably neglected, stand of olive trees. The smallest had the diameter of a broomstick and was five feet high. Spencer was thinking that a little tree like that, watered and fertilized in a friendly yard, would grow at least six feet in a year and be ready to produce fruit.

He fixated on the tree, seeing the scraggly limbs becoming stout, reaching into the heavens, putting out tiny bunches of flowers to become tiny green fruits, no larger than a pea, in the summer, then swelling in the autumn, growing, growing, plump and green until the magic days of late December, when they started turning black and could be picked, sliced, brined, turned into impressive appetizers...

He became conscious of a rhythmic noise beneath him. He looked down and perceived a large Rottweiler, sitting just below him and looking up with joyous expectation, tongue lolling out, panting, but no intention of barking, as a stupid Shepherd would have done, just waiting for the moment when the intruder might drop down into his territory and provide the moment he had been trained for all his life.

"Bon chiot!" said Spencer in the friendliest tone he could muster. *Good puppy!* The Rottweiler cocked an ear, heard the unfamiliar accent, and just barely lifted a lip in a silent snarl. He shifted his hind feet as if seeking a firmer stance from which to leap up the wall.

"These damned French with their damned German dogs!" raged Spencer to Rosalind when he got home. "Haven't they ever heard of a Golden Retriever, a Lab, some nice dog like that?"

"It's the burglars, darling," said Rosalind, trying to calm him down. "We ourselves have twenty-thousand francs worth of burglar prevention with the alarm connection to the police. Most local French people can't afford that. So they have German dogs. It's a lot cheaper. And the dogs will wake up when a thief comes in the night, not like the lout our village calls a policeman."

"Wakes up! That's it, my sweet! Wakes up! You're a genius!" Spencer was on his feet dancing with joy. "We just have to make sure the dog doesn't wake up. Your pills! You must have something..."

and he went into the bathroom where Rosalind could hear him rooting through drawers. He emerged with a bottle of valium in one hand and several capsules of *Dormitol,* a French prescription sleeping pill, in the other.

"Remember your back pain? And the doctor in Apt said you'd sleep like a baby? How many of these do you think..."

"Well remember, a Rottweiler doesn't weigh what a human..."

"Oh come on! That bastard is sixty kilos if he's an ounce. He'll outweigh you ten pounds at least!"

"Maybe a couple...and some valium to relax him..." Rosalind was getting into the pharmaceutical spirit of things.

"And you remember," she added. "Andy left that pipe half full of hashish last May?"

"Do I remember! It was monstrous! I could barely walk after one puff. And I've been tempted to throw it away. But do you think a dog would eat hashish?"

"Christ, Spencer! Have you ever seen a big dog eat? He'll have half a can of dog food full of pills and hash down his throat in two seconds!" She giggled. "I wish I could see it."

"You mean you're not coming with me?"

"Sorry, Spence. I don't do olive trees."

"Well then. But you'll have to go get the dog food. Alright?"

"Fine. I can do dogfood."

But Rosalind began to wonder the next day at the village grocers. She had intended to go to the supermarket in Apt where she could buy dogfood anonymously but she'd been too busy and finally just walked down the block to Henri's little *épicerie* in the village. As usual Henri was talking, laughing, joking, gossiping with everyone in the store as he checked them out and her heart fell when he finally got around to her purchases. Out of the pile of coffee, rice, cereal, mineral water, and onions he immediately snatched the can of dogfood and gestured with it to the whole store, babbling away in French.

"Ah, Madame! You are buying a dog! A wise move. The thieves are everywhere these days!"

"No, no," interrupted Rosalind hastily, in her adequate French. *"I'm just picking up a canfor a friend."*

"You have a friend with a dog, then?" Rosalind was about to make up some other lie, but to her relief Henri, as usual, couldn't resist joking.

"Or maybe he's going to eat the dogfood himself? Ha ha! Better than the paté you get atsome stores. But you know, a woman came in, oh, last spring, and said she actually wanted dogfood for her husband."

The crowd in the store grew silent. They knew that Henri was going to tell one of his famous stories.

"She'd read that this certain dogfood would improve her husband's...you know what I mean!" And Henri grinned and winked shamelessly. There was a ripple of mirth in the crowd. Most of them had heard the story.

"So the next week she came back and bought two cases of the same dogfood. I thought, 'That man must be like a stallion by now!' But I didn't ask. How could I?

"Well, two weeks later she came in and you could see she'd been crying. So I ask, 'How is your husband with the dogfood, does it make him...you know?'

"But she just starts crying again, blubbering away, and finally says, 'He's...he's dead.'"

Henri did a good impression of a woman blubbering. *"So I said, 'I knew that much dogfood couldn't be healthy!' And she says 'No, no. It wasn't the food. Yesterday he was lying inthe street licking his balls and a bus ran over him.'"*

Rosalind escaped with her purchases in the general laughter, hoping that no one would remember she'd bought dogfood.

Spencer had been at his computer trading on the internet all morning. Along with his blue chips he had begun experimenting with selling upstart internet stocks short. A week ago he'd taken a big gamble. Today he redeemed the stock he had shorted at a third of its cost and came out over $14,000 ahead once he'd paid the commissions and the interest on his margin account. So he was in a good mood when Rosalind came home.

He laughed uproariously at the dogfood story. "Hey! That's a funny joke! I wonder where an imbecile like Henri heard it?"

"Probably in the French edition of *Playboy*," said Rosalind. "But the joke's surely as oldas the Hittites."

"Did the Hittites have dogfood?" asked Spencer and roared again at his own wit.

"I don't know, but you can explain, next time Henri runs into you and asks you how the stuff is working." Rosalind was grumpy, but cheered up at the news of the stock market coup andthey were soon in the kitchen, mixing dogfood with valium, *Dormitol*, and hashish, arguing over the ratio of ingredients.

"Maybe we shouldn't use the hash," said Rosalind. "If you got caught...you know how the French are about drugs."

"I think the French are even tougher about poisoning someone's dog," said Spencer. "Anyway, no one's going to catch me. I'm going to go out at one o'clock this morning. The moon's going to be almost full. You know this town. On a weeknight there's no one awake at eleven, let alone at one"

"If you say so, " said Rosalind. "But dress warmly. It's still cold these nights."

Spencer stayed up and watched a movie on the television, It was an American gangster movie dubbed into French and he understood only a bit of the dialogue but the movie was action driven and the plot was senseless anyway.

Inspired by the violence and fortified with several little glasses of Armagnac he set out silently a little after one A.M., wearing his good pigsuede jacket and a backpack containing a short spade and a sturdy hatchet normally used for firewood. In a plastic bag was the enchanted gobbet of dogfood.

The outer lanes of the village were completely deserted and a slight mist obscured the street lights. Spencer soon left the lights behind on the path up the hill and was gratified to see the forest ahead of him illuminated by the brilliance of the full moon. He soon reached the designated oak tree and began to climb carefully, making just enough noise to alert a guardian dog. This time he managed to evade the sadistic sharp limb that had pierced his thigh the last time. He found the long branch that reached out over the wall and was wondering whether the Rottweiller was on the job or not when a piercing bark from below nearly made him lose his grip. He peered frantically down into the gloom. There was the Rottweiller indeed, no longer mute but threatening to bark again.

"Bon chiot!" said Spencer in his most reassuring tone, struggling to extract the dog bait from the top of his pack. Luckily the big dog fell silent, looking upward now in anticipation. Spencer extracted the wad of dogfood, making a filthy mess of his right hand, and held it out. *"Bon appetit!"* he said, and let the ball fall to the ground.

The Rottweiller was on it in a second, but suddenly paused and looked up into the tree. Spencer was beginning to worry that this was a trained guard dog and would refuse any food except from its master. But he had nothing to fear. After the one suspicious glance the big dog took a single whiff of the morsel at its feet, wolfed it down in two swift gulps, and looked up eagerly for more. Now all Spencer had to do was wait.

He had actually not thought about the length of time it would take to suitably drug a large dog. The branch he was lying on got harder and rougher on his chest and stomach and the chill of the night began to pierce even through his leather jacket and wool sweater. Beneath him the dog continued to mount a vigil, now and then wandering off to the right or left as if to make sure that no other path of invasion had been left open. The creature did not bark again, fortunately.

It was close to three o'clock when Spencer finally saw the big head begin to lower, then jerk suddenly erect again, a reaction familiar to Spencer himself from his days in college lecture halls. Then the dog started wandering again, this time aimlessly. He looked confused and once tried to bark but it only came out as a muffled "woof" and finally he headed back towards the front of the estate, staggering once and with difficulty regaining his feet.

All was going as planned, Spencer thought. But he waited for another frozen ten minutes before wriggling to the end of the branch. First he took off the pack and dropped it to the ground. Then he laboriously turned himself around so he could lower himself enough to drop to the ground himself, which he did clumsily, falling noisily onto the underbrush. He held his breath for a moment, terrified that the dog would reappear.

But silence reigned and Spencer slowly got to his feet and tiptoed with the pack over to the olive orchard. As if an omen, the moon came out from behind a patch of mist and shone directly on the little tree he'd seen the other day. The silvery leaves gleamed in the moonlight. Spencer set to work as quietly as he could, shoveling the dirt away from the base of the tree until the clump of roots stopped his spade. From experience he knew that he could cut the outlying roots with a hatchet and then bend the tree this way and that until the roots at the bottom either broke or could be cut as well. The tree would recover quickly and grow new roots once back in the ground again.

He'd forgotten how time consuming it was to uproot an olive, particularly if one wished to preserve a fairly large root ball, so the sight of the moon dropping below the trees to the west just as the olive finally came free from the ground alarmed Spencer. He consulted his watch and saw that he'd been working for a half hour. He had no idea how long the dog would be suitably drugged. He therefore set to work quickly, filling the hole in the earth, smoothing the ground around it, and strewing leaves and brush at random until the site looked like the surrounding wilderness. Then he put spade and hatchet in his pack and lobbed it over the wall. There was a satisfying *clunk* on the other side. He now began to swing the tree with its heavy ball of roots and earth, planning to swing it to the top of the wall where he could lever it over.

But on the back swing Spencer suddenly heard the thunder of great paws behind him. In his apprehensive mood it sounded every bit like Ben Hur coming in his chariot. He frantically jumped sideways in time to see the huge dark shape of the Rottweiler surge past him and run directly headfirst into the wall. He was preparing to hurl himself up the wall, olive tree forgotten, when he saw that the dog was lying motionless. My God! Did I kill the poor thing? He thought, and rapidly began swinging the tree again. A-one, a-two, and a-three. He gave it a tremendous swing and the tree actually cleared the wall. He could hear it crash down on the other side.

Spencer now considered his last obstacle, to climb back across the wall. He had planned to leap up, seize the overhanging limb and use it to get a foot on top of the wall, avoiding the broken glass. His first two attempts failed as his shoe skidded off the edge of the wall. Then he had to let go the limb and take a few deep breaths to get his wind back. Finally he determined to put everything into the effort. *What am I?* he thought, *Some puny wimp? I used to be an athlete!*And he leaped up to grab the tree limb, swinging his left shoe up onto the wall. His heel dug in satisfactorily and now he started to twist, hugging the tree limb and trying to bring up his right leg. But his right leg wasn't coming up, caught on something, he thought, shaking it. Spencer was about to jump back down and he gave a quick glance to see what was preventing his leg from coming up. He cried out in dismay at the terrible sight.

There was the Rottweiler, at least partially revived, jaws locked around his running shoe. The dog was still obviously groggy and was sort of staggering around, but the strength of its jaws was there...and increasing. As Spencer desperately tried to shake his foot free the dog began to growl.

"Oh my God!" whimpered Spencer, and in a great spasm he jerked up on his right foot as hard as he could. His foot slipped right out of his shoe and suddenly he was free. But the momentum threw him onto the wall and he convulsed in pain as his left leg ground against the spikes of broken glass.

"Aarghh!" Spencer shrilled through clenced teeth. With a herculean effort he pulled himself back onto the oak limb. But his chest brushed against the top of the wall and he felt a puncture of sharp glass in his chest before he was able to rip his jacket free. Finally he could slither back down the tree on the other side of the wall to retrieve his treasure. The tree did not neglect to rip at his groin with the sharp broken stub on the way down.

Then all Spencer could do was look with horror at his olive tree. It was lying directly across the prostrate figure of a little old man whose face was obscured by Spencer's pack. It seemed obvious. Old Raymond had somehow heard or suspected him and had crept up on the outside of the wall, planning...what? To confront him with his theft? No, worse. There was a shotgun lying in the brush. So the old man had been going to trap him, maybe shoot him. And then Spencer had thrown the pack containing the hatchet and shovel over the wall and hit Raymond right on the head, knocking him unconscious. Then the dog had attacked. Then Spencer had thrown the tree over to land directly on the man's abdomen. Could he be alive?

Spencer gingerly felt a grimy wrist for a pulse, then almost collapsed in relief. There was a strong pulse and now he could hear labored breathing and smell the reek of poorly digested food and too much wine. Steeling his nerves, calming himself, Spencer now gathered up his pack and his tree. He could do nothing about his lost shoe so he began to creep carefully down the path towards town, hobbling on his one bare foot. As he was reaching the outskirts of the village he heard a dog on the hill behind him begin to bay in pain and despair, starting up a chorus from every other dog in town. But his back gate was near and he slipped quickly through it.

The clock in the 17th century cathedral was striking four o'clock in the morning when Rosalind finally finished bandaging Spencer's cuts from the broken glass. There were two small ones on his chest where the sharp points had gone right through his leather jacket. But there were three serious slashes on his left calf from when he'd heaved himself up onto the branch. He'd barely felt the cuts at the time but now they were smarting miserably in spite of liberal annointing with *Erythrogel,* a powerful prescription antibiotic.

"At least it won't get infected," said Rosalind. "But I really think you need some stitches." She'd shaved his leg all around the cuts, medicated them, and bandaged them tightly.

"God! They really hurt. Do give me another glass of the Armagnac, babe."

"Spence, I don't know—the ointment package says alcohol is *déconseillé*—it might cause an adverse reaction. You know, we could go to Dr. Beauvais tomorrow. He could put in a few stitches and maybe prescribe a painkiller..."

"Sure! And two minutes later everyone in town knows that I have glass cuts on my leg. And there's probably blood all over the top of the wall! Oh Christ, it stings so!" Spencer was being a baby, a condition Rosalind never discouraged.

"Oh, poor Spence! You'll have to tough it out then. At least we have some valium and *Dormitol* left."

"Thank God! Give me a few."

"Actually, they're mixed in with the dog food we didn't use. And there's the hashish in there too. That could be a plus. You know, they say the dog food's not bad at all, we could warm it up with a little oil and garlic…"

A few days later Spencer strolled down the main street of town through the towering plane trees to Jeannot's café, disguising the pain of walking on his torn leg with a studied lassitude, as if suddenly fully aware of the enchanting Provençal village.

Taking a table outside under the plane trees and talking to Jeannot, he could see into the bar where a ray of sun lightened Jeannot's trophy wall and the bloody jersey. It only reminded Spencer of his own wounds.

"So, you took the olive tree!" said Jeannot. "What luck! Now you are one of us!"

Spencer had told the whole story, knowing that Jeannot, alone of all the villagers, would never disclose a confidence, at least not while it remained a sensitive issue.

"Yes, but I'm worried sick. I know the police were up there at the *mas*, looking at the wall and everything else. And they've got my other shoe!" Spencer was whispering intently.

"The shoe? I don't know…fingerprints? Who knows? If you have never been fingerprinted in France there is no comparison, *hein*? And I talked to the police, being very concerned, of course. They told me they could find no crime, nothing stolen, only the blood on the wall, and they think old Raymond was just drunk and imagining things. The shoe? They said the dog probably found it somewhere and brought it home. What did you do with the hole from the olive tree?"

"I filled it in with dirt and scattered leaves around it."

"*Voilà!* No one knows there is an olive tree missing. So, my friend, I think you have a free olive tree, aside from the cost of your coat and your pants. How much did you pay for the leather coat, did you say?"

Spencer started grumbling about the ruined clothes but Jeannot's attention was distracted by the view down the street, seeing Raymond himself trudging toward them. The old man had a bandage tied around his head and he was holding a huge Rottweiler on a long leash, letting the dog circulate among the tables outside the two other cafés along the tree lined lane. Most arresting was the sight of the large running shoe in Raymond's other hand, which he frequently held out for the dog to sniff.

Should I say something? Jeannot thought. *Or maybe just let things take thei course. It is the Provençal way after all. And who knows what will happen?*

Timmy's in the Well

The dog started barking again around six, just when she'd poured herself a drink and sat down at the computer. It wasn't a normal *arf-arf*; he had a nervewracking scraping kind of yelp, fingernails on the blackboard, that kind of bark. Julia tried to keep working on her article but it was no use. She got up and yelled down the stairs, "Danny! He's driving me crazy! Go over there again, and this time..."

But something in the echo of her voice told her that Dan wasn't there, he must have gone down to the village butcher's to get dinner. She looked at her watch. Sixish. That was about normal if they didn't have leftovers to eat. He was going to cook something for dinner.

Dan had gotten a good contract for his proposed "Cooking of Provence" and they were over here in an eighteenth century stone house built into the medieval wall of a little farm village in the hills east of Avignon. His publisher knew the owner, who never used it. Dan had four good-selling cookbooks and he could have easily written this at home in Connecticut but he wanted the atmosphere and to be able to buy French food and cook it here in Provence. Julia had her own writing to do and was about to stay home but her publisher told her, no problem, we'll pay for a fax there in France, just keep sending the pages, we're all one electronic world now. So she'd been doing well on the three contracted articles—except for the fucking dog.

Dan had a theory about the barking dogs. "Every family in France has a dog," he'd said. "You have to get used to it. In the evening the first guy who gets home feeds his dog. All the other dogs a mile around can smell what's happening and they want to be fed too. So they bark. Listen," he said, waving down her objections "You know Jeannot, over there across the court? Works at the Total station out on the D 32? He starts work at seven so he comes home around five or so after a few drinks at the café. He's home first, so he calls that idiot boxer of his in his high voice..." Dan pursed his lips, sounded "Qui-NOU, Qui-NOU" almost like a bird call. Julia had to laugh, it was perfect. Dan went on, "Watch, I'll show you." And he went outside on the upstairs terrace and started calling, "Qui-NOU, Qui-NOU!" Immediately four dogs started barking in the neighborhood and the yelping of the dog next door was like an icepick in Julia's ears.

"Danny! Stop it...it drives me nuts!"

"So, I tell you what. When the dogs start barking everyday, late afternoon, we'll walk into the village, drink a pastis, talk to the locals and catch up on the town gossip. All the monsters get fed, we'll come home and we can both work for a while before dinner. Okay?"

She'd said it was okay, but it wasn't. For some weird reason she didn't usually like writing in the morning. But four or five o'clock in the afternoon, first drink of the day, she was charged. She could write seven or eight pages, hearing Dan cooking dinner downstairs, refreshing her drink now and then, coming down around eight, eight-thirty, really happy with what she'd written, knowing she could clean it up in the morning easily with that new word- processing program she'd put on the old Mac. But the problem was that in late afternoon the dogs started, and the next door neighbor's was the worst. The yelper. A widow lived there and never fed her dog until dark. So there were about two, two-and-a-half hours of barking, that awful yelp that made it impossible to concentrate.

Dan had gone over to talk to Madame Flacelière but his French wasn't very good and Madame was old and vague, purposely misunderstanding: *it is so difficult, my children want me to go to a home. I have so much to do, I must have a dog barking against the thieves, they rob every house these days...* Julia went over one day, out of her mind from the barking, wanting to see the awful creature making this noise. She'd expected to see one of the German killer dogs the French all seemed to love, or a neurotic little yapmeister. Instead it turned out to be a sweet- faced middle-sized dog, sort of reddish, long-haired, intelligent looking and immediately focusing on her there over the fence with a frown of worry, seeming to ask her, who's going to feed me, take care of me? Having seen the widow Flacelière tottering around she had to admit that the dog had a point. Julia was sure that many times Madame Flacelière had simply forgotten to feed her dog in the evening.

She heard Dan coming in downstairs. "Honey, I'm home!" he yelled, in his eternal parody of some old TV series. He'd been doing it for five years now and she still found it funny when she was in a good mood but the rest of the time she wanted to throw a pan of food in his face, if he liked old comedy that much. Trouble was, he was the cook--he was the guy with the pans of food, which she hardly ever touched. He did all the cooking, even all the cleaning up, if you could believe it. Julia went downstairs, still hearing the *"Yelp...yelp...yelp..."* from next door, just like clockwork.

"Dan, I'm really going crazy. And I thought I'd finish the travel article tonight. Can you go talk to that hag again? She'll listen to you."

Dan was shaking his head in sympathy, smiling. "It's awful, babe! I'm going right over there."

She loved him so much, he always knew what she really wanted, never gave her one of those we-men-know-what's-best kind of arguments. She felt a little misty, watching him stride next door, tan legs in his shorts, good bod, even eating all the great French food he cooked. She had her hands on her hips and couldn't help feeling to see if she was putting on inches. She knew she was. The scale told her.

A few minutes later the barking stopped, but Dan didn't come back for a bit. When he did he looked serious.

"The ambulance came for Madame today. She thought she was having a heart attack, I talked to her niece, you know, Monique? Had to come over from Mazan? Madame's in the hospital in Carpentras and they say she's resting okay now. Anyway, we fed the dog for tonight."

"Oh, God! That dog! The poor thing! I feel so guilty, it has such a sweet face. How can it make that awful sound? I was going out of my mind!"

"Well. I told Monique we'd feed the dog for a few days, however long it took. Maybe if we had it over here, in our yard, played with it or something, it wouldn't feel so helpless, like it had to bark all the time. You know?"

Julia knew she had no talent for playing with dogs and she thought it was a bad idea. "I'll go over and feed it. At least it won't have these anxiety attacks, for Christ's sake!"

"You remember," Dan said, "I have to go up to Mondragon tomorrow to review that restaurant. You know what French lunches are like. I probably won't be back till five or so. Sure you don't want to come?"

Julia always felt out of sorts when he asked her these questions. The problem was they were in maybe the biggest meat-eating country in the world and she was practically a vegetarian, maybe a little piece of salmon now and then. But she hid her irritation and nodded.

"I remembered. You just go and have fun. I'll keep an eye on the dog, feed it if it gets hungry. I could finish two assignments if I could work steady...what's the little asshole's name?" She had realized, guiltily, that she was calling the dog "it" and didn't even know its gender.

So the next morning, after Dan left, Julia went over and fed little Robert (Ro-BAIR, as the French said). She patted him and scratched his ears and he wiggled his behind and smiled, so she figured she could leave him alone. Then it was great in the morning for once. Her ideas were flowing and she finished her article and was most of the way through the second. She felt so good about it that she called her agent in New York, woke him up at seven in the morning and talked to him for an hour. Then it was past noon and she was getting hungry. Little Robert hadn't made a sound for an hour and she figured he was asleep so she went down into the village for a salad at the Café du Cours. She ran into the Wilders there and had a hilarious conversation about the mayor's sexy wife, who everyone knew was having it on with the *entraineur* of the local rugby team, a tall, slim, longhaired dreamboat. Back at the house the work continued well, but then she seemed to hear a dog barking again. RoBAIR! She'd forgotten all about him and went clumping down the stairs and out into the yard.

In their part of the village the backyards sloped downhill into the fields and vineyards. They faced west, and in the afternoon the sun could be much too bright and hot, reflecting white off the surrounding dusty fields. Years ago the crops had all depended on wells but now they had irrigation and the old wells skulked at the lower corners of the fields. She could just barely hear the yelping now so she walked across the little alley and let herself into Madame Flacelière's yard. No little dog came rushing to greet her so she stopped and stood completely still for a moment. After a bit she could hear the yelping again, weak sounding, and it seemed to be outside the yard, sounded like down in the vineyard, and she thought, the little monster is chasing a cat or something, how the hell did he get out?

She walked downhill following the last sound she'd heard of that familiar barking. There was a dirt path going around the vineyard and she paused there, listening. Then there was a yelp quite near, funny sounding, with a weird echo. Julia looked around. In the afternoon sun the world was still and frozen in heat and brightness. Above her the village of St. Gens shimmered in the heat but nothing moved, everyone seeking a nap in the shadiest rooms of their houses. The town looked like one of those dead villages up in the hills where no one had lived for fifty years.

She tried calling. "Ro-BAIR! Ro-BAIR!" Where the hell are you, you little bastard! Then there was another muffled yelp, almost gargled, and suddenly she focused on the low stone well to the east. Jesus! Was he in the well? She ran over, saw the rotten wooden cover that someone had pulled partly aside. She tried to look down but it was too dark. She was rewarded however with a passionate yelp from below. Christ! Robert was in the well! Struggling, cursing, she managed to push the cover mostly off the well head. There below was the little dog, grimly paddling in the murk. He gave another soft yelp and then sank under the surface of the water for a second, evidently from the exertion of calling.

The poor little guy! Julia looked frantically around for some man. Then she wondered if she should run up into the village and try to find someone awake. Would they all laugh at her? She had no confidence in a French village, she'd never felt close to anyone here, they all seemed so distant, preferring to talk to Dan, although her French was much better than his. Well, the hell with French men, was her reaction. Timmy's in the well! I don't have to send Lassie for help, or whatever. Attached to the side of the well was a sturdy wooden post that had once been part of the superstructure. There was an old rope looped around it, obviously part of the old pulley mechanism that had been removed years before. And there were two old mossy wooden steps that had been bolted to the stones on the side of the well God knew how long ago.

Julia thought rapidly. She had climbed mountains. She knew how to rappel down rock faces. She'd written an article about it for *Sunset.* She'd go down and save the dog, get him on her shoulders or something, then just pull her way back up again. What could it be down there, ten feet? Piece of cake!

The well face was made of mortared stones, which made it easy for her to grab the rope and begin to lower herself down, toehold by toehold. Halfway down the well face had been mortared over but the surface was still rough enough for her sandals to get a purchase and the last old piece of wood was right at water's edge. That was when she began to wonder, *why did I come down here in my sandals. At least I've only got on shorts and a halter. But I could have changed to my running shoes! Oh well. Too late now.*

The water was almost a relief when she entered it, after struggling down in the afternoon heat. It wasn't even cool, it was just plain cold, rising from the limestone below, fed by melting Alpine snows a hundred kilometers away. She knew, she'd written a story about the Fontaine de Vaucluse over the next hill. But she forgot all these thoughts at the relief of being able to hold the rope with one hand and then support the feeble little body of Robert with her other arm. The poor little bastard! He felt so weak! He must have been paddling down here for three hours or more. She could see his front paws, torn from trying to get a clawhold on the rough mortar, bleeding down her arm now as he tried to lick her face in pathetic gratitude.

"How the hell did you get down here, you little asshole?" she asked. "Did you chase a rat or something under the cover?" He whined softly.

"Okay, pal, now we're going back up. And you have to cooperate." She managed to get him around to where he could ride piggyback, his forepaws over her shoulders. He was trembling from the cold but he seemed to know what was needed, could sense the procedure.

"Okay, RoBAIR, here we go," and she gripped the rope hard and began to walk her way up the wall. For a second she was worried that she might not have the strength, with an extra what-- twenty pounds?--on her back. But then she thought, *I've done this with even a heavier pack on,* and she concentrated on the muscles she was using, keep it slow, nice and easy, hand over hand, a few inches at a time, keep the feet firmly planted.

As her hands reached up into the sunlight slanting down into the well she could feel Robert tensing against her back and she thought, *Oh great! He's going to leap up over me. Probably scratch the shit out of my back and knock me back into the well!* So she took an extra firm grip with both hands and pulled hard, getting ready.

The rotten rope suddenly gave way and they both plunged back into the well, Julia striking her head a glancing blow on the side of the shaft as she fell. Everything went black.

Julia's eyes opened and saw a wall. She was back in her house looking at the century-old stone wall of their bedroom. *It was a dream!* she thought. *God! What a terrible dream!* And then water entered her nose and she realized it wasn't a dream, she was back in the well.

She thrashed about for a few seconds before she was completely conscious again. And then she was pushed under one more time by little Robert trying to climb on her back. Sputtering, cursing, she kicked her way back up, treaded water, made Robert cling to her arm instead of climbing on her back. She looked around. There was that piece of wood. Could she climb up on that? But it was slimy with moss and without a rope to hold onto impossible to pull herself up. Then she wondered, *How deep is this well, maybe there's a bottom somewhere I could stand on.*

So she told little Robert, just hang in there a minute, buddy, took a breath and let herself sink down. Whoops. Out of luck! She didn't hit anything for about four feet and then it was some rusty machinery that someone had thrown in there and she was terrified of being caught in it and came scrambling and sputtering again to the surface to be mounted again by an almost hysterical Robert, whimpering and clawing.

So. She and Robert were going to have to wait until someone came by and heard her call. And when would that be? She thought of St. Gens asleep in the afternoon heat. When did anyone come out? There were workers in the vineyard, Arabs who could be seen in the morning but who also disappeared in the afternoon. She might have to wait until late afternoon. The once refreshing water was now quite cold and she began to worry, *Can I last a few hours in water thiscold? Will my fingers still be able to hold on to this slimy board?*

As she was thinking she suddenly heard the voices of children. Of course! Kids sometimes walked by here in the afternoon, it was a shortcut from the upper end of town to...where? Somewhere! She'd seen them before from the upstairs window. She'd just give them a call.

But nothing came out but an asthmatic croak. Her throat had swollen, as it often did under stress. Try as she would she could not get a sound that would carry out of her throat. In frustration she tried to scream at Robert, but it came out a hoarse whisper, "Bark! bark! you little fucker!" desperately willing him to start up his famous yelp. But Robert only nodded his head, smiling at her in a worried way, knowing that she, the big human, could handle this problem. He wouldn't make a sound. So she went crazy, trying to scream, splashing the water, cursing the stupid, senseless little kids going by, until she heard gargling and realized that she'd scared the shit out of Robert, that he'd tried to swim out of the way and was too tired to stay afloat and was now drowning on the other side of the well. She clawed her way over and lifted him up.

"Oh, RoBAIR! I'm so sorry!" He was coughing and spitting water in her face now. "RoBAIR! It's going to be alright, babe! You just hang on old Julia's arm and someone will find us!" He calmed down now, although he was still shivering and she realized, she was too, the water was mountain spring temperature, not like the eighty degree day overhead.

How did she ever get in this position, she wondered. They don't even have wells like this in the States, they have to fill them in. But she'd always wanted to live in France. Right after her degree in French at Stanford she'd come over to stay in Paris for a few months on a Ravage fellowship. That was her family's joke. Their name was Ravage and when she wanted to go places in the summer, taking summer courses, her dad would say, "Well, I guess we can manage another Ravage fellowship." The thing was, she was a serious student and everywhere she went she studied hard and learned what she was there for. The full-immersion French school. The computer school, where she learned how to type and produce desktop copy. And the postgrad semester in France was going to put her over the top in understanding French politics. The program almost promised a job as a journalist somewhere in France, following French affairs for some publication. And then she'd met Jean Claude at the embassy party. She'd fallen head over heels in about two minutes flat and her career was on hold. He'd been amazed that she wanted to make love the first night they were together. "Not like French women," he'd said. "They always want to get the rules established first." She didn't care about rules. She'd had a dizzying year following him around Europe on his assignments, going to all the parties, being his glamorous American companion, and on the vacations, wandering through the little villages in the Dordogne, lying on the beaches at St. Tropez, even the longer trips to Taormina, to Crete, and once, almost a dream, to the Seychelles, snorkeling in the unearthly blue lagoons, the *luxe* hotels, the endless sunsets with drinks and little bites of seafood hors d'oeuvres, the languorous lovemaking at night, or in the morning, or in the late afternoon before the nap, or after...

She'd never even hinted, only hoped and hoped and then one rainy evening back in Paris he'd asked, "Julia, my love, can we go to Tours this weekend, to see Papa and Mama again?"

And she'd asked, why, we were just there a few weeks ago, and he said, "Because I want to tell them we are getting married."

Just like that. What she'd always dreamed of. Married to a rich, handsome, French diplomat. A big flat in Paris, a vacation house near St. Raphael, right on the water, a condo at Courchevel, best skiing in Europe. And that was when she learned the difference between being a French mistress and a French wife. It was as if Jean-Claude disappeared from her life. She realized suddenly that now she was expected to stay home while the diplomat went on his trips. "But you have your friends here, cherie," he said, surprised when she protested. "Marie, and Avril? And you always said you didn't see Helene enough?" You are in Paris, my love! So many restaurants to try!" Is that what I'm supposed to be now? she wanted to know. One of the ladies who lunch? And I hardly eat anything. "And the clubs at night!" he went on. "The theatre! You know Henri would die of ecstasy to take you around. He told me." She had to tell him that going around the clubs and the theatre with a darling gay actor was not her idea of a hot date.

Maybe he'll miss me and take me with him again, she hoped over and over. And then there was his picture on the cover of the tabloid. On a yacht off St. Tropez with other beautiful people, the women fashionably topless. The photo taken from shore with a telescopic lens by one of the hundreds of papparazzi who haunted the place. He had his arm around that singer, his hand just touching her nude breast... She'd fled to Tours to see her mother-in-law, who'd been so kind to her, such a loving friend, nicer to her than her own mother, actually.

"My son is an idiot," his mother had said. "But this is what French husbands do, if they're rich and spoiled. "He will just laugh it off and deny everything. And he feels no guilt at all, I can assure you."

So she showed everyone what American wives do. She divorced him. "I'm so sorry, darling," her mother-in-law had said. "In France the property settlement can take decades!" But she didn't care. And the next week she met Dan and everything was...

She lost her grip on the wood and went under again. This time she swallowed quite a bit of water and coughed harshly, Robert whimpering and trying to lick her face. How long had she been here? Had she been drifting off to sleep in the cold water, her mind wandering in the past, like explorers caught in a blizzard? She knew all about hypothermia too and knew that she could be so numbed by the cold that she'd just give up and slip under the water. She looked up at the well head. The sun was no longer hitting the edge, in fact it was much darker down here in the well now. She shuddered. Robert was now trembling uncontrollably. Who's going to go first, she wondered, him or me?

Dan came out of nowhere into her life. Her mother-in-law dragged her to a party against her will and there were all the most privileged people in France, chatting, drinking, eating, laughing—and smoking, of course. And she knew they were talking about her, a dumb American who couldn't forgive her husband a tiny affair, a meaningless thing... "Do you mind if I talk to you a bit?" he'd said. "I thought I could speak French but everything's going too fast for me." And he gave her a wry smile. That was Dan. Julia thought her mother-in-law had arranged the meeting at first but Madame was as surprised as everyone else. An American author who thinks he can cook French food, if you can imagine. Michel brought him, my dear. Maybe he'll cook something for you. And he did, and it was delicious, and when they visited important restaurants and Dan went out to talk to the chef she could see that they respected his knowledge and asked him serious questions, nodded their heads when he explained his approach to certain dishes. *Eh voilà. Ça y'est. Vous comprenez!*

She heard French voices in the distance. Was someone coming? Once again she tried to call. Nothing. A croak no one would hear. "RoBAIR," she whispered. "Bark, bark, bark!" But he just nodded his head, looking at her wide-eyed, waiting for her to do something. The voices grew louder and she realized they weren't French, it was guttural, maybe Arabic, some farmworkers going home from the fields in the evening. From the sound they were abreast the well now and then the voices began to recede. Julia began to cry soundlessly and at that moment she thought of Dan, how she'd never see him again, how heartbroken he'd be, and she remembered one of the last times she'd seen him, standing there on the terrace, pursing his mouth and pretending to be the neighbor calling his dog, "Quin-NOU..."

And then suddenly she was shaking Robert and croaking to him as loudly as she could, "Qui-NOU! Qui-NOU! Qui-NOU!" And he yelped! "Yelp, yelp!"

"Yes! Yes!" she grunted hoarsely, "Qui-NOU! Qui-NOU! Quinou is eating dinner, you little fucker, and here you are in the well!" And he yelped again, and then again and again and there was a noise above and dark faces looking in and then there were shouts going up the path to the village and all she could murmur, sobbing, holding the piece of wood grimly now, was "Quinou... Quinou...Quinou..."

A Scent of Thai

They kept noticing each other at this little Thai lunchroom just off Wall. The place had no illusions about being a restaurant, with counters around three walls and stools to sit on. You'd stand in line at one window and order from the limited menu and day's specials, then pick up your plastic plate and beverage at the other window. It was made to order for the financial district. You could order and eat something that actually resembled food in less than twenty minutes and get back to work. Secretaries and mailroom boys stood in line with million dollar brokers and lawyers, waiting for their Pad Thai or green curry, very democratic.

The first time their eyes met, standing there in line, it was magic. Maybe the perfumed air had something to do with it, the cumin and garlic and cardamom, star anise, lemon grass and Thai basil and ginger and *nam pla* wafting out of the kitchen. If you closed your eyes you could be in an exotic world, slow and sensuous, where pleasure replaced commerce as the daily fare. Her name was Susan and he was Matt, but it took some time before they knew each other. The allure built each day they saw each other there—maybe a slight trembling of the thighs, or a sudden sensitivity of the skin—and when one of them might miss lunch for some reason the other felt such a...deflation, that it was almost impossible to work that afternoon. Perhaps they both felt that an actual contact, even a spoken word might break the spell. Who knows? At any rate it was more than three weeks, the anticipation, the flesh overheated, the mind exploring fantasies of touching, undressing, slow wonder of small caresses, skin to skin, lips locked, all emotions simmered in a tropical steamy broth of spiced air in a cheap lunchroom, before they finally sat next to each other, toying with their noodles, and—"I see you here all the time."

"Yes. You know, when I don't see you...ha ha, isn't it ridiculous...I almost worry that—"

"I feel the same."

Their eyes met again. What else they said we'll never know. But phones were used and instead of going back to work they were in a cab going to her place, not far. They didn't dare touch each other in the cab. They went up in the elevator, walked down the hall to her apartment, where her cat, surprised at the change of schedule, jumped down off the kitchen table to greet them. But they had no time for her, swerving into the bedroom and falling on each other. Pleasure's promise was fulfilled, many times over, the fantasies lived out and then again with new improvisations. They ordered in for supper that night and no doubt had one of those magical conversations between two souls that had suddenly merged as one. And then there was the whole night ahead of them. She forgot to change her day-by-day Garfield calendar. It still said September 10.

Mulkey gave up trying to find a cab. The buses weren't running and the subway—at least in this part of town— wasn't running, might never run again, he thought. So he walked the fourteen blocks to the precinct house, his arthritic hips hurting him the whole way, and trudged up those familiar steps. A stale, airless room confronted him. At first he thought no one was there, the whole squad room deserted. He was turning to go out when he heard a voice behind him.

"Mulkey? Dan...what the hell are you doing here?"

"Cappy. Just thought I'd come around, see if I could help. You're probably short-handed, right?"

"Christ, Danny! You retired three years ago!" Mulkey had never seen Captain Brady cry, never imagined it. But there were tears on the broad, fleshy face.

"We're eleven short, Danny. And they're not coming back."

Wordlessly the two old men clutched each other's shoulders.

"What in God's name is the world come to?"

"And Danny, it's worse in some of the other precincts. One lost the whole watch."

"Jesus! Cappy, I don't know what to say. You got anything I can do here, fill in? I been following it on the TV. Then I thought, Cappy can use some help. Never could run a computer, but some leg work, whatever..."

Just saying "leg work" his hips twinged again. He looked around the vast empty room, at this time of day usually full of angry people, the early hookers being booked, neighborhood people complaining about something, thieves and dealers being processed.

Captain Brady saw him looking around. "Yeah, Danny. Empty. We're deserted. A silver lining or something? Today, no crime. They took the day off."

"Mother of God...! I don't believe it."

"It's true. Me and Gomez stayed here to hold down the station. And only one real call came in."

"One? Only one? In the last six hours?"

"Something like that. Here's what, go figure. Some Arab creeps kill three, four thousand people—who knows—and the crooks have a heart. They take the day off. Oh, but I'm sorry. There's one guy, one miserable bastard, who can't rest. He has to kill a nice girl right here in our precinct. And we got no one to send. Homicide's there already, who they could spare. Danny, you can help me out."

There was a skeleton crime scene crew there from Homicide. A uniform stopped Mulkey at the door, then let him in when he saw the badge. Unfamiliar faces, but Mulkey recognized the M.E., an old fart like himself.

"Herschel," he called. "Anything yet?"

The stocky man in the black suit turned around. "Danny? I thought you were retired."

"Three years ago. Just helping out for the moment."

"Bless you. It's a terrible time."

"Why I came in. I kept thinking, what can I do? And then I thought, what you used to do. Keep busy anyway."

"Keep busy. Right. And you know, right here we have a terrible murder of a sweet girl— " The M.E. choked a bit and Danny had never seen that before either. "A sweet girl, and some creep feels he has to bash her head in." Dr. Herschel Mendel shook his head and the two men, not wanting to talk about what was going on outside just then, finding a refuge in the familiar, turned to the inside of the apartment and looked down at a dear girl. Pardon me, woman, but she was still a little girl, a slim naked body, lying on her stomach, unmarked, but her face turned sideways to the left, eyes open and full of wonder.

"Not shot, not cut," said Mulkey.

"No. You can't see it, but he hit her a hell of a wallop with that." He pointed to a blackish green jade statue of a cat lying on the floor. "Weighs about three pounds, harder than hell, and he swung it up and down from behind her, hit her right on the crown. Lights out. She never knew what hit her."

"A rape, you think?"

"Sexual activity. But consensual. There's the usual evidence in the bed. She knew him. What we can tell, she liked him. Liked him a lot."

A homicide detective moved over to where they were talking and Mulkey identified himself. The detective's badge, hanging out of his breast pocket identified him as Fred Corral.

"You're taking over for the precinct?" Mulkey and Corral talked over the procedure for a moment.

"This guy knew what he was doing," Corral said. "Up to a point. He wiped down the apartment. No prints, except hers, where you'd expect them. Then he showered. There's no wet towel, so he took it. He took the garbage, so he knows– they ate a meal, maybe takeout—that his saliva could be on the plate. Smell in the kitchen, musta been Chinese. We'll check the local restaurants, we ever get any staff back working."

"How do you know, the garbage?"

"Cabinet down there. A roll of black plastic bags. They fit that can over there, but there's no bag in it. Guy probably left with it. Stuffed the towel, anything else in it. We'll check the dumpsters around here, but like I say, lotsa luck, day like today."

"Her clothes? Purse?"

"Clothes right here. She takes them off, maybe in a hurry, leaves them in the chair right here. No purse. Maybe this guy thinks he's going to fake it as a robbery. Maybe not. Anyway."

Danny Mulkey looked around the bedroom. On the little dresser was a Garfield calendar with yesterday's date still up. Then he examined the pile of discarded clothing. Undies on top, dark gray panty hose, a pale beige brassiere, pale beige slip, and underneath a beige blouse and a crumpled dark gray pinstripe suit. A pair of conservative black heels under the chair, one on its side. The suit looked expensive.

"She works down here. Maybe a brokerage, lawyer's office, something like that," Mulkey said.

"We're talking to the neighbors right now. We'll know all that pretty quick. Yeah. Nice apartment, rent's up there over three thousand. She had a good job."

Standing there, Danny caught just the faintest hint of a strange odor. He leaned over the pile of clothes. Spices. Something unusual. He straightened up.

"They ordered in Chinese?"

"That's what we get from the kitchen. You know, all that soy, bean sprouts, your oyster sauce, MSG, whatever. Can't miss it. Go sniff in the kitchen."

Mulkey didn't want to get another smell in his nostrils. He bent over the clothes again. Stood up, thinking, still wrinkling his nose.

"Okay, Corral, try this out. She comes in with this romeo, maybe. First thing on the agenda is get the clothes off. So they have a little fling. Then they order in Chinese, eat it in the kitchen maybe? But earlier, when she came in wearing this suit, she'd been in another kind of restaurant. Here...take a whiff."

Corral leaned over, sniffing vigorously. He stood up, trying to identify what he'd smelled. "You're right. Not Chinese. Not, uh, Cuban, Puerto Rican. That's home cookin' for me. But something the same. Comino...?"

"Cumin. Right. Could be Indian, but I'm saying Thai. Marie and I used to love the stuff, eat it every Sunday. Since she...I still go to this same place now and then. Yeah. This is Thai."

They found out a little more about her. Susan Blackwell, an executive assistant at a prominent Wall Street law firm. The body had been found by a neighbor, an elderly widow. She'd been waiting in the hall off and on, for hours. And now Mulkey got to talk to her.

"Musta been around noon. Naturally I'm upset, who wouldn't...and then I'm in the hall and I hear her cat. Frisco, that's her name. Meowing? You know? First thing I think, 'Oh my God! Susan was over in the Towers...and her cat's starving.' I was gonna call the super but I felt the door knob and it was ajar, so I went in...and there she was in the bedroom. I...oh Jesus!"

Mulkey calmed her down and after a while she went on. "She didn't work in the Towers. Maybe someplace closer to Wall, I dunno. But she was, you know, somebody. A big firm, a law firm I think."

While the crime scene people were finishing up Mulkey just stood contemplating the window from which Susan Blackwell had been staring, standing there naked and defenseless. The approximate time of death left no doubt about what had transfixed her. What could have possessed her killer? Sudden insanity because of the horror out the window? No, Mulkey counseled himself, thinking of the scores of murderers he had put away. *The scene here is more exotic than most, but murder is usually simple. Jealous rage, or*—And then he had it. He turned back to Corral.

"I know who it is."

"Man, that's fast! Who are you, Poirot or something?"

"I don't know his name, but we'll find him. Just good police work from now on, although at the moment I take no pleasure in it."

* * *

November was lovely on the California central coast that year. On sunny days Mark Haddon liked to stroll from his office to the El Paseo for lunch. The restaurant occupied a large courtyard that could be any plaza in, say, Puerta Vallarta or San Miguel, with the servers dressed to match. And the food was adequate. Mark liked to start with the guacamole and tortilla chips and then, if he was hungry that day, go on to the steak taco with black beans and rice, with chipotle salsa, whatever that was. Recently he'd been lunching with the pretty paralegal from the law offices next to his, with the idea that she might fill a void in his life.

They were chatting amiably today when another couple came through the wrought-iron gate. An older man with a limp and a much younger woman in a business suit. They met a Hispanic-looking man in a suit, who was waiting at the desk, maybe the *maître d'*, thought Mark, who was used to checking out his surroundings, wherever he was. And now the three approached his table.

"Hate to interrupt your lunch, I know it's rude, but I was looking for a financial consultant, and your girl said I could find you here. This won't take a minute."

The older man was so friendly that Mark urged them to sit down for a bit. "I don't do business at lunch, but I can tell you the market is moving up again and it's a good time to get back in. If you can come round the office a little later, We can —" and he offered the couple a business card.

"That's great." But the old man made no move to leave just yet. "In fact we're looking for some valuable securities."

Mark stiffened, managed a tense smile. "I'm sorry, I said I don't to business at—"

Now the young woman spoke up. "We're talking about eighty million or so in securities missing from the New England Educators Pension Fund."

Mark's lady friend got up abruptly. "Excuse me. I have to go to the ladies' room," she said, taking her purse. But she must have lost her way because she went straight out the gate.

Mark Haddon reddened and his hands gripped the edge of the table as if it might get away from him. "I don't know what you're talking about." He turned to the Hispanic man. "Do you let people off the street bother your diners like this?"

The three intruders looked at each other and tried not to smile. Then the Hispanic man opened his jacket to show a detective's shield.

"Sorry. I didn't introduce myself. I'm Detective Lopez, Santa Barbara PD. This is Detective Mulkey, NYPD, and the big gun here is Janet Florio, Justice Department—

"It's great to meet you all," Mark broke in, "but—

"But this is my jurisdiction," interrupted Lopez, "so here goes, 'You have the right to remain silent...'" All the familiar, soul-deadening phrases.

Haddon elected to remain silent during the ride to the police station. Mulkey wondered what thoughts, protests, just plain lies were coursing through his head. In the interview room he uttered only the necessary words.

"I want a lawyer."

So it was nearly an hour later when the group assembled once more, now joined by the District Attorney herself. Haddon had named a famous and expensive defense lawyer, one of this city's courthouse mandarins, an elegant full-bearded man named Gordon. He spent a few minutes quietly conferring with Haddon in private. Then with all the joy of combat playing across his features, he leaned forward and addressed Ms. Florio, the highest ranking law enforcement person in the room.

"Would it be impertinent to ask what heinous crimes my client is supposed to have committed?"

Ms. Florio consulted a sheaf of legal-sized documents.

"From the point of view of the Department of Justice, the suspect, whom we prefer to identify as Matthew Harper, is accused of fraud, intent to commit fraud, multiple counts, grand larceny, and flight to avoid prosecution, all felonies." She then began naming a list of pension funds, hedge funds, and other impressive repositories of money.

Haddon ignored her the moment she started and began to whisper in his lawyer's ear. The others in the room waited him out. Gordon finally made a few notes, faced the woman from Justice.

"Yes. Well, you have a complicated story of financial shenanigans here. I'm sure that there are some grounds for suspicion, but you can't even identify my client with any certainty. I'm going to request bail, and low bail, until your prosecutor can arraign with something indictable." He nodded politely to the DA and started to get up, collecting his papers, when Mulkey cleared his throat.

"Uh, counselor...there's just one more thing."

Gordon looked impatiently at his watch.

"Your client may not have been entirely candid with you, I'm afraid. I have here a New York warrant for the arrest of Matthew Harper for the murder of Susan Blackwell on the morning of September 11 of this year."

"It was just police work," said Mulkey. "At least my part." He and the others were sitting in the staff lounge having coffee. Gordon had left hurriedly and somewhere across the street a door was going "clang" behind Mr. Haddon-slash-Harper. "I just started going to Thai restaurants, starting in a circle from Susan Blackwell's law offices, showing her ID photo blown up. The third one, a little hole in the wall, the lady says, 'Oh yes, I see her all the time.' And she had noticed the guy too. She says they were always checking each other out, but it was a while before they left together."

Mulkey chuckled. "She said, 'I know my customers, in Bangkok we don' wait so long.' So we sat her down with a police artist and he comes up with a picture, looks like a composite of every stockbroker you ever saw. I had no hopes."

"But here you are," laughed the DA. "What happened?" "I narrowed it down." Mulkey shifted in his chair, cleared his throat. "I was trying to imagine those few moments just before he killed her. They hear explosions, they rush to the window and they could see the Towers. I know, I could see where they'd been. And when the North Tower went down, he's thinking, 'Everybody in the world thinks I'm in the tower today. Everyone but—"

"Everyone but Susan Blackwell," Janet Florio cut in. "Right! And it took that cold bastard one second to realize all his embezzling was now safe. Because no one would even be looking for him. He grabs the nearest blunt object and...and, well—"

"You narrowed it down," said the DA. "How exactly?" "We showed his portrait to the North Tower people who also didn't go to work that day, or who got out. You have to realize that there were thousands of people helping to trace the dead, the missing, the lost. We put the portrait on the special internet site and in one day we had three hits. 'Oh, that's Matthew Harper. New England Educators Pension Fund.' Wife and kids in Scarsdale. That's when we called the Feds to help out. Janet, your turn."

"Harper was managing dozens of pension fund portfolios. And he was skimming with both hands. It might have taken years for anyone to catch on that there were a few million missing from a multi-billion-dollar fund. But once we knew the thief we could backtrack."

"And then there's the wife in Scarsdale," added Mulkey. "She's in mourning, actually planning the memorial service. But when she hears the whole story...and finally believes it, she lets us go through all his home computer. And here are a bunch of emails to this city in California. All very innocent, but we figured here was where he was setting up. For months, it looked like.

"Did he have anything to say to you, just before we locked him up?" asked the DA.

Mulkey shook his head sadly, thinking of the last conversation, one he didn't want. "I wanted to say something, and all I could think of was so trivial. I asked, 'Here in this town, there's a Thai place right near your office. We looked there first. I thought you liked Thai.' You know what? For the first time he hangs his head. He says, 'I can't even touch the stuff now.'"

Quartzsite

The powerful Buick flew northward across the Arizona desert chasing its own shadow with the low winter sun dead behind it, saguaro and ocotillo flashing by.

"Vernon, you're driving too fast, it's making me nervous."

Vern Babcock grumbled a bit but he slowed down. "Just trying to find a place for lunch.

It's almost twelve thirty."

In Yuma the Denny's had been closed for repairs and they'd been counting on it for lunch. They had a map of the southwest with all the Denny's marked on it for when they travelled out of the Phoenix area, which wasn't often. Estelle thought that Denny's was the safest place to eat, they were all so clean. They would always get there before noon, for the early-bird price, and have the hot turkey sandwich on the seniors' menu, or sometimes Vern would have the roast beef sandwich if he felt daring and he could get Estelle to shut up about his cholesterol.

"Is there another Denny's up ahead?" Estelle asked.

"There might be." Vern Babcock knew there wasn't. His wife couldn't read a roadmap for beans so he knew she wouldn't check on him. There wasn't as much as a flyspeck on the map until Quartzsite. He'd never been there but he figured there had to be some kind of hamburger joint he could get Estelle to take a chance on. Maybe even a family restaurant like Denny's. He was getting hungry.

The Babcocks had bought a condo on a golf course outside Phoenix three years ago. Vern Babcock used to own a factory back in Ohio. He'd built it up from just a little workshop after he'd got out of the army in the World War. Made specialty auto parts, kept up with the technology, and by the time he retired and sold out they had seven or eight annual contracts with General Motors, regular as rain, and he had a good bundle to retire on.

That's why he couldn't figure why they always had to get the early-bird rate, the senior menu, save a few bucks. They had plenty of money, what with the IRA and the factory sale money in a muni-bond fund. But he went along with Estelle and her thrifty ways. Woman'd pull out fifty of those coupons at the supermarket, fifteen cents off the big jar of Miracle Whip and like that, it was embarrassing.

"That must be the next town up ahead," said Estelle. She had sharp eyes. Vern was looking for buildings and couldn't see any. Just white shadows on the desert ahead. Then they started passing motorhomes here and there, and trailers, just all stuck out there on the desert in no order at all. Vern had to slow down behind a massive Winnebago and he could begin to see the trailers and motorhomes parked more densely now along the road. It was getting commercial. There were big lots, looked like swap meets, telling you, "Free Parking, Check it Out," signs inviting people to park their RVs, only $4 a day, and then $5, $6 as they went under the I-10 and got into the crowded part of town and by now they seemed to be right in the middle of Quartzsite and there were finally real buildings and street signs and a restaurant up ahead, Harry's, it said, family dining, senior prices. Vern let his wife spot it first, and she did, right on.

"Oh look, Vernon! They got a senior menu!"

Estelle liked the prices on the senior menu, but she crabbed all through lunch about how dirty the place was, she didn't dare order a salad, who knew who'd had their hands on it, so she only had the bean and bacon soup because it'd been cooked enough to kill the germs. *But not enough to kill that gas you'll be passing for a couple days,* thought Vern. He himself had a club steak sandwich, Estelle so immersed in her own food choices that he was able to get away with ordering a real piece of meat. It turned out overcooked and flavorless but his fries were good and Vern felt full and satisfied after his second cup of coffee.

He asked the waitress, old skinny lady, how come there was nothing but trailers and RVs here.

"They all started coming about ten, fifteen years ago, just a gas station and a couple buildings here then," she said, sounding like a local. "Then somebody started a rock swap meet, other people parked next door and started selling rocks and soon they all just started parking out there in the desert. No laws against that here in Arizona, not like California." Her tone of voice spoke volumes about the fancy folk of California.

"S'mostly rock shops here now, but you'll find real estate for sale too. Some land here actually belongs to someone." She gave them a smile full of big teeth.

When they started out walking around Quartzsite, looking at the rock shops, Vern knew this was going to drive him nuts. A year ago, Estelle had gotten interested in rock hunting because of some of the women in her group at the clubhouse. They'd shown her agates and crystals and stuff like that they found out in the desert and how they had them mounted on cards in boxes. To Estelle, it became a substitute for organizing all those photos of the grandkids in the albums, with the names and the dates, and where the picture was taken, except there weren't going to be many more pictures of the grandkids, them being all grownup and one of them actually in prison...but the rocks found in the desert meant something to her that she could keep doing, meant something new every day, stuff she could show her friends. And then she heard, at Quartzsite you could find super rocks, and the best prices.

So now she was oohing and aahing at the little baubles they had on all these swap meet kinds of long plank tables you could find, one after another, there in Quartzsite, and she could tell Vern was getting bored so she finally said, "Vernon, why don't you just wander around by yourself, see if there's anything you want, like a knife, or something." Vern had bought a fancy bowie knife with a turquoise inlaid handle a year ago and she was always telling him, "Go look for another knife," as if she figured that was his big deal, knives. It was like with the factory in the old days. Estelle had no idea what they made and when Vern started to tell her about some major sale they'd made of their new electronic cruise control module, she'd always change the subject. Now and then she'd say, "Vern, you take such good care of us!"

So they made an arrangement, meet back at the car in an hour and a half, and Vern went walking back the other direction.

Quartzsite really didn't have streets or blocks, except the main street that paralleled the I- 10, but there were sort of alleys between all the RVs and the trailers, and now and then a real trailer home. Vern was looking at rocks, rocks, rocks, here was a big hanging of dayglow Elvis on black velvet, now and then a skinned rattler with the fangs wide open, here and there a lady showing paintings she'd made of the desert and the mountains, Vern thinking he'd rather have Elvis on velvet than her painting in his front room... and now he ran into a nice looking little elderly guy in front of a place called Get your Rocks, who stopped him with a big smile.

"Hey, partner, you look like you're tired of looking at rocks. Wanta take a look in my shop?"

The guy was so friendly, so welcoming that Vern had to follow him in. Vern had sold stuff all his life and he tended to trust good salesmen.

They were in a narrow trailer, looking down at a display of rocks, crystals, looked like every other one Vern had seen. He was just about to complain to the proprietor when the little guy put his hands up and said, "Listen, I gotta go for lunch, I'll let Doreen give you the pitch," and Doreen came from the back of the trailer.

Vern thought at first that the woman just had a slip on. Then he could see that it was a very thin, light dress, thin straps over the shoulders, and very short. Doreen had dark, curly hair and full, sensuous lips. Vern had trouble keeping his eyes off the area between her long bare legs and the clear impression of her nipples under the top of the dress where she didn't seem to be wearing a brassiere. Her whole middle area just seemed to keep moving around. As a prudent man his first reaction was to make his excuses and get out of there. But Doreen moved first. She put a finger under the front of his shirt.

"You've been looking at a lot of rocks?" "Well, yeah..."

"Let me ask you, did you *get* any rocks yet?' "Well, no..."

"Okay, big guy, how'd you like to *get your rocks off?*"

Her offer was explicit, and so surprising that Vern looked around rapidly in all directions.

"Hey! Nobody's watching. We'll just go in back there and have a good time. You remember? You remember the last time you really got your rocks off?"

Vern, a businessman, suddenly realized that he was getting a business proposition. It was so surprising that his first reaction was to laugh. But next, obviously, he had to know the price. So he asked.

"Hey, no big deal, big guy!" she responded. "Hundred bucks, which is two, three under Vegas prices. And we take major credit cards."

"Credit cards?" he asked in amazement. "What's your business name?"

"Get your Rocks Off," she said, giggling. "It's a legitimate business name. We take Visa, Mastercard, no American Express."

The giggle did it.

Vern's life was flashing before his eyes. He figured he hadn't had it on with Estelle for more than twenty years, maybe a lot more. He'd had a quick affair with a waitress back in Tungsten, Ohio maybe ten years back, but that was it as far as actually doing it with a woman. At the age of seventy he'd thought that part of his life was over. But this curvy woman with the laughing lips sort of put him in a time machine and before he knew it he was in the back of the trailer taking his clothes off.

It was so much better than he remembered that afterwards he was lying there thinking, *take me Lord Jesus now!* But the practical side of his nature, which was mostly what he was, took over and he started thinking. *I'll have to try to get up here more often!*

So later on, when he met Estelle back at the Buick, and she asked him where he'd been, he said the real estate picture was interesting here, as a businessman he thought he should look into it. Usually when he'd mentioned business he could count on Estelle's eyes getting glazed, but now she looked a little worried.

"You wouldn't invest any of our nest egg, would you Vernon?" That's what she called the million six in tax-exempt muni bonds, their nest egg.

"Nah, wouldn't touch that. Parcels up here we could make a down payment out of the cash account. Nobody knows what they're doing here. A good businessman could really make a profit. You know, start selling something everybody wants, do some promotion, discount..." and now Estelle's eyes were getting glazed.

Vern made three trips up to Quartzsite, to see Doreen, and he thought he'd found just the thing to make his life perfect. He loved Estelle, and he liked just puttering around the retirement community and playing golf now and then but he'd been getting bored and his romps with Doreen were just the thing. They put some spice in his life, some spring in his step, even Estelle and some of their friends were saying he looked younger.

So he was crushed the last time when he came into the trailer and found the guy, Ralph was his name, and Doreen sitting there with long faces.

"Hey, Vern, good to see you. How about a cup of coffee?" Ralph tried to look a little more cheerful. But Doreen didn't seem ready to invite him in back. In fact, she looked like she'd been crying.

"Hey yourself! What's going on here?" Vern knew something was wrong.

"Well, partner, we're just closin' up shop. Gonna move on somewhere, fewer hassles, you know."

"Fewer hassles! Christ, Ralph, I never seen anywhere with fewer hassles than Quartzsite!"

"Yeah. Well. Tell him Doreen." Ralph just looked defeated, worn out.

"They're raising our rent," she said looking up at Vern, begging for understanding.

"Raising! They're doubling it!" Ralph broke in. "Bastards told us they can sell the property, so we gotta buy it or pay double rent!"

Vern was thinking quickly. "The owners know the business you're running here?"

"No, no!" Both Ralph and Doreen were shaking their heads. "No. Got nothin' to do with that. Just that we got some prime downtown Quartzsite land here and they got a good deal, they can sell it."

"So how much we talking about, prime Quartzsite land?" Vern was amazed, crummy little place like this out in the desert.

Ralph didn't answer him directly. "Vern, you got three thousand you could get easy, not have to borrow?"

"Why hell, yeah! Why you asking?"

"Vern, why don't you buy this place?"

Well, Vern Babcock just blew up at that. The idea of buying six thousand square feet, not even a quarter acre, and he was going on and on, how he didn't just fall off the turnip truck, when Ralph added, "And I'll throw in Doreen here."

Vern was going to say he thought they were married and all but Doreen, now looking a little brighter told him, no, it's just a business thing. You'd probably run it better. And it turned out, she owned the existing trailer herself and that was part of the deal.

Later that afternoon Ralph got in his pickup, after they'd been to the bank and done all the business. He waved goodbye and he was gone and Vern realized he'd bought a whorehouse with one employee. He didn't want to think about that just yet so he and Doreen went in back to celebrate.

Afterwards she started in with the ideas and wouldn't shut up, most of them good ideas. Doreen told him she knew a double wide, real cheap, for sale down the block. They could move it to the lot here and really have a crib, room for four, maybe even five girls. Instead of four, five hundred a day they could be scoring two K, three on a good day.

Vern did the math in his head. Not as good as Doreen was thinking, but it sounded good. They could amortize the land and the double wide in a couple weeks, everything after that would be profit.

"But where're we going to get the other girls?" he asked.

"Don't worry your sweet head about that, baby," Doreen said. "I'll go up to Vegas this week, pick up some girls I know, they'd love it here working with old guys like you."

"They'd like old guys?" It didn't make sense to Vern.

"Hell yeah! I been here with Ralph six weeks, not one old guy didn't have clean underwear and real polite. You think the girls like being there in Vegas, macho creeps smacking them around, pimps beating them up? Some of them are real dopers, like to be around the action, but I know ten girls at least, would love to get out of Vegas and start building up some savings, no pimps to pay off, no weirdos... Besides," she said, giving him a naughty smirk, "Wouldn't you like a little variety once in a while, all on the house?"

Well, that convinced Vern. He went back to Phoenix but the next week he was back there in Quartzsite supervising the double wide being moved onto his new property. And a couple of days later when he went in back with Trixie, one of the new girls, he knew he'd made the deal of his life.

They had an old retired prospector, Dusty, had worked for Ralph before, who would roam the streets and pick up the more prosperous looking old men, guys stepping out of new Buicks, with their lime green polyester sansabelt slacks. He'd follow them and their wives down the street a bit and when they split up to follow their own interests, which was usually inevitable, he'd give the geezer the pitch. Amazing how many of the old dudes would come back to life, follow the prospector back to the double wide hesitantly, but then, their business done, their rocks properly off, go prancing back the road, their nostrils flaring. Now and then some uptight old bastard would threaten to call the cops, but they didn't know where the place was and Dusty would tell them, "Suit yourself pal. But I ain't seen a cop in this town the last ten years. Hee hee!" And he'd skeedaddle off.

Besides Trixie, a frisky strawberry blonde who needed to fatten up a bit, Vern thought, they had Georgia, a buxom girl with big hair, a black woman named Shawneena, and two sassy little Salvadoran girls, looked like teenagers, who claimed to be twins, but weren't. They could get two-fifty or more for their two-on-one act. Deal was, the girls all kept half of what they made, plus the tips, which Doreen had told Vern was twice or more what their pimps let them keep in Vegas. And Doreen kept all she made, for running the place and keeping order.

It was a funny thing. The girls were really happy not to be working in Vegas anymore, but all their days off they'd head right back there to see their friends and party and gamble. Vern was happy with them gambling because it meant they'd all be broke after a couple of days and back working. He had a firm rule about drugs, though--so the girls just didn't tell him and kept it cool. Everyone else knew that Georgia and Shawneena were junkies and that Trixie was on speed most of the time she wasn't doing coke. There was some funny cigarette smoke around now and then but Vern didn't know what it was, he'd never smelled weed in his life, and he accepted the story that they were trying to stop smoking with herbal cigarettes.

Dusty once said there were lots of younger guys wandering around Quartzsite and would they like some of that trade and all the girls said, "No way, José!" which was Vern's opinion too. He had the normal seventy-year-old's distrust of any male under fifty and was glad to find out the girls had some common sense.

Get Your Rocks Off was a solid success for a month, six weeks, and Vern could tell Estelle he was doing great on those rental properties up there. But it couldn't last. First thing was a big tubby, happy guy named Harley, a little too young, who visited two, three times and Caridad, one of the Salvadoran girls was upset.

"Tha' guy, he's the heat, man! I can always tell!" And Shawneena was getting the same vibes. Next thing you know Caridad disappeared.

Her "twin sister" Maria came to see Vern, next time he was up there. "Vernon, Caridad she had to spleet, 'cause joo know she's illegal, joo know what I'm sayeeng? Dey catch her, dey gone send her back to Salvador. Focking bostards dere, police, dey already kill her modder and fadder!" Maria started crying.

Vern nodded. He figured he was going to lose Maria too.

"So she went to LA, joo know. An' I gotta go help her dere. We can get work, I know, but I know the eenglish better. Joo know what I mean?"

Vern had always been very fond of Caridad. Now he took out a roll of bills and counted out five hundred, what the hell, a thousand dollars.

"Maria, you go take care of Caridad. And don't let her get arrested, you hear?"

Maria burst into tears again.

"Vernon, you de nicest mon I ever met, my whole life!" She smiled through the tears. Then she looked at him with pure love in her eyes. "Joo want a queek one, 'fore I go?"

Vern turned it down and drove Maria with her bags to the bus stop before he went back to Phoenix. The whole way home, he had this warm, good feeling about himself and he was humming an old song, Patti Page used to sing it, he thought.

But the next week Doreen looked worried. "I really gotta go to Vegas, get some new staff." She said. "I told Dusty already, don't bring anybody around today."

"Why? What's going on?"

"Well. Georgia and Shawneena finally took off. Y'know, I always figured they needed their...they needed that Vegas atmosphere too much. So now it's only Trixie, and she's up there now, her day off."

"Goddam! We're almost out of business! You better start recruiting fast, hon." Vern wondered if this business was getting too volatile.

"And another thing. That guy Harley was around today, wanting Shawneena. I tell him she's on a break, he goes 'What are you guys anyway, an LA operation?' And I'm like, 'Hey, is that your business or what?' and he started laughing and saying he's sorry, pretending he's embarrassed or something, but I think he's trouble. What do you think?"

Vern was worried. Doreen had already told him Quartzsite would get too hot in the spring for them to keep going but he'd been counting on maybe another three months anyway.

"Maybe we should taper off for a bit, see what's going on. Overhead's not that high with the girls gone. Why don't you go on up to Vegas and look around. But don't bring any new staff back until I call you. What's your number up there?"

Doreen told him and drove off, looking relieved. Vern cleaned up the place a little because the girls always left it a goddamn mess and then he was about to leave himself when the door burst open and two men came rushing in.

The first one was Harley, not looking happy any more but hard and mean. He put a hand in the middle of Vern's chest and pushed him backwards. Well, Vern had always reacted badly to things like that so he just popped Harley one, knocked him on his ass. Next thing he knew, the next man through hit him on the side of his head with a pistol barrel and he wound up sitting on the floor, looking up at this guy in a black suit, holding a big automatic on him.

"Okay, that's enough of that shit. Now let's talk some sense." The man was talking very calmly for an armed thug, Vern was thinking, painfully trying to get his head back together.

Harley was getting up now and he was steamed but the other man just told him to shut up and sit down.

"What kind of sense we talking here?" asked Vern. "You want to rob this place? There's some ladies' clothes, probably dirty. Dishes in the sink, there's a little shit TV and a VCR. The girls are all..."

But the man shushed him. "Forget it, pal, this is business." Vern was going to say something but then he told himself, just shut up and find out who these guys are, what they want.

"We want to know, is this an LA operation?" Vern didn't say anything, looked like he was puzzled.

"You know, are you the LA people?" And Vern realized, this guy thinks this is a mob business.

"No." he said, "We're sort of the Phoenix people."

The black suit looked at Harley, who shrugged.

"Well, here's what's going on. We're taking over."

"The hell you're taking over!" Vern was getting hot and thinking about taking away the guy's gun and feeding it to him like he did to a union punk back in Ohio thirty years ago.

"Back off, buddy. We're paying you off. Harley's been around a few times, watched the trade going in, he says it's maybe worth twenty."

Now Vern felt more at home, doing business. He looked outraged. "Twenty! We got at least forty K sunk in this place, not counting next week's payroll!"

Black suit pondered this. He looked at Harley and back, then made up his mind. He took out a roll of bills. "Forget about next week's payroll. We'll take care of that. I'm giving you twenty-five and that's it. You even open your mouth again and you're in trouble. Tell Phoenix not to come squawking. It's not their jurisdiction. Got that?" Vern grumbled, but he took the money and put his coat on, getting ready to go. "And remember this," said Black Suit. "Harley here's a cop, with state CID. Just so you know we're covered, all ways." Harley smirked.

* * *

Vern spread out the two-hundred-and-fifty hundred dollar bills on the breakfast nook table in front of Estelle.

"See, hon? I told you I could make some good real estate deals up there in Quartzsite. About a thousand percent profit!"

"Oh, Vernon! That's...that's...are you sure this is legal? And what about the taxes?" Estelle went on and on, but Vern knew she was already spending it in her mind, maybe not have to go early for the senior menu next time, or buy an agate or something. So then he put down on the table the turquoise and silver squashblossom necklace she'd been admiring at the gift shop downtown but wouldn't buy because she thought seven hundred was a fortune and they could never afford it. And he couldn't remember when he'd seen Estelle so happy.

He phoned Doreen, let her know. Then he gave the new owners time to get started in business up there in Quartzsite. He figured a couple of weeks would do it. And then he made an indignant phone call to a Mormon bishop he'd met out on the links, told him about being propositioned in Quartzsite, of all places, and did he know anyone in the law?

A few days later he had to chuckle at the photo in the *Republic* of good old Harley being led off in handcuffs. "State Police Implicated in Prostitution Ring," said the headline. Then a feature story on the same page caught his eye. It seemed that a trailer town had grown up almost overnight on a secondary road outside of Tombstone. Rockshops, antiques, and old gunslinger memorabilia were selling like hotcakes. The photo of the jumble out in the desert looked just like Quartzsite. When Estelle went off to play bridge Vern called Doreen in Las Vegas.

"Hey there, old timer!" she said. "I was wondering if you'd forgotten little Doreen. You probably remembered you were going to split the Quartzsite sale with me, didn't you!"

"That too. But I also think we're back in business again. You game?"

STARTING ALL OVER AGAIN

The doctor got there right away when he called. Then the doctor called the funeral home, and they came, got ready to take her away. The doctor—Vines, that was his name—asked if he had relatives, children, whatever, where he could stay for the rest of the night. No, he said, he wouldn't wake them up this time of night. Then, the doc asked if he wanted a tranquilizer. Dr. Vines was very concerned about his state of mind. No, he said. I knew it was coming. I can get along tonight, the rest of tonight, what's left. Doctor Vines left in his car, the funeral home van left, the sheriff car left; he had no idea why the sheriff had come. Maybe just proving they were always on hand, justify their budget.

He sat in his comfortable leather chair, there in the living room, for maybe an hour, trying to figure out what he thought about his loss, losing Florence, finally putting a name to her. Florence. She was gone now.

A light was beginning to fill the room, coming from over the hill to the east. He'd lost track of time, but it was the sun coming up, it was almost six in the morning and the sun was rising. The yellow light illuminated the living room through the blinds, coming from the high windows facing the east. He could make out the big desk in the corner, the paintings on the wall. The bookshelves, all around the room, jammed with the collections of forty years.

As the light hit the first rose in the garden he rose, slowly, putting his hands on his hips and creaking his back, getting ready to move. Out through the back door he trudged in his slippers and picked up the hose. Turned it on, gently. He walked through the garden, watering Florence's roses. They wouldn't last a day, she'd said, not in this climate, unless you water them, lay down a pool around the roots. Don't ever spray on the leaves, you'll make mildew. He could smell the pretty smelling ones, not even being near them. They all had names but he didn't know them, roses was roses. The sun from the east was beginning to pick them out and as the rays hit each bud, the perfume got stronger. And then suddenly he felt hungry. He'd filled the little basins under the roses fairly well so he went in, trying to think what he'd have for breakfast.

In the kitchen he turned on one burner, reached below for a non-stick pan. He'd butter a piece of bread, put it in the pan for a few minutes and have a piece of fried bread, always tastier than just plain toast from the toaster. Butter. He could put on as much as he liked now and he grinned a little at the thought.

Reaching to his left toward the silverware drawer his hand encountered the begonia in the pot that Florence had established on the kitchen counter. He usually did a lot of the cooking, but Florence had rules about where things went and she liked the begonia pot right there, to the left of the stove. It seemed anything he wanted to do he was sticking his hand in the begonia.

He picked up the begonia pot, moved to the kitchen door, and threw the begonia pot out into the yard. After all, he thought, Florence doesn't care where her begonia is now. As he closed the door he heard a familiar sound at his feet. Little Jasper was there, meowing, looking up at him imploringly. The little cat never got to go out. Their last cat, Climber, had been an outdoor cat but had disappeared. Everyone in the neighborhood knew what had happened. When the drought started the coyotes had begun to move into town, moving up the little stream bed that ran through their neighborhood. Some coyote had eaten Climber. They'd called her Climber because she was such a sweet, clinging cat, would climb up your leg if you didn't pay attention and go to sleep on your lap.

He reached down and patted Jasper, then put out some canned catfood for him. But he'd seen the door open and he ignored his food, went over to the door and meowed again. Poor cat, he'd never been out but he never gave up hope, looking out there in the garden, seeing the birds pecking around on the ground.

"Okay, Jasper," he said. "You're an outdoor cat from now on." And he opened the door and let him out. He figured he could get one of those cat doors, put it in the kitchen door so he could go in and out. He could smell the bread toasting and he took it out of the pan, smeared on some honey and ate it. It was the best honey, Florence's cousin had sent it from some part of France where it was special and she never wanted to use it, save it. For what? he thought.

The phone rang. He looked at the clock instinctively. If anyone phoned before eight Florence would really get mad, tell them immediately where they'd gone wrong, even her best friends. It was only six twenty-five. Even as he was moving toward the phone he realized, he didn't have to answer. That's what the machine was for. The phone shrilled five times, then intoned Florence's voice. "We're not able to answer the phone right now. Leave your name and number and a message." Years ago someone had told Florence not to say they weren't home, because it was only burglars, checking, so they could come and rob you. So she never said "We're not home." It shocked him to hear her voice, as if it was an offense to nature, once she was gone, to leave an echo. Right away he was determined to change the message and he picked up the folder with the directions for the answering machine. But he couldn't understand anything it said, she'd always done the message, and besides, he had nothing to say to people who phoned. So he just unplugged the answering machine and plugged the phone right into the wall. The way it used to be, most of his life, before answering machines.

As if challenging him, the phone rang again. His instinct told him to pick it up, but he was stubborn. He thought that if you gave him an hour he couldn't think of anyone he wanted to talk to just now. So he let it ring, ten, twenty times, then he got mad, just picked up the receiver and put it down again. The dim light on the shades in the living room bothered him. Florence had installed shades on the tall windows so the sun never came in. The sun would bleach the rugs, she said, and the books in the bookcase. He'd always liked to see the trees outside so he pulled up the blinds and let the world come in. It was great.

When he sank back in his chair again the sun was glinting off the plaque on the wall. It was his familiar plaque, hanging up, the dark green plush with his memorabilia mounted on it. It always gave him a good feeling. In the left upper corner was an old photo of him waving a AK 47, one he'd taken out of the bunker that day, the day he'd won the medal. Next was his combat infantry badge, the long blue rectangle with the silver rifle in it. Then his Bronze Star--the medal for bravery. Underneath were a few other old photos, sort of yellowed now, him and his buddies over there. Mostly they were drinking, waving at the camera. Florence hated his plaque. The war's over, she'd say. We could put a nice picture there. But that was his life, he'd told her, his life before real estate. There were his sergeant stripes, cut out and pasted on the plaque. A sergeant. Who knows what a sergeant is these days, he thought. And then he realized he'd forgotten to make coffee.

Sitting there he remembered there were no beans left. He'd meant to go to Coffee Roasters yesterday, get a couple of pounds of espresso. But he'd forgotten. Florence always wanted him to get the mocha blend, it was lighter and the espresso was too strong for her. But she drank mostly tea and he loved the dark espresso. He thought about going to Coffee Roasters now. There was this cute girl there, Laurie, who always made such a big deal when he came in. "Henry! I missed you honey! Two pounds of espresso again?" She was so...perky. Perky, that was the word. Once, she had patted him on the face. Her little hands, her delicate little fingers had sent a shock through his cheek. He'd had fantasies ever since then about Laurie. What if he asked her to go to Las Vegas for the weekend. He'd give her lots of money to gamble, maybe go shopping, buy a wardrobe. What would she do when they were alone in the hotel room, maybe one of those rooms you could get with a jacuzzi, steam coming up, floating in there together naked? He was imagining it, just in the back of his mind. He thought, sure go to Las Vegas with Laurie! How about going to Mars with Madonna? Just about as likely! But why should he be negative?

Henry stared at the wall facing him, looking for inspiration. He could see the desert stretching before them on the I-15, the road to Vegas, he'd gone there before, ages ago with Florence. Okay, forget Florence, this is about Laurie. Let's see, she had a, not a great figure, but petite, you could see the little nenes in there against her T shirt, even a little nipple, he remembered, the last time he'd been there in the coffee shop and wondered if she had a bra on. Laurie in Las Vegas! He stared at the wall, seeing the long empty freeway, the desert, the light tan mountains in the distance with the light on them from the sun behind him. And the road kept going up and up...

There was a sound of a car coming in on the gravel outside in the driveway. A car door slammed. Then there were heavy footsteps in the gravel, then clacking on the concrete walk. A key turned in the door and Florence walked in.

"Henry? Why is the cat outside? Are you crazy? You know what happened to Climber!" There was the sound of parcels being put down on the kitchen counter. "And what's my begonia doing out in the garden? Henry? And you got the blinds up! Don't you know what that'll do to the rugs? I've been telling you and telling you..."

Florence stopped in front of Henry in his chair. He was a man at peace, his eyes open staring at the wall in front of him, a little smile on his face.

"Oh my God!" said Florence. She looked at Henry, then looked at the wall he was staring at. Her eyes focused on the plaque.

She looked back at Henry, then at the plaque again. She frowned. Then she quickly took the plaque off the wall and jammed it down into the waste basket at the side of Henry's chair.

The phone rang. Florence picked it up.

"Hello?...Yes. Hi, Betty!...You did?...and then he hung up?... Listen, Betty! You're not going to believe this!" Her face was alive with excitement.

THE LONG WAY TO TUSCANY

It had rained during the night but the day dawned impossibly beautiful, the bluest of blue Mediterranean skies, perfectly clear with the new sun just peeking over the Alps to the northeast. *Maybe it's just because we're never up at this hour,* thought Jane. They'd come into Milan on the plane last night from Frankfurt, and JFK before that. They'd fallen into bed at the hotel like dead people and woke promptly at five o'clock, victims of jet lag. So they decided to go for a walk at six and it was marvellous, hardly any traffic in the streets, air still fresh, smelling like the orange blossoms on the trees along the boulevard, the streets clean from the rain.

By eight-thirty they'd breakfasted, packed up, and were on the autostrada heading south in their little rental car, the green Fiat, luggage in the trunk where it couldn't be seen by thieves, as the agent had advised them

They were driving through green fields, immature in the springtime. The farmhouses were funny looking, not like little family farm homes back in America, but massive, looking almost like warehouses, but centuries old, peach-colored, with tiled roofs, tractors standing in the yards, fields and houses protected by rows of poplar trees.

Jane was eating it up with her eyes. The strangeness, the beauty. Neither of them had been in Europe before and now Dick had five weeks of sick leave after being badly hurt on the job.

Dick's friend Tony had said, "You guys gotta go to Italy, man! You'll love it!" And he'd recommended an agency that specialized in rentals in Tuscany. Villas, they called them, but they were really cottages, by the week, a good price before the summer season really started. The agency gave them a package: airfare, rental car, and a month in this villa. Dick was actually Italian, their name was Santi, but he'd never been here and his parents hadn't let the kids learn Italian. "We're Americans now," they'd told Dick, and he'd regretted it ever since, especially on his job, with so many Italians to deal with there in New York.

As Jane was looking at Dick sitting there in the driver's seat with a smile on his face two, three cars with German license plates went screaming by them in the fast lane.

"I don't believe those guys!" said Dick. "I thought we were going fast, but they must have been going a hundred or more! I wonder if it's just Germans, or if all the Europeans drive that way?"

"I read that it's all the same speed limit now, a hundred-and-thirty kilometers an hour everywhere, now that they're all like one country, don't even need passports, or anything," said Jane.

Dick's face instantly froze in terror.

"My God! What's wrong, babe?"

"When you said passports! I just realized. I gave my passport to the hotel clerk last night and I forgot to get it back this morning. Oh shit!"

"Well, it's no big deal, Dicky! Next exit get off, go on back. We'll still get to Pienza by lunch, if we hurry!"

But Dick had seen a police turnaround on the autostrada. "I'll do it even quicker," he said

"I don't know if we're supposed to use this..." Jane was saying, but Dick had already whipped the little car around the turn and was going back the other way on the autostrada.

The ticket taker at the offramp on the outskirts of Milan was not helpful. He looked with disbelief at their toll ticket which was supposed to be going in the other direction and pointed them at a parking slot by the police office. There, they had to wait over a quarter of an hour. Dick finally peeked around the door and saw three policemen in snappy uniforms watching what seemed to be a daytime soap opera on the television. He cleared his throat, got annoyed looks and a babble of argument among the three men. Finally the evident loser of the argument got to his feet and came outside. The ticket taker yelled something from his booth and the policeman nodded. Dick tried to explain what had happened in his few words of Italian. The policeman obviously had no intention of understanding.

"Passport," he demanded.

"Ah! Passport! In hotel! Milano!" said Dick desperately, pointing towards the center of the city in the distance.

The policeman said nothing but strode over to the little coffee shop next to the toll booths. He was some time before returning with an old man wearing an apron. He indicated that Dick should tell his story again to the old man.

"Aha! Americans," said the old man. "How you doin'? I worked in Trenton, New Jersey. Twenty years. So you leave the passport in hotel! Old problem!" And he cackled. "You have to go back, no?"

"We have to go back, yes," said Jane, with growing irritation. "So, will they let us go now?"

The old man rapidly explained the situation to the policeman, who burst explosively into a long tirade directed at the old man, then looked grimly at the Santis.

"He say, you gotta pay lost ticket."

"But we didn't lose the ticket," said Jane. "It's right here in your hand!"

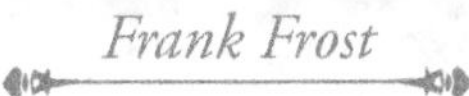

"No. Lost ticket from Firenze—Florence. You coming from direction Florence, you have to pay ticket from Florence!"

They both protested, but the policeman was adamant. Finally Dick pulled out his wallet with resignation and asked how much.

"Jesus!" he said to Jane, after figuring it out. "That's almost forty dollars! And I don't have enough liras."

"*Cambio qua*," said the policeman, pointing at the coffee shop.

"Yes, we change money. Good rates," said the old man, leading them to the shop. "This rate is terrible," said Jane, looking at the handwritten chart over the coffee shop cash register. "It's about two-thirds what we should be getting for a hundred dollar travelers check! Thirteen hundred? It should be about two thousand at least!"

"Screw it," said Dick. "Let's pay up and get outta here." But back at their car there was no sign of a policeman. The attraction of the soap opera had won out.

Jane looked around rapidly. The ticket taker was bogged down with a long line of cars. "Come on, babe. Let's just go. We're really not stealing or anything. We were on their dumb highway about five minutes, is all. We head back to the hotel, we can still be back on the road in a half hour." And they took off back down the offramp towards Milan.

But it was not to be so. The one-way streets that had been so helpful leading them directly to the autostrada now took them every direction except back to their hotel. Finally Dick managed a shortcut by backing up one one-way street and then brazenly driving the wrong way up another street for four blocks, ignoring oncoming cars blaring their horns and swerving up onto the sidewalk when necessary.

They parked in the unloading zone at their hotel and Jane ran in to get Dick's passport.

"Oh, Signora, I'm so sorry!" said the clerk. "I was not on duty last night, I didn't know the passport was yours. The police come every morning and we cannot keep passports. They take them downtown if there is no person."

"Oh my God!" said Jane. "We'll have to drive down to the police station?"

"No, no!" the clerk was firm. "Impossible to drive. The *centro*, the center of town is crazy. And nowhere at all to park. You must take taxi! Tell him, the *Questura*"

Jane and Dick conferred. "I'll take a cab to the police station, the *Questura*, whatever,"he said. "You stay here and keep an eye on the car and the luggage, babe."

A taxi obligingly turned into their street, Dick hailed it and, with a grin and a wave, was off to the crazy *centro*.

Jane sat in the car for a bit, looking at the roadmap and trying to figure how far they would get by lunchtime if Dick took half an hour, or an hour, or more. Then she realized there was a big Mercedes right behind her and that their little Fiat was right in the middle of the unloading zone. So she moved to the driver's seat and pulled the car up almost to the street. It wasn't enough. In a minute the clerk came out.

"I'm so sorry signora!" We have many people coming. Could you maybe find some other place to park?"

Jane looked at the street. It was jammed with parked cars, even double-parked in places. "I...I don't think there is anyplace. Look, I'll just move the car when people pull in.

Okay?"

The clerk looked dubious but he went back into the hotel. Then, about five minutes later, a slender, elegant man in a beautiful light tan suit came out of the hotel and right over to the car.

"Signora," he said. "Carlo told me of your difficulty. But I think we can help you. A special favor. We have a private parking behind the hotel. I have told Carlo it is perfectly alright for you to park there. It is very safe, with a locked gate, and then you can sit in the hotel."

"Oh, that's wonderful!" said Jane. "Just point me out the direction."

"Well, up there, at the end of the block, there is a *senso unico*, how you say?"

"One-way street." said Jane. It was one of the phrases they had been told to memorize.

"Yes. One-way. So you have to go left, instead of right at the corner, then the next block it is again a one-way..."

The gentleman was obviously thinking hard. Then he made up his mind.

"Is simple if I drive the car, okay? No problem then. I meet you at the back of the hotel. There is a door to the parking."

Jane was relieved. She hadn't driven in Italy yet and wasn't sure she wanted to, what she'd seen so far. She handed over the keys gratefully. There was just a moment of apprehension as she saw their little green Fiat, and all their luggage, going off down the street with a man whose name she didn't even know. Then she chided herself for her mistrust. He had an elegant suit, he'd just come out of the hotel, he must be a manager or something. So she walked back into the hotel, down the long hall leading to the back, and found a blind intersection, short halls leading to left and right, no obvious door to the parking outside. She ventured down one hall and found a dead end. Then, pulse rate mounting, to the end of the other branch, where she encountered two maids with their cart, one a dusky brunette, the other very black. They were busily cleaning a recently occupied room.

"*Prego*," she said, using one of her fifteen Italian words. "Where is the door to the parking?"

The two ladies were friendly, trying to help, but it was obvious that there was little comprehension.

"Parking, parking!" she repeated, pointing towards the back wall, willing her finger to penetrate the wall and register some understanding. She'd seen signs in Milan already that said "PARKING" and knew that it was a universal word.

The ladies looked at the back wall, conferred rapidly with each other in a babble of Italian, then the older, matronly lady left the cart, took her by the arm and led her back up to the entrance, saying firmly, "Reception, reception, signora," smiling in a exaggerated way, as if reassuring an idiot.

There she met the clerk with a face so devoid of understanding that she somehow knew what had happened. But she asked the question anyway.

"Where is the door to the hotel parking, in back?"

She knew, she knew, before the words were said. *There is no hotel parking. Where didshe leave her car?*

When she finally admitted that she had given the keys to their car to a stranger, the words coming out with hopeless resignation, the clerk could not at first believe his ears.

"You gave the keys to your car to a strange person?"

"Yes, but he came out of the hotel. And he had on a light tan suit. I thought he was the manager or something."

"Signora! You cannot give your keys to someone you do not know!"

His tone made her a little mad. "But he came out of the hotel. You must have seen him! A thin man, older, good looking, with a nice tan suit?"

By this time there were several hotel employees gathered, listening in on what promised to be an entertaining conversation. The clerk turned to them and started a long, explosive dialogue. Jane could see the gestures, the height of the man, his slimness, the fine suit, all explained in staccato Italian and accompanying sign language. At least everyone nodded. They knew the man.

The clerk turned back to her, sighing. "Yes, signora, the man came out of the hotel. But he was only asking to reserve a room. We told him we were, how you say, *complet*, and he left."

Jane thought quickly. "But how did he know what I was doing out there on the driveway?"

Once more, conferring. "Yes. Yes, signora. He said he wished to bring his car up and we told him you would have to move out of the way."

Jane was a big girl so she didn't collapse in tears. But she had to grope her way back to the little lounge in the reception area and sit down with her head in her hands. She was trying to figure out what to do but the situation was so impossible that she was beyond thought. All she could do was inventory the contents of the suitcases. The clothes, the books, the few kitchen items and favorite knives she had brought along to cook marvelous Tuscan food—and then she remembered the attache case that was in there, with the thousands of dollars in travelers checks, and...all the rental papers for the villa...and her passport, now in the same limbo as Dick's. She wondered, idly, if it was worth trying to get the clerk to call the central police station, to try to intercept Dick, but it just seemed all so hopeless, so hopeless...

* * *

Dick looked up at the large dirty faceless building in the noisy madness of downtown Milan. He didn't know where to start so he just walked in and looked for a directory, the kind they would have in New York in any public building. Nothing. There was a man at a small desk by the entrance who was looking at him curiously so he walked over and asked if he spoke English. The man unleashed a long sentence of Italian that seemed to mean that he didn't, but that he would try to find someone who could. At least he was smiling and pleasant.

A small man in a suit eventually turned up. He didn't speak English either, but Dick managed to say "Passport, passport," with enough feeling to make the man nod, take his arm, and guide him to an elevator.

"Five. Five!" said the little man. But he wouldn't get on the elevator with Dick.

On what Dick would have thought of as the sixth floor the elevator stopped and he got out facing a long counter, familiar in every bureaucracy in the civilized world, manned by too few personnel, with too many people standing in line.

Dick obediently took a place in what he thought was the shortest line and waited, and waited and waited. After about a half hour he'd had enough. Jane had often cautioned him about his temper but in his line of work he often found that it helped. He walked over to the counter and made his own line.

"Hey!" he shouted with some force. "I'm looking for my passport!"

The man at the counter at whom he was yelling looked at him with contempt and gestured at the back of the line.

"No!" Dick shouted. "You people have my passport and I want it now!"

The commotion triggered an appearance of several uniformed officers from a back room.

They rapidly surrounded Dick and he realized he was being treated like any other disruptive person wandering into a structured environment. A mean-faced cop looked him in the eye and demanded, "Passport! Give me passport!"

"I don't have my passport. *You* have my passport!" Dick was doing his best to point back into the office, where he hoped his passport lay somewhere.

The policemen conferred. Then one stepped forward.

"You have other identification?" he said in labored English.

Dick had been told that American driver's licences meant nothing in Europe. But he did have credit cards. So he pulled out his old leather wallet, put it on the counter, opened it and heard a gasp of amazement.

It took him a second to realize that they were all looking at his buzzer—at the badge in his wallet that was inscribed: NYPD.

A moment of silence was broken by a question from the circle of onlookers. "You are *En Why Pee Dee?*"

Dick heard the disbelief in the questioner's voice and wondered if he was in bigger trouble. First, no passport, then impersonating a police officer. And now from an inner office came a short, broad man in civilian clothes. He had a hard, flat face under sparse, curly dark hair. The short sleeves of his shirt revealed massive, hairy forearms. And he was angry. He shouted what were obvious obscenities at the crowd that was being entertained, then turned on Dick.

"What is your business here? Are you making trouble?"

Dick started to explain about his passport, relieved to find an English speaker, but a babble of Italian from the other policemen interrupted him.

The newcomer now scrutinized the open wallet and the detective's badge. He looked up with suspicion.

"You are policeman?"

"Well, yeah. Detective."

"You have other identification? Everyone here watches this NYPD show on television. You think no one ever pretends to be NYPD cop?"

As usual Dick just got mad himself. Looking around he spotted one of the other skeptics laughing, a man in semi-uniform with a handcuff holder on his belt. Time for action.

"Yeah. I have ID. Let me show you." He turned to the man with the handcuffs and held out his hand. "Could I see those for a minute?" he asked with studied politeness. Surprised, the policeman handed him the cuffs. In a split second Dick slapped one cuff on one of the man's hands, spun him around, and cuffed both hands behind his back, yelling, "You have the right to remain silent..." the litany of the Miranda warning.

Once again there was a moment of silence. Then everyone started speaking at once, some of them yelling humorous abuse at the handcuffed cop, the victim shouting back at them to release him. There was now a huge audience of civilians who had been standing in line, now forming an appreciative circle, glad to postpone their business for a show.

Hairy forearms just smirked. "That was a good move, or maybe you practised a lot. What brings you to Italy, Mr...." and he consulted the wallet..."Mr. Santi? Santi? You're Italian? And you don't speak Italian? Or maybe you just have Mr. Santi's wallet? Eh?"

Jane had gone into the small ladies' toilet in the lobby of the hotel to wash her face and try to pull herself together. It wasn't working very well. She had a moment of panic and collapsed in tears on the tiny settee. She lost track of time until a voice began to register in her consciousness. "Signora...please, signora?"

She looked up. It was the black maid, reaching out hesitantly to touch her shoulder.

"I'm...I'm sorry. I didn't hear you?"

"Signora. I should tell you something..."

"But...you speak English?"

"Yes. I learn in school back in...back where I come from."

Jane couldn't imagine how a black woman in Italy would know English. Or why there was a black woman in Italy, for that matter. "Where...where did you come from?"

"Ethiopia. Was part of Italy. you know, long time ago, so my mother came to Italy. More jobs. And we learn English back in Ethiopia. Everyone wants to know English, go to America, England." Her face was alive. Jane felt a sudden relaxation of tension, having someone to talk to in English.

"Uh, I'm so relieved there's somebody I can talk to...tell me, what's your name?" "Is Miriam. You know, like in Bible?"

"Miriam. Yes. Okay. Also like in America, Miriam. A nice name. My name is Jane. And what...?"

"Miss Jane? I heard Carlo say, about the passport, about the car?"

Jane suddenly realized that this woman knew something about her big problem.

"Yes? What do you know? Please tell me!"

"It's very simple," Dick was saying. He had taken a business card out of his wallet and was holding it out to his inquisitor. "You call my precinct at this number and ask who Dick Santi is. They'll tell you. And here..." he pulled a wad of lire out of his pocket, the same lire he had avoided paying out at the toll booth on the autostrada. "Here, this should cover your phone bill."

The Italian policemen looked at each other questioningly and one pointed at his watch and started to say it was the middle of the night in New York.

"Excuse me!?" Dick burst out. "You close up here at night? I'm sorry, pal. The bad guys don't close up in New York. I can tell you my watch commander who's on duty right now..." he consulted his watch..."One thirty in the morning, it's Sergeant Blomberg. So go ahead, call, and ask him about Dick Santi!"

The head cop gave Dick a hard stare, then, carefully, instead of phoning the number on Dick's card he called New York information, got the same number, spoke with Sergeant Blomberg and then entertained the whole office with a long story. He accompanied his tale with many gestures, including obvious discharges of firearms. Then he pushed the money back at Dick "No charge for the phone, detective. So tell us all about the shooting. Your sergeant says you were a hero."

* * *

The Ethiopian woman was in turmoil, Jane could tell. Her face was contorted, turned to the restroom door, anticipating a sudden interruption to their conversation. Finally she summoned her courage.

"I think Carlo is bad man. I think he helps the other man steal cars."

Jane was shocked. "Steal? He helped steal my car?"

"Yes, signora. I know he did something like this two times this week. Both times foreign, like you. Some story about parking. And with that other man."

Jane was trying to comprehend. Could there actually be collusion between the clerk and the car thief? When she thought about it it seemed logical. But the passport? What could they have done…"

"And the passport, signora, I have to tell you, the police do not come to take the passports."

Jane came quickly to life. Now she had an idea of what was going on she could do something about it.

"Miriam, can we call the police station, whatever they call it, the *Questura*, see if my husband is there? Will you help me?"

"I said I would help you, signora. I was afraid I will lose my job. That's why I didn't speak before. But now I know I must tell the truth." She came to Jane, took both her hands.

"Signora, I maybe lose my job, but don't let them hurt me, will you?"

Jane was getting steamed up. "Miriam, you just stick with me. Nobody's going to hurt you!" And she stormed out of the bathroom, headed for the reception desk.

Down at the *Questura* Dick was surrounded by a crowd of admirers. He had his shirt pulled up and he was explaining the eight inch, angry red scar on his left side.

"See, my partner Tony kicked in the door...BOOM! he's a big dude, know what I mean?...then I'm first in the room and I'm yelling 'Police! Police! Freeze!' and everyone freezes, except this one guy, cool as a cucumber, lifts up his niner and it's like I can even see the fucking bullet coming. WHAM! It hits me in the side and I'm like, 'This is it, I'm fucking dead, after all these years!' And I'm on the floor. And then I hear BOOM, and it's Tony blowing away the sucker with his shotgun. So they got me to the hospital and they're trying to fix the hole it went in when the doctor goes, 'Wait a minute,' and they turn me over and he finds the hole it went out and there was like major damage. But I gotta hand it to those guys. They put me back together like I was the six million dollar man, you know what I'm saying?"

The guy with hairy forearms, whose name turned out to be Mario, was translating for the rapt audience when a woman came out of the inner office and called him away. Now Mario returned with a puzzled look on his face.

"Detective..."

"Uh, call me Dick, please..."

"Okay. Detective Dick, the carabinieri just called from the autostrada. They say they have a rental car in the name of Richard Santi, they stopped it and arrested the man driving it. They were looking for the car because... Did you drive off without paying earlier today?"

"Well. Yeah. Maybe. Listen, it's a long story. But what the hell is my car doing out there? Listen, I gotta find out what happened to my wife!" Dick was getting panicky. "Can we call the hotel from here?"

"Come, we call from the car. They recognize the man, a thief. And much valises with your name in back. We go!"

Jane and Miriam were coming out of the bathroom preparing to confront Carlo at the desk when they saw him on the telephone. Whatever he was hearing made him go pale and without a word he hung up and walked out the hotel door.

"What was that all about?" Jane started to ask, but just then the phone rang again. Miriam sprinted across the lobby and answered in Italian. Jane could her her saying "Si, si, signore..." and then she handed the phone to her. It was Dick.

"Babe! Thank God!" he was saying. "I just found out about our car. And I thought something had happened to you. So how the hell...?"

But Jane interrupted. "YOU found out about the car? What about the car?" And finally they both slowed down and explained their adventures, Jane rather sheepishly about giving her car keys to a stranger.

"No, no, babe, don't feel bad," Dick was saying. It's an old con and a good one and lotsa smarter people than you been taken that way, right on the streets of New York."

"But what if...what if I'd stayed in the car with him?"

"He've found a way to get you out. Fender bender, ask you to get out, check the damage, anything, he drives off! I've seen this before, the guy's not inventing the wheel, you know! Now what you gotta do is go out to the autostrada. I'm on the police car phone right now. Mario here is taking me with him but he says there's no time to pick you up. Wrong direction. So can you grab a cab and meet us out there? We can finally leave, get to Tuscany this afternoon. Mario says it's hard to get a cab this time of morning, but I'll just wait here if you have trouble."

"But what about your passport?"

"Mario says the cops never pick up the passports any more, if they ever did. Are you standing at the desk? Look through any drawers they got there. I saw the guy put it in last night."

Jane rummaged quickly through the drawers in front of her. She found one full of passports, but no Richard Santi.

"Yours isn't here. Carlo must have taken off with it."

"Well. No big deal. Now the locals know our story we can get another from the consul before we leave. How about your passport?"

"I just hope it's still in the car, with our luggage."

"Our luggage. Jesus, let's hope so. Anyway, gotta go. See you out on the autostrada."

As Jane hung up she realized she'd been hearing a horn honking persistently for the last few minutes. Now the source of the noise entered the lobby, a large man with a red face, wearing a black suit. He zeroed in on her, there behind the counter.

"Vere is ze bellboy? I am vaiting a half hour already!"

Jane had a sudden inspiration. "Oh signore, I am so sorry," she said, hoping her Italian accent wasn't too over the top.

"Miriam!" she called. "Please to carry the signore's bags. And I make Carlo to park the gentleman's car in our parking.",

Why the hell should I try to find a taxi, she was thinking. *We've wasted enough timealready.*

The Man with the Veal Medallions

The chef peeked through the little window in the kitchen door to check the crowd. He should have started the show five minutes ago but there were still only two couples waiting. And a garrulous old lady, Mrs. Rodeheaver, who was talking away as usual, waving her hands. He figured that if he didn't get going pretty soon she might drive the other customers away.

The poster out there in the dining room said,

WEDNESDAY, 3 PM.
KITCHEN TOUR WITH CHEF EUGENE.
DISCOVER THE SECRETS BEHIND OUR FABULOUS
MENUS

It was the manager's idea. With the hiking, the mountain climbing, the horseback riding, canoeing, and so forth, some clients had asked for something relaxing to do there at the lodge in the afternoon. So the manager thought this was a natural. Everyone loved the food so much, people from New York, San Francisco, *raving* about the menus, spending so much time talking to Chef Eugene when he toured the dining room every evening. Not just asking, of course, but wanting him to realize that *they* knew what a *beurre blanc* was...where did you ever find *morilles* in Idaho?...Not even Jean-Georges, or Thomas, or Alice ever made ginger catfish, truffled quail ravioli, caramelized- pear-lamb shanks—and so on, take your pick—like this!

It was a high-powered crowd. If they weren't here from the big cities, it was Aspen, or the Vineyard, or Santa Barbara. They knew that the five hundred and fifty dollars they were paying per couple every day gave them a little log cabin, with no TV (the lodge *advertised* that) and unlimited riding, hiking, whatever. They could figure out the rest was going into their two meals a day, breakfast and dinner—so they'd better be good.

The meals were much better than good, and so the manager— *call me Herb*, he said—Herb thought people would love to spend some real time with the chef, look at the kitchen, all that sparkling stainless steel, maybe watch someone chopping onions.

Which was why Chef Eugene couldn't figure out how come there were only five people? He was just opening the kitchen door when a sixth client came in, a slender man, medium height, wearing jeans, beautiful snakeskin boots, a denim work shirt and a suede jacket.

"Hi! I'm sorry I'm late. Did I miss anything?"

He was a pleasant-sounding man, middle age. He spoke quietly, relaxed and at ease, but Eugene was thinking he was the kind of quiet guy who could suddenly make people laugh.

The others turned to look, turned back to greet the chef. The clients all knew each other—just to nod to in the dining room— but they tended not to get too clubby. You didn't spend five and a half bills a day to get stuck with a bore, which was why someone like Mrs. Rodeheaver generally felt surrounded by peoples' backs. Judge Rodeheaver himself was always up in the mountains all day, painting. Three guesses.

"Hi, hi! Thanks for coming, everyone! I hope you realize you're the first group ever to tour the Clanton Lake Lodge kitchen. No sir, you didn't miss a thing. Uh...you were the veal medallions with chanterelles last night?"

Everyone chuckled, and the newcomer was surprised.

"How did you—?"

"You know, I see the whole crowd every night. There's only fifty-two of you, so after a few dinners, I've got everyone figured out. I'm real busy back there but I've still got time to play this little game, you know? Like, 'That guy took the trout last night; I bet he goes for some real meat tonight.' Or, 'That lady ate every course last night. And two desserts. Today she's going to take the clear soup, skip the first course, and order the crawfish tails *à la nage*.'" Everybody laughed.

"Now—" He was going to continue but Mrs. Rodeheaver started to interrupt. Chef Eugene had escaped from her in the dining room before and didn't want to get bogged down, so he just held up a hand, smiling, and said," You know what? We should get started. There's plenty of time for questions as we do the tour."

Everyone gladly moved through the double doors into the kitchen. Chef Eugene turned, his back to a long metal counter. "Here's the last stop folks, just before you get your food." He gestured with his hands in both directions, like a symphony conductor acknowledging his musicians.

Everyone's attention was on Chef Eugene. He was a fairly young man, maybe thirty-eight or so, but looking younger, with his very short blondish hair, his round, very open freckled face. A stocky frame, not at all fat, but an appropriate build for a good cook. He was a naturally friendly man, full of good cheer, and they all had talked to him in the dining room, if only briefly.

"Every plate comes out here and I look at it, check to see if it's just right. You may not notice all the little garnishes, the fresh herbs, the parsley oil—"

There were murmurs, objections, almost indignant denials... they *had* noticed.

"Okay! okay, great. But it's not just the garnish. You don't want a little slop of sauce on the edge of the plate..."

No they didn't.

"Or maybe even forget the potatoes!" They all laughed, shaking their heads. As if!

"So I check the order very carefully and enter it on the computer right here—table number and a little code for the dish. Just a 'V-M' for your veal medallions, sir. That way I can take ten minutes, end of the evening, sit down at the computer and *boom* it's all there, exactly how much of every ingredient—"

"What was my elk chop?" Mrs. Rodeheaver asked. Someone groaned, quickly turned it into a throat- clearing.

"Your elk chop on the green peppercorn cream coulis? Just an L-K. Elk."

"We musta seen a hundred elk yesterday, driving around," said Mr. Nilwater, and his wife nodded. "No problem getting elk chops here, I bet."

"You know the darnedest thing? I get my elk from New Zealand. Venison too. It's farmed there." There was a chorus of disbelief.

"No. Listen, you wouldn't believe the Park regulations, what we can serve or not. And my trout? With all the trout streams and lakes around here? That has to be flown in too. Not so far though, Wisconsin."

"You probably get consistent supply that way," said Mr. Biddle, sounding knowedgable. "And no waste."

"You got it! No waste. And you got your portion control. If we butchered a whole elk here we'd have about nine hundred pounds of elk meat left over. What are you gonna do with that?"

"Host the Elks' Club convention?" Everyone laughed. It was the man with the veal medallions.

"Ha ha, that's good. Now folks, if you'll just follow me...?"

They wound in and out of the counters in the kitchen, observing the sauté line, the wood-fired grill, the two sous-chef stations, the prep tables, the walk-in cold rooms. The conversation was spirited. The two couples were obviously both foodies, knew how to cook, went to good restaurants. Mrs. Rodeheaver was even a bit intimidated by the expert flow of food conversation. She would just start to say something about a meal she had in Des Moines and someone would break in...

"The smoked duck breast? You brine that first?"

"Yes sir. Just overnight. Firms up the outer meat a bit, keeps it juicy. Got a little backyard smoker right out back."

They had circled back to the kitchen door again and the subject of memorable dishes had come up. They were going on and on. Mrs. Rodeheaver even finally got in her meal in Des Moines, and Chef Eugene thought maybe he'd ask the man with the veal medallions to say something and then he could shoo them out the door.

"You sir? You've been pretty quiet. Are you a great cook like the rest of these folks?"

"Not really. I do fool around in the kitchen now and then. Right now I'm trying to duplicate a recipe I had at this hunt club back in New Jersey. Just a simple linguine with eggplant, but I think there's something missing."

Everyone looked to Chef Eugene, expecting him to volunteer some surefire trick, but he had suddenly frozen in his tracks.

Finally, he looked at his watch. "Whoa! The time! Gotta get movin' folks, or dinner'll be late." He abruptly turned away and walked toward the back of the kitchen.

Later he found the man with the veal medallions out in the lounge having a cup of coffee. It was the quiet time before cocktails and no on else was in the lounge. Late afternoon sun was streaming through the windows. Eugene came out and sat down across from him.

"Brown. Nathan Brown. That's what the register says."

"That's really my name, too, Gino."

"You didn't look like a wiseguy to me. Man, you startled me like that. I almost had a heart attack. I been expecting, you know, a couple of years, some bent nose is gonna walk in and that's it."

Nathan Brown chuckled. "Gino, I'm a lawyer. They asked me to see if I could find you."

"A lawyer...? Does that mean Vinnie...Mr. Castle might—"

"Might settle for what you owe him?"

"That's what I meant, Mr.—"

"And the vig?"

Chef Eugene's face fell. "Mr. Brown. I been saving up some money. I been planning all along to make good. I'm close to what I owed, you know? But if I have to pay the vig...what's it been now, almost three years? I could never—"

Nathan Brown smiled, waved his hand dismissively. "Just kidding, Gino. No. Vinnie always liked you. When you disappeared he almost cried, you know why? The food at the club. It just went downhill. And especially the linguine siciliana. The one with the eggplant?"

"I know. Every Friday lunch. I offered to put it on the menu twice a week, but Mr. Castle said, no, he liked getting hungry for it in the middle of the week— anticipating—you know what I mean?" Eugene was silent for a moment, just thinking it over. "You mind telling me how you found me?"

Mr. Brown smiled. "It's not like it was a full-time job, Gino, you know? Vinnie goes, 'You think you can find him?' And I go, 'I'll have some people look into it.' Basically it was just checking lists. I figured you'd be at a private club somewhere, a resort, not a restaurant where you might show up in restaurant reviews. I told my people, 'Check every place within fifty miles of a casino. This guy gambles. Has to gamble.'"

The chef was shaking his head, rubbing his jaw, a rueful expression on his broad face.

"Mr. Brown, you figured me out all right." He looked up, confident now.

"But you know what? How I used to throw all my money away on the tables, the horses? I got out here, I spent some time in therapy. Like in AA, which I did that too ten years ago. They can treat gambling the same way. Not just gambling, but, you know, gamblaholics, I used to be? I got rid of all that insanity—gotta catch up, bigger and bigger bets. Now I can just walk up to the tables, win a little, lose a little, walk away. Besides, it's different here! The Indians, got that casino the other side of the lake? It's a great casino, and you know what? Babes in the woods, comes to real gaming. They been trying to hire people from Nevada, but they can't get enough. They really don't know what they're doing, how to rob people!" He was becoming animated.

Nathan Brown was looking skeptical, so Eugene kept talking even faster.

"What I been doing, every week, is going over there and playing the safe games, blackjack, sometimes poker...you know I could always play poker. Almost every night it's been a hundred, two hundred, one night over a thousand, even—"

The lawyer was holding up a hand, laughing. "Enough, enough. That sounds great, Gino. We're talking about seventeen large, now. You think you can come up with a good down payment on that?"

Eugene leaned forward, confident now. "Mr. Brown. Couple of years ago I just figured one day I'd be dead. But I still started planning, maybe if I could make a deal, I don't know. I put aside half my salary every month. And then I just started adding whatever I won. I've got everything in this leather bank envelope, you know, like I was just thinking something like this could happen? I *got* that money! Really. I got that much saved up, I could show you!"

Nathan Brown got up, filled his coffee cup at the big coffee maker. Chef Eugene was on his feet in a second.

"Mr. Brown, why don't you let me get you a nice espresso? I'll just holler to Mike in the kitchen—"

The lawyer smiled, waved him off. "I just wanted another mouthful, Gino. You know everything you're telling me is good news. Vinnie's going to be a happy man. But what about this casino. Maybe we should take a look at it, just from a business point of view. What time you get off tonight?"

It was ten-thirty when they drove around to the other side of the lake. There in the remote Idaho mountains the Indian casino had been carved into the pine forest, its garish lights blinding the stars and its parking lot jammed with hundreds of cars. They had to park in the trees, off the asphalt, and walk for over a hundred yards. A light wind was stirring the trees and they could smell the pines, the wood smoke—and then look at the absurdity of this trashy casino. Two stolid, silent bouncers gave them a glance and waved them through into a cacaphonous alley of beeping, booping, flashing slots. Eugene pointed to the back of the main room.

"Poker tonight. See if we can find a game. There's some guys drive here all the way from Boise to get taken, you know the type? It used to be me. Just watch."

Eugene wandered a bit through the poker tables. It was obvious he was known. He soon found a table of four where he was enthusiastically welcomed. Nathan Brown said that he was just going to poke around, maybe have a drink. From the bar he could see the players he figured Gino was targeting, a younger man, flushed, talking too much. And a stolid old Indian, it looked like, never said a word, just looked at his cards, made his bets. In less than an hour Gino came back to the bar, counting chips.

"You saw me sandbag that guy? I let him catch me bluffing one hand, he wins a few bucks. Then, eight hundred or so on the table, I've got two pair, but I've been counting cards and I don't figure there's bupkus out there. He stayed in until he caught on and then it was too late. Bingo!"

"Also," said Nathan Brown, "I notice every time the Indian deals you win, or almost."

"Well. That too." Eugene was sheepish. "They call him Chief Many Chips here. He's a real Blackfoot, you know, but he was a dealer in Tahoe for thirty years.

Nobody here knows that. We hooked up a long time ago. I gotta pay him off tomorrow."

They cashed in and the chef tucked his winnings into the large leather envelope. "You see, Mr. Brown? I learned a lesson here. I never take a drink anymore, always quit while it still feels too early, win or lose. You'll give this to Mr. Castle, let him know I want to come back?"

They paused at the lounge. Dark reddish light, only a few tables occupied, everyone else out where the action was.

The lawyer looked around. "There's just one other thing, Gino. The linguine. Vinnie wants the exact recipe. Can we sit down a minute? You just reel it off and I'll jot it down." A waitress in a miniskirt and net stockings came to take their orders. Eugene ordered a coke, Nathan Brown a bourbon-rocks.

Later Gino was talking and laughing non-stop all the way back to the woods where they'd parked the car. He was going on about how he'd always loved the hunt club, didn't have to do anything but cook, but here at the lodge he had to be the kitchen accountant too and he'd always hated that side of it.

"You know what I mean?" he asked, his hand on the door of the car. "You know what it's like, having to do two different jobs at the same time?"

"I surely do," said Nathan Brown.

It was a warm day for fall and the luncheon crowd was out on the terrace of the hunt club overlooking the forested slope leading down to the Delaware river. Nathan Brown joined Vincent Castle at a table for two.

"Nate, Nate! Great to see you back." He put up a big meaty hand. "Now don't tell me... First of all, you got the recipe?"

Smiling, Nathan Brown pulled a note pad out of his jacket. Today he was wearing dark grey flannel slacks, a black faux turtleneck, and a light grey silk herringbone jacket.

"Wait, wait just a minute!" Castle gestured to a waiter. "Aldo, go get Aristide, quick." He turned back to Brown. "You gotta catch this guy, this cook. My cousin discovered him in a hotel in Marsala two months ago, now he cooks the whole menu, French, American, you name it."

A quiet man came out of the kitchen wearing a chef's jacket and checkered pants, wiping his hands on his apron, a question on his face. He pulled up a chair, straddled it.

"Aristide! This is my lawyer, Mr. Brown. He brought back that recipe I told you about, the linguine?"

Aristide nodded politely. "Okay, Nate, let'er rip."

Brown checked his notes, wanting to get everything in the right order.

"Okay, the whole secret, Gino says, is how you do the eggplant. First thing, you gotta crush some garlic, chop some rosemary and basil and put it in your olive oil, maybe a cup, the best you got, let it steep. Then after an hour or so, you slice your eggplant and just brush the oil on, both sides. Then—and this is important—you gotta grill the eggplant on a wood fire, real hot. Other than that, just cook your linguine, toss it with the left over oil—that has the garlic and stuff in it—use a fresh tomato sauce not cooked too much, fresh chopped basil, top it all with your eggplant and of course the *caciocavallo* to grate at the table. How's that sound?"

"You get that all, chef?" asked Castle, anxiously.

There was a brief exchange in Sicilian, Aristide nodded again, even smiled, and went back to the kitchen.

"What Gino said, the oil the eggplant is grilled with, crisp, a little black even—it calls to the oil on the pasta, almost a spiritual thing.

"Fabulous, fabulous." said Vincent Castle. He looked around, lowered his voice. "So. How was the rest of your trip? Gino look like he could pay anything off?"

The lawyer shook his head. "He wanted to show me how well he was doing. Took me out to this Indian casino out in the woods and dropped a bundle. He's still a loser. So I took care of it. How about lunch, shall we order, or what?"

New York Jews

New York Jews who are writers are always writing about what it's like to be a Jewish writer in New York. Well, as all the books say, write what you know about. Anyway, since half the magazines in the country are published in New York I have this picture in my mind of editors looking at stories set in Santa Monica, or Dallas, or anywhere, Spearfish, South Dakota, you name it, and they read one paragraph and say, Nah! Where's the Angst? It's a tough market to crack. I got the rejection slips to prove it. So when I was explaining this to a woman friend she said, "Well then, Petey, instead of just complaining why don't you write about what it's like being a gentile writer here in the Valley? Maybe there's a market for that." So I go, "Sure! How many people you know here in the Valley read anything?" and she goes, "Women do, dummy! Don't you know that women buy eighty percent of the books in this country?" And I'm like "Come on!" so she goes, "*Cosmo*'s got a circulation of around three million. *Esquire*? 750,000, I looked it up. That's only one quarter of..."

"Hah!" I break in, "How about *Playboy*?" and she goes "Men don't buy *Playboy* to read, they buy it to beat off." Well I wasn't going to argue with that so we discussed it some more and finally I agreed I'd write something about what it was like being a writer in the Valley.

I always wanted to write. Actually what I originally wanted when I first started was not so much to do the writing part of it, but to be a Writer and be famous and meet babes at parties because my friend Mort told me his older brother was a screenwriter and once they were shooting his script and this sort of minor actress wanted a bigger part and more dialogue and heacted dumb and said, "Uh, what lines would you want where?" and she said come on to my trailer and I'll give you some ideas. And Mort's brother gives us a knowing look and rolls his eyes around meaning we're supposed to believe he got awesomely laid, which I don't believe because between his bald spot and his big gut he could've given her twenty pages of Tennessee Williams and still not gotten laid. But anyway. Anyone can write, but being a Writer means that at a party if you're introduced to a woman as a Writer and she asks "Oh yeah? What have you written?" you can say, "Well, Harper Collins published my *Last Offramp to Redondo* and Bantam is dickering for the paperback rights but if they can't do better than a mil five I'll go to auction." Actually, I couldn't say that because I'm publishing almost exclusively these days in only two magazines and if I told any reasonably intelligent female at a party what the magazines are they'd find they had to go out to the kitchen to get some more onion dip. But I do make a pretty good living. Fifteen years ago when I dropped out of Cal State Northridge to try writing full time I sent stories everywhere, from *The New Yorker* and *Atlantic Monthly* to *Christian Maturity*. I'd hang out at this big bookstore in the magazine section and read all the mags and getan idea what kind of material they wanted and then try to adapt my style. I really did sell a story to *Christian Maturity* (that used to be *Young Christian* but their subscribers were really loyal) and believe it or not, one to *Romance and Gourmet* under the name Felicia Pandolfi. That was after *Dating Scene* was bought by *Dining World*. But I never cracked the big ticket mags and I was getting more and more published at these two other magazines so I just decided that's where my future was.

So now I guess I have to confess that the two magazines I mainly write for are *BIKER!* and *Big Breasted Babes*. Okay, I know you're not going to believe that bikers actually read magazines or that there's a mag called *Big Breasted Babes,* either one. But just look up the headings in *Periodical Markets for the Modern*

Writer and there they are. You see, I was going through that book alphabetically, mainly to see what they were paying per word or per page and under the Bs I found those two and they paid pretty well and I sold the first submissions I sent in. So I finally decided to specialize and by now *they* phone *me* up and say, "Got anything new, Petey?" Best thing is, they're both bi-weeklies so they always need material. For *BIKER!* you have to tell stories about guys with Harleys who are either heroes in some violent situation or who score with awesome babes in some totally unrealistic scenario. *Periodical Markets* tells the aspiring writer that *BIKER!* wants violent heroics or erotica, no fantasy or sci fi, but I'm telling you that what these guys want is really fantasy, something that'll convince a biker with a huge hairy gut and six months worth of B.O. that if he beats up a guy wearing a suit who is supposedly "bothering" a waitress with ten ton tits that he can score some steamy sex because of her gratitude. Is that science fiction or what? Real fantasy, you get a look at some of those guys. *Big Breasted Babes* has a lot of photographs of you know what and they want just a few stories everyweek to suggest some imaginative situations you could get into with a big breasted babe because most of the guys who read this mag don't have much imagination and so they look at the photos until their mouths are flapping open and then here's this story right next to the photo that starts, "Gavin let his tongue roll around Chantal's erect nipples until her moaning got too intense..." and then these guys think, "Hey, I could do that!" and they actually read the story, which has got to be pretty short and to the point. I can write about three of those in an afternoon and at four hundred bucks a story it's easy work.

A funny thing. One day a woman phoned me up and asked for Monique. At first I thought it was a wrong number and then I remembered I had written a story under the name Monique Glide. It started out with a guy in a typical Valley singles bar asking a babe what her sign was and she said, Slippery When Wet, and went on from there. Anyway, I wasn't going to admit that I was Monique Glide but this woman was very insistent and I wanted to find out what kind of woman wanted to talk to the author of a dumb story about a big breasted babe who said her sign was Slippery

When Wet so I finally confessed that I was Monique Glide. And she hollered, "I knew it, only a man could write bullshit like that! Aren't you ashamed of yourself?" And I said, like I say to relatives, it's a living and it's only fantasy and I'm sorry you were offended, because believe it, she was offended, you know what I mean? I thought she'd hang up but she kept going on, what kind of a chauvinist pig can write garbage like this for a living and I told her that I'm actually considered a nice guy and that I could give her referrals from several women who know me. And she goes, "Sure! and do they all have big tits?" So I got a little hot myself and I go, "What I do for a living has nothing to do with who I am," and then I asked, "What do you do for a living?" and it turned out she was a paralegal working for a big personal injury law firm there in the Valley and I said, "Well, there you go!" and I could tell she was trying to decide whether to hang up or laugh but we talked about it a bit and she finally laughed and that's how I met Barbara and we had some great times.

But about then the big crisis in my life came along. In my professional life that is, because I got two letters the same day. One was from the publisher of *BIKER!* and the other wasfrom my editor at *Big Breasted Babes* and the letters were identical because actually they were just a printed handout and they said, "To all vendors, advertisers, creditors, and contributors. Be advised that of August 31st the two magazines *BIKER!* and *Big Breasted Babes* have been purchased by Finian Mudrick Publications. Because of excessive overhead the publishers have decided to combine the two magazines, provisionally under the title of *BIG BREASTED BIKER BABES!*" And in my envelope there was a note from my editor at *Babes* saying, "Petey, this title sucks! Can you come up with some other idea? We're not publishing until October." So you can imagine the pressure on me. Because this guy Finian Mudrick is a billionaire from Scotland who already owns about twenty American newspapers and magazines and a dozen TV stations and a movie studio and I can just imagine while I am trying to write a story about big breasted biker babes he's going to acquire *Arthritis Update* and *Koi Owner* and put them into the same magazine too. Bottom line, what I'm looking at is my income cut in half because there's no way I could write *all* the dumb stories in the new combined magazine.

The whole scene was getting complicated in other ways. Just a week before I got this letter the editors of *BIKER!* hired me to come out to sign T shirts in Laughlin, Nevada, where the Harley guys have a convention every year. It was amazing, seeing two thousand Harleys parked in one place and these guys wandering the streets in all their getups and with their babes and the hotel clerk said they were the least trouble of any convention they ever had. It surprised me but it turned out some of the *BIKER* readers had actually written in and said they liked the stories by Matt Barstow, or Doc Ramblin, or Mame Frazee, or some of the other names I used and I could sit at a table and actually admit I was all those people and autograph black T shirts with a silver ink felt pen for five bucks apiece. And that's where I realized the market was changing. Because I was hanging out in the bar with a couple of old-time bikers, guys with long grey ponytails and beards, listening to their old stories, to get ideas, you know, keeping the Cuervo Gold flowing, and some dudes came up to the booth with humungous arms hanging out of their cutoff jackets, tatoos and all that, and it turned out they were like engineers and computer programmers and they were saying, hey man, we like the stuff you write but why don't you do some stories where bikers accidentally hack into some secret government computer, find out that there's a conspiracy to take over the country, so they get all their biker buddies together and attack the headquarters before it can get going, using laptops and cyber- sabotage and downloading viruses into the bad guys' main frame, stuff like that. We're all sitting around in the bar of the Paddlewheel Radisson and these guys are getting more and more enthusiastic and I go, "But that's just the plot of your *Saturday Night Movie* on Channel Thirteen!" and this bald guy, wearing all black leather, goes, "Hey! I'm the *producer* of *Saturday Night Movie* on Thirteen, fuhchrissakes! I'm dying for a good biker hero, all we get now are sci-fi or crud that went directly to video!" Well, you know he got my attention in a hurry. So I asked this guy, if I get a story published can you find a producer to make a TV movie of it? And he says, if I like the story, and I like all your stories. Thats how I met Mike Radulescu, who really looked more like a biker than a Channel Thirteen movie producer, although the tatoos washed off, which is really sort of Channel Thirteenish.

Anyway, I wrote the story and the bikers had cell phones and laptops built into their Harleys so they could communicate and solve complex situations and their informants were some waitresses at a Hooters bar in D.C. who had overheard some slimy guys conspiring to take over the government. And the final scene was when the bikers attacked a secret installation in Virginia and they had disabled the bad guys' electronics with their computers and as you might guess, the waitresses from Hooters had already infiltrated, pretending to be models who were going to show a good time to the bad guys and their clients, who were rotten foreigners. And the hero at the last second cracked the code of the bad guy's mainframe, which was about to set off a nuclear bomb under the Pentagon. And you can bet your ass that *Big Breasted BikerBabes!* published that story in their first issue

So that's how I happened to be sitting in the office of Finian Mudrick one day, having been called to consult on making a movie of this piece of crap for his movie studio. He's a little wiry guy, doesn't talk very much. And he surprised me, he really did, because I figured him for a fast buck guy, but he's saying, why don't we budget this film at around 90 mil, top stars, and lots of great special effects. You'll get billing as top writer.

But my reaction was, the subject matter will sell it to those dummies out there. So how about only *fifteen* mil, get network TV stars who've never been on the big screen to do it for next to nothing, everybody knows their names, spend the extra money on promotion, all the mouth breathers who watch TV will come to the movie and then you can bring out a line of laptop computers based on the movie and even some designer biker clothes.

This guy Mudrick is staring at me through his yellow glasses he wears all the time and he doesn't say a thing for almost five minutes and I'm thinking I'm going to have to go back to short stories for a living and in my mind I'm going over the plot for the next thing I might write for *Gay Christian Maturity*, which was a spinoff after the original mag failed. But then Mudrick goes, "If we go low budget, could we set the final scene in Malibu, it's a lot cheaper than Virginia?" and I go sure, and he goes, "Can the bomb be under Hollywood, it'd be a lot more relevant?" and I nodded, yeah, you got that one right, and then he asked the big question, "Could the bikers invading the secret installation have to work their way around pools full of deadly Koi?"

And you know what? The son of a bitch had actually gone and bought *Koi Owner* and I should just be grateful he didn't buy *Arthritis* whatever too because I sure wouldn't have known how to work that in. What really bothered me was that now I had to write new material for Koi instead of starlets who might've done major favors for extra lines.

So that's why I'm writing this here in my hilltop villa in Bel Air that I bought with what I scored on the movie which I lucked into because Finian Mudrick didn't think one percent of the gross was going to be very much. And there's a dividend I have to tell you about. If you're trying to sneak into this place . Don't get near the Koi ponds. Because Mudrick had them bred special, just for the movie, which as you know grossed over a hundred mil here, where we like our bikers and big breasted babes, but *three hundred* million in Japan, where they know their Koi.

That last scene in the movie still haunts me.

THE COLLECTORS

Professor Mason was standing outside his office trying to remember. Had he gone down the hall to the bathroom deciding to come back and finish some work? Or had he finished, locked up, and only gone to the bathroom to avoid urgency on the way home. He couldn't remember. There was no light under his door and it didn't seem important to him so he walked to the stairway door and began the long spiral down through the stairwell.

Professor Mason always used the stairs even though his office was on the sixth floor. He reasoned that he got no other exercise. He certainly wasn't going to run around in his underwear, as some of his younger—and even older—colleagues were doing. Nor did he wish to visit a club where he could use strange machines to raise his heartbeat and smell the sweat of many other people. Besides, he was a historian of science and was aware that until about 1965 no intellectuals had ever exercised. Yet their age at death was quite a bit later than other statistical groups, including military personnel, professional athletes, and criminals, all of whom had obviously been required to exercise repeatedly during the course of their lives.

Nevertheless, the professor enjoyed taking the stairs twice a day, or several more times a day if he went to the library or to lunch with a friend or graduate student. The tall, dimly lit tower of the stairwell was featureless concrete, had no associations with any other part of his life and therefore was conducive to concentrated thought as he slowly plodded up and down. He was accustomed to setting himself some specific problem of finite duration, usually the phrasing of a footnote or a slight change in a syllabus, to contemplate on the journey up or down. He was rarely disturbed in his solitary stairwell because the students at his university, although glowing with vigorous Southern California health and wearing expensive running shoes and sportswear, all seemed to prefer the elevator, even to the Sociology department on the second floor.

It was rather unusual therefore when he heard a door open on the next landing, echoing up and down the concrete tower. He had lost track of the floor he was approaching, having been distracted by trying to remember whether the Library computer read umlauts as *fuer* instead of *für* or simply ignored them. Actually, come to think of it, he had been descending for some time.

He rounded the corner of the stairs and there below him were Morgenstern and Cathcart, one Political Science and the other Anthropology. It wasn't second floor Sociology then. Or not necessarily. They were both looking at him.

"Hello there, Mason," said Morgenstern. "Good to see you, John," said Cathcart. "Shall we walk down together for a bit."

"Yes, hello, hello. Please join me," answered Mason. "Although it's hard to talk here in the stairwell, it always echoes so."

In fact it was not echoing now at all. *"Something atmospheric,"* thought Mason.

And then, as his two companions chatted, he remembered something about Morgenstern. Hadn't he died recently? A sudden stroke on the golf course? Or had that been Morganson, Physics? And Cathcart. He hadn't seen him for weeks, even months? He realized he had come to a halt. So had Morgenstern and Cathcart and they were regarding him gravely.

"I've had a sudden terrible thought," he said.

His companions only looked at him. They seemed unusually sympathetic and concerned for fellow academics.

"I'm dead. That's what, isn't it?" he said.

His companions were silent for a moment. Then Cathcart spoke.

"We've come to walk with you for a while, John. In case you had some questions."

"It's the exercise thing, isn't it. I knew I should have been jogging or something; everyone seemed to be doing it. Although I don't remember anything but standing outside my office. Is it always that way? You don't remember?"

"Not at all, John," said Morgenstern. "You were in perfect health for a man of sixty-two."

"It was quite unexpected. An accident," added Cathcart. "Do you know Drake in your department well?"

"Yes, of course, Renaissance. And the big course in Western Civ. Good Lord! Is he dead too?"

"No," said Morgenstern, "But he should be."

"Yes," went on Cathcart, "He had a crazy student named Cogelshatz, who got a "D" from his teaching assistant. Cogelshatz phoned Drake in an absolute rage and demanded a grade change. Drake firmly refused."

"And with his usual bad grace," said Morgenstern. Drake adored children but famously had no patience with lazy college students.

"But what did that have to do with me?"

"It didn't, of course."

"Cogelshatz, you see, got off the elevator on the wrong floor. Drake's office is right below yours. Cogelshatz burst in the right door, but on your floor."

Morgenstern took up the story. "He had picked up a fire axe walking down the hall and he sank it deep into your skull."

Mason's hands flew to his head.

"No, no! There are no marks!"

"There never are," Cathcart added helpfully.

"But that's terrible!" cried Mason. "And Cogelshatz! What's happened to him?"

"Well. He tried to turn the axe on himself."

"Not at all as easy as with a firearm," added Cathcart with a wry smile.

"No," said Morgenstern. "Poor Cogelshatz made a mess of everything. Western Civ., you, and himself. He will need extensive cosmetic surgery before his eventual journey to an institution for the criminally insane."

Mason stood silent there in the hall. For they had evidently emerged from the stairway onto a long hall, wood paneled, with soft gray carpeting and concealed lighting. He was trying to figure out what he thought of all this. His wife would have been hysterical, but she had died several years ago. His two children lived far away with their own families and called rarely, usually to advise him on investment strategies, advice he never took. He had no research burning to be published, only his long actuarial study of academic lifespans in various scientific disciplines. He had long ago admitted to himself that he didn't care what patterns emerged. But, but, but...

"But what happens now?" he stuttered.

"Ah," his companions said together.

"We're getting to that."

* * *

They were walking down the long hall. Now and then there was a door, as if to an office. Once, in an alcove, there was a telephone. As they passed it rang.

Morgenstern picked it up.

"Hello?...Yes, yes....everything is fine—or at least as it ought to beNo, no, he took it very well." He turned to Mason. "I've told them you took it well."

Mason felt a bit cross. "I'm not so sure I've taken it well. You haven't given me much time to think about it. And who in the world are 'them'? And if 'they' are so all important, why did they let Cogelshatz off at the wrong floor!" He felt himself flush.

"John I'm sorry. I shouldn't have taken the liberty of assuming anything about your attitude." Morgenstern looked honestly contrite, almost pained, and Mason's anger waned as rapidly as it had risen.

"We'll be off in a bit," said Cathcart. "And the last thing we wanted was to have you upset."

"No, no, I'm quite alright now. It's just that I have no idea what I'm doing, or if I'm going to be doing anything at all."

"Oh yes, John. In fact you're going to be doing quite a lot."

They had arrived at a glass door looking out at a bus stop. Cathcart was no longer with them.

"Cathcart's off now, John, he's done his bit. And after a little while I'll be taking off too. That's the way it works."

"Could you explain the rules?" asked Mason. "It would help me do whatever it is I'm supposed to be doing."

"John," said Morgenstern, "All we're supposed to do is help our friends over the shock. Then, I assume, everyone's best instincts take over and we act as we always have--ladies and gentlemen helping past friends get used to the idea of..."

"But what happens? I mean, for instance, what happened to Cathcart?" John Mason was a little annoyed at himself for sounding nervous and high strung. He wasn't quite sure when his best instincts were going to click in.

"I have no idea," said Morgenstern. "I just know that during our brief time helping our friends adjust we get this feeling that in some way we are finishing a long, long job and that some marvelous new life is about to start. John, you're about to start your part of the job. Don't you feel it a bit?"

* * *

Mason strolled down a path into the park. He was evidently to serve for a little while as a Collector. A sort of interim guide. He had to admit that his colleagues had made the transition less upsetting than it might have been. The trees were in full spring foliage, squirrels scurried across the lawns, and birds hovered above the luxuriant flower beds. Not far away he could see a small lake with swans and ducks going about their business on the surface. A small girl was now approaching from the left along a long avenue of plane trees. When she saw him she started skipping until she was facing him. She studied his face seriously.

"What's your name?" she asked.

"John," said Mason, thinking that "Professor Mason" would be a little formal. "And what is yours?"

"Um. It used to be Debbie. But that's all over. And I'm so happy!" She gave a little hop, then twirled around twice.

Mason had expected someone, probably male, of his age and station, and he had no idea how he was expected to console a little girl, especially one who needed no consoling and who seemed to know exactly where she was. But she didn't need his help to keep the conversation going..

"This is just like I used to dream!" she said. "Back then I had these awful, heavy leg braces. And thick, thick glasses. And my tongue hung out and looked all yucky." She demonstrated, not very successfully. "I was 'suh-verely dee-velop-mentally dis-abled,'" she said carefully, pronouncing every syllable. "I could hear, you know, and see a little bit, and feel, mostly hurting. I knew people, like the nurses and my mother when she came to visit. She cried a lot," she confided. Then she tried another twirl.

"But I used to dream and in my dream I was like this, pretty, and...am I pretty, John?"

"You're the prettiest little girl I've ever seen," said Mason. And indeed the little girl had the sweetest face, with long brown hair pulled back in a ponytail. She was wearing a light yellow summer dress in a small flowered pattern that was a little too short for her long coltish legs.

"I was always pretty in my dream, and it was sunny and I was in a meadow with flowers, and I could dance and sing. It was marvelous. I always had the same dream. And then this one time I was in my dream and when I woke up I was here. And it's funny, you know, that I know all those words—like 'dee-velop... op...' you know what I mean—and even 'meadow.' I know I never saw a meadow. And now I'm here and I even know what I'm going to be doing!"

Mason wished he knew what *he* was doing. He wasn't sure he'd be able to speak at all what with the lump in his throat, thinking about the awful past life of this little girl, and thinking about his own little girl when she was seven or eight—the girl who was now a thirty-five-year- old mother of three in Portland, Oregon and whom he'd never see again now. But Debbie gave him no chance to speak. She pointed to a hill in the distance.

"Here comes another girl," she said. "She's going to need help. Her mother's boyfriend hit her until she was dead. Isn't that terrible!" she said matter-of-factly, as if a picnic had been interrupted by rain. "And there are supposed to be others. Can you help me when they get here? We can get them all talking, or in a game or something"

Now Mason knew there was something wrong. And as he looked wildly around he suddenly saw a telephone set into a square recess in an oak tree. He'd never seen a telephone in a tree before, except maybe in a comic strip once, but now it seemed entirely natural and he immediately walked over and picked up the receiver.

"Hello, Professor," he heard a pleasant woman's voice say. "How are we getting along?" He had always been annoyed by the patronizing "we" used by persons who were in no way involved in one's problems but now he was too concerned to notice.

"I'm afraid there's been a terrible mixup," he said. "I thought we were to 'collect' people we had something in common with, people we could sympathize with and help through their dismay and confusion. But..."

"It's odd you should say that, Professor, what with all your work with children. Could you explain..."

But Mason suddenly knew what had happened. The poor maniac Cogelshatz was supposed to have killed Drake all along! Drake was to have been the designated Collector. Drake, who adored children. Drake, who volunteered hours every week counseling abused children. Drake, who read aloud to a mesmerized audience of children every Saturday morning in the public library, readings that had been glowingly described in a Sunday *Times* feature story.

"You know, I'm positive it's Professor Drake who's supposed to be here all along!" he said with some urgency. "All these little girls! When they get here I'll probably just get all upset and choked up and not be able to say a thing! This is absolutely a job for Drake!"

"Well, you know," said the woman. "We *have* been having trouble with this new software... Let me check back at the last window. Hm. I'm not really sure how to get there from here."

"Maybe I can help," said Mason eagerly. Eight years ago he had learned, slowly and painfully, to operate the computer programs so necessary to his statistical studies and now he could even help colleagues with relatively simple problems.

"Oh, I wish you would!" said the woman, with relief. "The person who's supposed to be running this program is away for a while and I only know how to do it when it's running smoothly."

"First of all," asked Mason. "Is your computer a Mac?"

"A what?"

"A Macintosh. Uh, does it have a little picture of an apple on it?"

"Oh, I know what you mean. The apple with a bite out of it. No. They didn't think that would be appropriate. But this doesn't have any name on it. Ah! There! I got back to the last window. Now what was the name? Drake? Uh oh! It looks like you're right, Professor. His file is highlighted for uploading. But to upload him I'm going to have to delete..."

"No, no, no!" said Mason, hastily. "Don't touch anything for a moment. Let me think..." And he pondered the various programs he knew, the alternative and never very certain scenarios for taking back an action and substituting the right one. Years ago in a fury he had cursed the computer geniuses who had designed programs with no tolerance for wrong steps and he had wished them all dead. Now, he realized, they *were* dead and were here doing the same thing.

"All right," he announced. "Let's move carefully here. First, drag the current window off a bit so you can see Drake's file."

"Okay, I see what you mean."

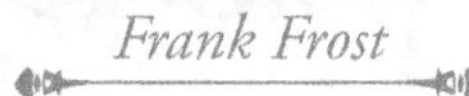

"Now activate my file, just click on it anywhere."

He could see Debbie skipping across the grass, going to meet the newcomer. There was a pair of butterflies flirting above her head.

"All right, I've done that."

"Now. What do you get when you pull down your File menu? It should be up at the top there somewhere."

"Let's see. Okay. It says, *new, open, close, save, finalize...*"

Mason was sure he didn't want to be finalized. "Try clicking on *save,*" he said.

"Okay," she said. "This is great, Professor. I'm sure glad you know what you're doing!" Mason was by no means as sure, but he went on doggedly.

"What options do you have under *save*?" he asked.

Up the hill two more girls now appeared, one white, one black. The white girl seemed to be crying.

"It says, *save changes* or *cancel* or *restore.*"

Mason realized he was going to take an awful chance. *Save changes* probably meant that he was stuck here. *Cancel* just plain worried him. *Restore*, if the programmers had any wits at all, *should* restore him back outside his office, where this all started.

"All right," he said, trying to sound confident. "Listen carefully. Your first step is to bring up *save*. Then click on *restore*. Then when my window disappears, you click on Drake's file and activate him. That should do it. Is that all clear."

"Oh it certainly is, and it all makes sense, too, Professor! I can't thank you enough! Okay! Here goes!" Mason saw that Debbie now had two of the new girls by the hands and was leading them his way. They were all smiling and the other girls were tagging along. It was a beautiful day and he almost wished he could stay for just a bit.

* * *

Professor Mason stood outside his office trying to remember. He'd just gone down the hall to the bathroom but he couldn't remember whether he was coming back to finish something or just to go home. The office seemed to be dark under the door so he concluded that he had already locked up. Hard to remember when you're trying to recall how the Library has catalogued German titles.

He was trudging down the stairwell when he heard a roar and a terrible shriek from the floor just below his. "*Students make more noise every year,*" he thought. And he went home.

ON THE BEACH

It was a truck driver who first saw him standing there by the side of the road, sun coming up in Orange county. Jimmy Morin had started to drive around five in the morning from Temecula in his Dodge pickup with a load of produce for the farmers' markets up north. He was going to hit San Luis Obispo, then work south for a few days, until most of his load was gone. Arroyo Grande on Friday, and the big market in Santa Barbara on Saturday ought to do it. Jimmy always liked some company on a long drive, so he pulled over, pushed the passenger door open.

"Hey, pal, get in. How far you going?"

The young man didn't say anything, didn't seem to have any kind of pack or bag with him, got right in and pulled the door to, then just stared out the windshield. Jimmy let out the clutch and the truck moved on out down the highway.

"You comin' from the Vets' hospital back there?" Jimmy asked. "'Cause I picked up a few guys there now and then. 'Ghanistan, Iraq, even some from the old Gulf War. They got some stories!" Jimmy was grinning, inviting whatever memories his guest wanted to share. But the youngman—maybe not so young, Jimmy thought, just young looking—didn't respond, didn't even look at him, just relaxed against the old sprung seat with the fruit stains on it, and looked straight ahead. He had clean clothes, at least, jeans, a long-sleeved plaid shirt. Hair was combed and he didn't look crazy.

"So. You seen some bad shit, I guess. Don't want to talk about it. Well, that's okay, man. I understand. Would've gone myself back then, the Gulf war, but I had three kids, you know? They're big now, two in high school even. Funny, that war didn't seem that long ago. Anyway..."

Jimmy kept talking all the way up the coast. After about two hours he pulled off the freeway to a convenience store.

"Always stop here for a coffee. Can I get you one, pal?" The man looked at him but didn't answer.

"Okay, I'll take that for a yes. I'm guessing cream and sugar. Right?"

But when Jimmy came back, juggling two steaming foam cups, his rider was gone.

He walked down a long two-lane road, something pulling him that way, toward the ocean. There were hills on both sides of the road, a few houses up there peeking behind the trees on the slopes from time to time. A cold foggy day, and not much traffic to the beach.

The county park entrance beckoned and he walked into the parking lot and to the low bluff overlooking the beach. Grey waves were rolling in. A few brave surfers in full wet suits were challenging the cold water of early spring. To his right were the empty tables of a seaside restaurant, deserted this morning in the wind and fog.

He walked down the steps to the beach, looked both directions, and then started west, into the wind. It was a long beach beneath high cliffs. Seabirds thronged the wet sand, dodging the foaming breakers as they kept rolling in. There were piles of seaweed here and there, torn up and washed ashore by the last storm. He was a almost a mile from the park and the restaurant when a cleft in the cliffs attracted him. A tall stand of reeds almost concealed the shadowed opening. He stood in the narrow space for a moment, protected from the wind. Then he sat down and rested, his back to the cliff. He sat there for several hours, not moving, not sleeping. A few gulls wandered into the cleft, curious. One approached, cocked its head in all directions, hopped a little closer, finally gave a gentle peck to an exposed ankle.

He didn't move. But the gull was aware that the thing was alive, not ready to eat, and it flew away with its followers.

In the afternoon he emerged from the cleft and looked up and down the beach. At the foot of the cliffs were mounds of driftwood, from little sticks to huge eucalyptus trunks. Every size and shape. He began collecting sticks, first longer ones that he held upright and pressed down into the sand. Then he gathered smaller branches and piled them up against the uprights, with no artistry, just making a screen from the beach. Then he made a hollow in the sand behind his screen and lay down, curling up on his side. In a few minutes he was asleep.

The moon was out over the ocean when he woke from pangs of hunger, shivering with a sleeper's chill. He stood, brushed the sand off, and walked back down the beach to the restaurant. They were turning the lights off inside and the last guests were leaving. The kitchen door was in back right up against the cliff. He stood there, smelling the food. There were several garbage cans and he lifted a lid. This was mostly a seafood restaurant and the remains of fish and shellfish had been sitting in there all day. They stank. So he put back the lid and just waited. A young dishwasher came out of the kitchen door with a bag of garbage and almost ran into him.

"*Eee-ho*! Man, you scare the sheet out of me, you know?" The dishwasher looked closely at him, frowning. "You a 'omeless guy?"

He didn't answer, just turned his expressionless face to the little dishwasher.

"Man, I bet you focking 'ongry, Jus' a minute, you way." The little man went back into the restaurant, came right out with a plastic bag. "I got some old 'amburger buns. Lotsa fish off the plates, you know. Piece of steak the guy don' finish." He put a hand on the man's arm, looked around, lowered his voice.

"Leesen, you slippin' on the beach? You better go down long ways. Focking sheriff, they been rousting pipples."

He started to walk away, but the little dishwasher followed him a few steps.

"An' you want some water? Bat'rooms right over there. Take it easy, man."

He walked back up the beach, putting his hand in the bag, pullin out old stale buns, pieces of fish, whatever, and gnawing on them. Halfway to his shelter he realized he was thirsty, really thirsty, so he backtracked to the restaurant and found the restrooms. He drank water out of his cupped hands for almost a minute, then resumed his trek up the beach. Someone had left a dirty old beach blanket crumpled up and he took it, shook the sand out of it. Back at his hole in the cliff he rolled the blanket around himself and lay back down in the depression he had made in the sand.

Voices woke him instantly in the morning and he sat bolt upright. Some people were calling to each other. Then he saw that early morning surfers were down at the edge of the water, inspecting the waves. He relaxed, and after a moment looked around for the plastic bag. There were still a couple of buns and a cold greasy piece of steak. He finished everything in the bag. After his breakfast he began walking up the beach westward, away from the restaurant. When he reached a promontory poking out into the ocean the tide was high and breakers were rolling up to the base of the cliff. Without hesitation he walked through the shallow waves around the point. From here the beach was deserted as far as he could see. He sat for quite some time on the sand, then came to a decision. He took all his clothes off, squatted next to the cliff and relieved himself. Then he walked across the sand and into the ocean, pausing when breakers came in, and finally wading out beyond the breaker line. He swam strongly and easily, at home in the sea. The water was frigid, but he gave no sign of feeling it.

After putting his clothes back on he continued up the beach. He had reached an affluent part of the coastline and there were large homes with luxuriant landscaping perched on the high cliffs above. A woman came down the beach from the other direction, accompanied by two large dogs, a Lab and some other kind of retriever, both off the leash. He kept walking, not looking at her or the dogs.

The woman stopped. She was in her fifties, dressed in warmups and running shoes. Strands of silver hair escaped the scarf around her head. She gave him a hostile glance, not worried, confident with her two big dogs.

"This is a private beach, you know..."

He paid no attention, kept walking. The two dogs now circled him, lowering their heads to sniff at his shoes.

"There's nothing but private homes up here, you know, you'd better go back." Her voice was angry and the dogs picked up the vibrations, backing up now, and confronting him.

He stopped and looked at the woman. The two dogs were immediately alert, looking toward their mistress, waiting for instructions. Then he turned and walked back down the beach toward the distant restaurant. One of the dogs ran along beside him for a few steps and he stopped, reached down and patted the dog, who wagged his tail and bumped up against his leg.

"Bruiser! Come back!" Now for the first time the woman's voice betrayed fear. "Bruiser, Mindy! Come here!" The dogs obediently ran back to their mistress, who crouched down to hold their collars. She looked terrified.

"You! You get out of here! I'll sic my dogs on you."

But he ignored her and just kept walking slowly back down the beach. The tide was beginning to go out and swarms of shore birds were feeding on the wet sand, running inland to avoid the last tiny waves of foam from the breakers offshore, then chasing them back to snatch the little creatures the water had brought to the surface.

Late that afternoon he walked back to the restaurant and the park ranger station as the day was dying. Behind the ranger station there was a lawn, reclaimed and cultivated out of the surrounding wild underbrush. Three older women were feeding cats on the lawn. They were carefully spooning out little lumps of catfood from cans, spacing the lumps so that many cats could come eat without fighting over the food. One of the women looked over her shoulder and saw him.

"We feed them every night," she confided. "People get rid of their unwanted kittens here. It's terrible, just dumping a little cat like that. We pick up some, little kittens that are sick and weak, you know? Have to put them down, only humane. If they're healthy we have them fixed, take them to the Humane Society. But the grownups are too wild, won't come near us."

He could see the cats cautiously coming out of the underbrush, the young ones running for the food, the older ones cautious, looking in all directions. They were joined by a puppy, a short-haired mongrel, chestnut with white patches, who came trotting out of the brush and tried to join the cats eating the catfood. But he was met by snarls and was batted on the nose by the cats already at their food. He sat back on his haunches and whined.

One of the women told him, "You see that puppy? Someone abandoned him here too. He's been here for over a month. Now he thinks he's a cat."

He watched the cats eating for a while, seeing the dog steal a bite now and then, wagging its tail, trying to convince the cats that he was one of them.

The women had now noticed that he was strange. One of them whispered to the others and they sidled over closer to the ranger station. He paid no attention, watching the cats eat and the dog trying to convince the cats to share.

After a while he walked over behind the restaurant, used the men's restroom, then just waited outside the kitchen door. After a while the same kitchen helper came out to dump garbage.

"Shee! You still here? Hol' on man...see wha' I can fin'" A few minutes later he came out with a foam container. "Lady lef' half a cheecken, som' feesh'n cheeps, copple rolls...You getta way now, boss see you I'm fock, you know?"

Instead of going back up the beach, he went back to the lawn where the cats were eating. The dog was forlorn, lying down with his head between his paws, watching the cats clean up the last scraps.

He reached in the bag and pulled out the chicken breast. The dog's ears perked up, his head lifted, and he looked around quickly. Some of the cats smelled the chicken and started to mill around his feet. But he held the chicken out until the dog sidled closer. He lofted the chicken breast to the lawn in front of the dog. Two cats pounced on it immediately and the dog backed up, whining. But the piece of meat was too big for cats to drag away and while they were contemplating their next move the dog moved in quickly, grabbed the chicken and wolfed it down, then looked up rapidly.

He reached in the plastic bag and came up with a handful of fishy fried potatoes. The cats were not interested and the dog came closer, gobbled a pile of fries off the lawn, looked up now and wagged its tail, smiling.

"It won't come near you," one of the braver women said, over by the ranger house. "We've been trying to catch it for a week, take it to the Humane Society."

If he heard her he gave no notice, but turned back to the beach, carrying his greasy bag. The dog watched him go, and after a moment's thought trotted after him. The women saw him walking up the beach, the setting sun casting his shadow against the cliffs, the smaller shadow just behind.

"I think he's a nut case," said one of them.

"Homeless," said another. "And most of them are mental. I saw on Channel Three, a week ago."

"Well, the poor guys have to live somewhere. Better than downtown, begging all the time," said the third.

"Why in our town? And here on the beach? They should give them all a bus ticket somewhere else...inland, somewhere. Fresno, or something."

"Bakersfield," said another and they all laughed. "No. Let's be reasonable." They laughed again, watching the two small figures walk out of sight around the cliff.

He woke up in the night and felt the dog sleeping against his leg.

The next few days he continued his routine, walking up the beach, swimming, returning in the evening back to the restaurant and waiting by the kitchen door. But now he was trailed constantly by the dog. One day, along the beach, the dog ran ahead and picked up a stick, then ran back and crouched playfully in front of him, dropping the stick, wagging his whole rear end and waiting for him to notice the game. But he paid no attention and continued walking up the beach.

Another day the younger ranger, the guy on the early shift, caught him walking with the dog down to the eastern part of the beach, toward the town and the harbor.

"Hold it a second," the ranger called, and came trotting out with a large black plastic garbage bag. He gave him the bag.

"You know, you're going to be around here, give me a hand with the cleanup. County cut our budget fifty percent. Just pick up the cans and paper down there and toss 'em in the dumpster there. Okay?"

He took the bag without any expression and walked down the beach, just holding the neck of the garbage bag as if it was his luggage. It was low tide and there were some large rocks exposed along the beach. He was walking along the tide line when a soft drink can washed up in front of him on a wave, sparkling in the sun, resting there on the sand in front of him. He paused, and the dog ran over to sniff the can, then looked back curiously, to see what he would do.

He picked up the can, put it in the bag, and continued down the beach. After a quarter mile the beach rounded a corner and he could see steps in the cliff coming down and people on the beach. So he turned and walked back. Now he saw a candy wrapper, picked it up and put it in the bag, then another can, and a plastic bag. The dog now understood the game, and all the way back up the beach he would run and crouch at every piece of human refuse, looking back and barking, until it was picked up and put in the bag. Back at the restaurant and ranger station he hesitated, looking around, finally just standing there motionless. The ranger spotted him, came out and yelled.

"Over there in the dumpster."

He put the bag in the dumpster and was walking back down the beach when the ranger caught up with him.

"You know, you pick up like that every day? I'll get you something from the restaurant, okay?"

But he didn't listen, and continued down the beach.

The next two days he accepted the garbage bag from the ranger and went up and down the beach. One day the ranger just brought him a bag with a burger and fries in it. He took it and looked at the dog at his feet.

"Oh, I got them to put in an extra patty. For your dog. Okay?

He didn't look at the ranger, just took the bag back up the beach with him.

They came in the night, the sheriff deputies. There were two of them, and he woke to find his arms pinioned in back of him and then roughly handcuffed. He jerked wildly for a moment, then gave up all resistance. The dog was dancing around the perimeter of his little shelter, barking madly.

One of the deputies, an older man, told his younger partner, "Give him a whiff of Mace, quiet him down."

"Hell, he quit fighting, Duffy. He'll go easy."

And they walked their prisoner down the sandy beach, one on each side holding an arm, the dog following behind, only barking once in a while now.

Parked in the entrance to the county beach was a large black van. The older deputy unlocked the rear door, then stood back with his pistol in his hands.

"Okay, Reese, put his ass in the van."

There were almost a dozen prisoners on the benches lining the sides of the van, all cuffed, no one struggling. They looked with mild curiosity at the newcomer.

He stepped up into the van without urging and sat down next to the last man on the bench. The deputies slammed the back door and locked it and the van moved off.

"Where'd they get you? The beach?" asked his seat mate, a large Latino.

He made no response, just sat there, looking down at his feet.

"Shee-it, he crazy, man," said a small black man on the other side of the van. "He like Bonzo over there." And he gestured with his head at a motionless figure seated opposite. "Bonzo don' say shit either. Right, Bonzo?" And he kicked the man gently on the leg. There was no response.

"See? We gotta get these two dudes together. Maybe they talk to each other. Some 'planetary language, know what I mean?" He laughed and most of the men in the van laughed with him. Somebody started whistling the "Twilight Zone" theme.

They drove away from the beach, took a ramp onto the freeway for a few miles, then off and up a hill to the county jail. There was a television van waiting there in the night, the reporter and the cameraman ready to roll. Deputy Duffy stepped to the rear of the sheriff's van and started to open the doors.

"Just a minute," said the TV guy. "Let me interview you, just a few questions, then we'll shoot them coming out of the van, okay?

"You got it."

"Rolling..." said the cameraman, and a glare lit up the two deputies and the back of the van.

It seemed there had been numerous complaints in this prosperous seaside community about the homeless, sleeping in doorways, in parks, or on the beach. It hurt tourism, they said, and business of all kinds. So the sheriff had decided to do a sweep and call the media to show how well he was protecting property values. He hated the paperwork it would generate but he thought maybe once every six months would cut down on the complaints.

The bums, drifters, drunks and others caught "camping illegally" were led out of the van and booked.

"What's your name?" they asked him. But he just stood staring at the wall as they took his picture. He was searched, but he had nothing in any of his pockets.

"We can send his prints to the Feds," suggested a jail deputy.

"Can't afford it, every bum like this."

"But you know? He looks like a vet to me. I was in the Gulf, you know. Just something about him says Army to me. Maybe Marines. Maybe he needs help. Whadya think?"

"Sure! The asshole supervisors cut our budget, then make us go on homeless patrol! You wanna fill out more reports?"

"No, but—"

"Okay. Then call Mental Health. See if they want him."

There was a lone woman on the desk at County Mental Health at that hour. She was not enthusiastic.

"If he's a danger to himself or others, we can take him for a seventy-two hour hold. That's it. You wanna fill out the forms?"

"No, but—"

"Why don't you just let him go? You got tons of extra room at the jail?"

Everyone knew they didn't. He was marched with his fellow campers to a large cell already crowded with over twenty detainees from the evening's drunk driving, bar fights, gang disturbances, domestic complaints. The new arrivals were greeted with groans and curses.

"Shit! There's no fucking place to sit already!" And so on.

Most of the newcomers sought out a vacant space on the floor and just flopped. He stood just inside the gate, where the jailers had left him, until he was noticed.

"Hey man! Grab some floor. We can fit you in."

"Nah! Look at him. Fucker's nuts."

"Got a nice shirt, man. Maybe he'll give it to me." A bearded man with a large gut advanced on him. "Leave him alone."

The bearded man whirled. "Who the fuck you talkin' to, burrito breath?"

An Hispanic man stood up. "I'm talkin' to you, asshole. The guy looks like a vet. And we vets stick together."

Half a dozen other prisoners stood up. "Just forget about it," one of them said. "Leave him the fuck alone."

After a while he sat down with his back to the bars.

In the morning he was the subject of argument in the booking office.

"He's got no name, we don't know if he has a record, Mental Health won't take him, what does that leave us?"

An older deputy was in charge of OR—*release on own recognizance.* "We just let him go, tell him not to sleep on the beach again."

"But he'll just be back—"

"Yeah, if you wanna walk a mile down the beach in the middle of the night to bust him again. What the fuck you wanna do, make us more work?"

"Not me, Sarge!"

He walked out of the jail doors at seven that morning. He looked around briefly, then headed down hill. On the frontage road leading east from the jail he felt the sea air to his right so he crossed the first overpass over the freeway and found his way to the road out to the county beach park. It was still early in the morning, foggy at the beach and only a few tourists were braving breakfast outdoors at the beach café. A different group of women were feeding the cats and they paid him no attention. There was no sign of the dog. After a while he walked over to one of the benches by the beach and sat down looking out to sea. The ranger found him there, still sitting, in the middle of the morning.

"Your dog's not here. You know what, the sheriffs called Animal Control and they came and got him. Probably out at the

Humane Society." The ranger looked dubious. "If you can get out there, they're going to charge you twenty five bucks to get him out."

He didn't acknowledge the information. Later in the day he walked back up the beach. He looked out to sea for a long time before finally taking his clothes off and entering the water. He walked through the surf, not avoiding the waves, just letting them smack him, until he was out beyond the wave line, where he began to swim. Today he kept swimming, out past the first patches of kelp, not slowing down until he reached the heavy belt of kelp almost a quarter mile out. Here he paused, exhausted. There was a slight overcast, no wind, and the surface of the sea was glassy. He looked back at the shore. A flight of pelicans went by, on their way up the coast. Some gulls were attracted by the unusual presence of a land animal this far out to sea and they landed in a small circle to the west. He stayed there, treading water, as if waiting to come to some decision. Finally he turned slowly in the water so that he was facing out to sea again. He started to bring his legs up in order to swim when suddenly, ten feet in front of him, a seal broke the surface and stared at him, whiskers twitching. Neither made a move for a handful of seconds. The seal examined him with large brown eyes, its sleek black head dog-like in expression, before it sank slowly back beneath the oily swell and disappeared.

He turned once more to face the land and began to swim slowly back the way he had come. Once on shore he got dressed and walked to his shelter in the cliff. The sheriffs had partially kicked it apart, so he spent some time rebuilding it. As dusk began to fall he walked back toward the restaurant but this time kept going toward the entrance of the county park. As he reached the gate a white pickup stopped in front of him.

"Hey, pal?" It was Reese, the younger of the two deputies who had arrested him, but now out of uniform, wearing jeans and a T shirt.

"Hey, I got a friend of yours here." He opened the driver's door and a brown shape leaped over his lap and to the ground, barking and then leaping up on the man, who finally leaned down and tried to pat him, as the dog gyrated around him and kept jumping up to lick his face.

"I heard Animal Control got your dog, so I was going by there anyway and picked him up for you. Figured you might not have a ride."

Neither man nor dog paid attention so the deputy closed the truck door, leaned out the window.

"I know you won't be sleeping on the beach again," he grinned. "Take her easy, guys." And he drove off.

After the dog calmed down they walked together toward the restaurant. Two women were watching the stray cats. In the twilight some kittens had come out and were playing, dashing back and forth, as the grownups started to assemble, expecting their evening feeding. The women noticed him coming with the dog.

"Now, don't you let your dog chase the kitties," one woman warned.

He stood still for a moment watching the cats, then looked down at his dog.

"It's okay," he said. "He likes cats."

www.ingramcontent.com/pod-product-compliance
Lightning Source LLC
Chambersburg PA
CBHW072119300726

48975CB00003B/862